Hugh I. Strang, A. J Moore

English Literature for 1890, for University and departmental Examinations

Byron's Prisoner of Chillon, and Childe Harold's Pilgrimage

Hugh I. Strang, A. J Moore

English Literature for 1890, for University and departmental Examinations
Byron's Prisoner of Chillon, and Childe Harold's Pilgrimage

ISBN/EAN: 9783337149239

Printed in Europe, USA, Canada, Australia, Japan

Cover: Foto ©Andreas Hilbeck / pixelio.de

More available books at **www.hansebooks.com**

ENGLISH LITERATURE FOR 1890,

FOR

UNIVERSITY AND DEPARTMENTAL EXAMINATIONS.

BYRON'S

PRISONER OF CHILLON,

AND

CHILDE HAROLD'S PILGRIMAGE,

II. 73 TO III. 51 ;

AND

TWENTY OF ADDISON'S ESSAYS,

(SELECTED FROM " THE SPECTATOR,")

WITH

BIOGRAPHICAL AND CRITICAL NOTICES OF THE WRITERS,

NOTES, &c.,

BY

H. I. STRANG, B.A., AND A. J. MOORE, B.A.,

GODERICH HIGH SCHOOL.

Toronto:

THE COPP, CLARK COMPANY, LIMITED.

1889.

PREFACE.

As this is the third time that the editors have undertaken to provide a school edition of the English Literature for University and Departmental examinations, it is hardly necessary to do more than to say that this edition has been prepared on the same plan and the work divided between the editors in the same way as in the two previous ones.

The object of the introduction in each case is to enable students to understand clearly what manner of man the writer was, under what circumstances he wrote the work to be studied, and by what influences he was likely to be affected, and also to call attention to some of the leading characteristics of his style : that of the notes to lighten the labor of both teachers and students, and to lead the latter to observe and to judge for themselves. If the notes err on the side of fulness it is because the editors have kept in mind the case of candidates studying by themselves and of others who may not have ready access to good works of reference.

The text of the poetry has been, with, perhaps, two or three variations, made to conform to that of Murray's edition of *Byron's Poetical Works*.

In the case of the prose the text followed was that of Morley's edition of *The Spectator*. While, however, the first of the essays selected has been printed just as it stands in his edition, that students may see how English looked as it was spelled and printed in Addison's day, it has been thought best to modernize the orthography of the rest, the editors being, with Arnold, "unable to see that anything is gained by sub-

" stituting for the anomalies of our present spelling, which are
" sufficiently deplorable, a set of anomalies which were in use
" among our forefathers a hundred and sixty years ago, besides
"reproducing typographical absurdities and solecisms in punctua-
" tion, from which we have in a great measure delivered
" ourselves."

In preparing both the introductions and the notes free use
has been made of the Clarendon Press edition of *Childe Harold*,
and of Morley's and Arnold's editions of *The Spectator*.

The editors hope that they have profited by experience, but
at the same time they regret that owing to circumstances (for
which the publisher, however, is in no way responsible) the
work has been more hurriedly done and the book later in being
issued than is desirable.

GODERICH, June, 1889.

Byron's ancestry was undoubtedly ancient, if not illustrious. A Ralph Byron is down in Doomsday Book as holding lands in Derby. They can be traced through every reign. One ancestor, "Little Sir John with the great beard," was made by Henry VIII Lieutenant of Sherwood Forest, and got as his part of the spoiling of the monasteries the Priory of Newstead. At Edgehill there were seven Byrons for the King, and just after the first battle of Newbury, the first peer was created as Bar n of Rochdale. The fifth Lord, in the year 1765, murdered his neighbour and kinsman, Mr. Chaworth, in a room in Pall Mall. His brother peers, after a two days' trial, found him guilty of manslaughter, but Byron pleaded his privilege as a peer and was set at liberty. But the shadow of this crime never left him. He roamed about under strange names, spurned by high and low, sometimes mewing himself in the Abbey for months, making his appearance only to become the subject of some wild story. That he shot two coachmen, that he tried to drown his wife, that he was attended by devils, were current beliefs, and he very naturally got the distinctive title of "the wicked lord Byron." He hated his heirs, sold the Rochdale estates, and cut down the trees at Newstead to disappoint them, but survived them all, leaving the impoverished title to the subject of our sketch in 1798.

The poet's grandfather, the brother of the "wicked lord," entered the navy and led an especially adventurous and danger-ous life. In 1750, in one of Anson's ships, he was wrecked in the straits of Magellan, was a prisoner with the Patagonians and Chilians, and only got back to England in 1746.

His own account of his adventures, published in 1768 is "remarkable for freshness of scenery, like that of our first traveller, Sir John Mandeville, and a force of description that rivals Defoe." His grandson, the poet, refers to it and makes use of it in his account of the shipwreck in Don Juan. "Mad Jack," the poet's father, was his eldest son, was educated at Westminster, and became a Captain in the Guards. He turned out a licentious and heartless rake, gamester and spendthrift. He seduced the wife of the Marquis of Caermarthen, and openly boasted of his conquest, but afterwards married her for her money. He squandered her fortune and led her such a wretched life, that her death in 1784 must have been a happy release. She left a daughter Augusta, afterwards Mrs. Leigh, the half-sister of the poet, and his good angel and friend through every trial and calumny.

Captain Byron very soon retrieved his fortunes by marrying Catherine Gordon, an Aberdeen heiress, also of undoubted descent from James I. The lady is described to us as violently passionate, wilful and fretful, and with more than the usual Highland pride of ancestry. They went abroad and in little more than a year, her fortune of £20,000 was gone. In the last days of 1787, the family, consisting of the Captain, his wife, Augusta and a servant or two, returned from France, and took up their residence in London, in Cavendish Square. Here on the 22nd January 1788, George Gordon Byron was born, and unfortunately with a club or twisted foot.

The worthless father abandoned wife and child soon after, and died in France in 1791, and the mother withdrew to Aberdeen with a mere pittance saved from the wreck of her fortune.

The boy was sent to various schools and masters, but seems to have been backward at his books and to have had no ambition to stand high in his class. His mental training seems to have been indifferent, while his moral training was positively bad.

The poor boy had no doubt inherited a passionate and wayward nature, but every fault was aggravated by the alternate indulgence and severity, petting and abuse of his foolish mother. He was morbidly sensitive as to his deformity, in fact it was largely the foundation of that after misanthrophy which colors and mars his poetry. In her fits of passion his mother would call him "a lame brat" and "every inch a Byron wicked as his father."

In 1798, Byron having succeeded to the title and estates of the "wicked lord," they moved south to England, and lived successively at Newstead, Nottingham and London. In time he went to Harrow, then under the mastership of Dr. Drury The master he loved, but the school he hated. He never liked its studies and was never an accurate scholar in his classics. French he read well, but spoke clumsily, of German he had the merest smattering, of Italian alone had he afterwards any real mastery. But the extent and the variety of his English reading were something wonderful for a boy. "His list of books, drawn up in 1807, includes more history and biography than most men read in a life time:"—Philosophy, the poets *en masse*, divinity largely, including Blair, Tillotson, Hooker, with the English Essayists and all the standard English and French fiction. He says of himself that he read eating, read in bed, read when no one else read. He was a favorite with his classmates, and when there was a change of masters, the leader in various acts of mutiny and rebellion. His most eminent schoolfellow was Sir Robert Peel, born indeed in the same year.

It was during the Harrow period that an event happened which gave another tinge of dark color to his life. On a visit to the Abbey, he saw Mary Chaworth, a daughter of the Chaworth whom his great uncle, the "mad lord," had murdered. His love for her was the grand passion of Byron's life. She encouraged his stolen visits, but she was two years his senior, laughed at his ardent letters, and looked upon him as a mere boy. Even the cruel question he overheard to her waiting maid, " Do you think I could care for that lame boy ?" did not seem to affect the intensity of his passion. She was a common-place, lively girl who could see no promise of greatness or celebrity in *him*, but to Byron, such was his passionate and imaginative nature, *she* was an angel. " She was my beau ideal," he says, " of all my youthful fancy could paint of beautiful." He calls her " the bright morning star of Annesley." He refers to her in various parts of his writings. This boyish idolatry no doubt nursed the spirit of poetry within him. It was the source of those beautiful lines in the *Dream* :

> " I saw two beings in the hues of youth,
> Standing upon a hill, a gentle hill,
> Green and of mild declivity—
> These two, a maiden and a youth were there
> Gazing—the one on all that was beneath
> Fair as herself—but the boy gazed on her ;
> And both were young, and one was beautiful ;
> And both were young—yet not alike in youth.
> As the sweet morn on the horizon's verge,
> The maid was on the eve of womanhood ;
> The boy had fewer summers, but his heart
> Had far outgrown his years, and to his eye
> There was but one beloved face on earth,
> And that was shining on him."

Her future was in some senses sadder than Byron's. Her marriage with the humdrum country squire she preferred was an ill-assorted one. After a few unhappy years they separated. Finally she went partially insane and died so in 1832.

In October 1805, being then nearly eighteen, Byron although preferring Oxford, was sent to Cambridge. He disliked both mathematics and classics, and, as at Harrow, was an idle and irregular student, doing a large amount of reading not set down in the course, and doing even that in a desultory, aimless way. However he got his degree, a poor one, in 1808.

Two of his best friends, while at Cambridge were John Cam Hobhouse, afterwards Lord Broughton, and the Rev. Francis Hodgson. The first was the steadfast friend of Byron's whole life, the companion of his travels and defender of his fame ; the second by his judicious and charitable treatment of Byron's religious doubts largely helped to lead him back to fixed belief, and was also one of the earliest to recognize the merit of his poems and to encourage him to persevere.

Some juvenile poems had already been praised by his friends and printed for private circulation, but in March, 1807, he appealed to a wider audience, and, mended and pruned, they appeared as the *Hours of Idleness*. A year later in the *Edinburgh Review* appeared Lord Brougham's caustic critique, pointing out its evident faults, its mawkishness, its weak imitations and commonplaces. Yet there are some stanzas, *e.g.* in *Lochnagar*, and in the *Elegy on Newstead* that might have saved a youthful venture from such merciless criticism. But it was then a chief object in criticism and seemingly a point of honour, to admit as little merit as possible, and the duty of a critic was to impale the wretched author on his shafts of sarcasm and ridicule for the amusement of the reading public and his own literary glory.

Byron, although he loved his title of Lord and its aristocratic influence quite as much as Congreve did that of a fine gentleman, was, quite unlike him, really sensitive as to his literary reputation. He was not made of the stuff to die of an article. The old Norse fighting blood of the Byrons was roused. To a man of his temperament it was much more endurable to be hated than to be despised. He took a year to study the masters of satire, especially Pope, whom he particularly admired, and in the spring of 1809 appeared *English Bards and Scotch Reviewers*. This vigorous satire was the beginning of his fame. The first edition was sold in a month and a second quickly followed. As to the critics nobody pitied them, but he was felt to be unjust with regard to many of the poets, especially the Lakists. The vituperation is too general. Many of his verdicts he afterwards recanted and deplored.

During his College life and since, he had indulged in a good deal of dissipation, not what might be called dishonorable—*i.e.* according to the code of the fashionable world. "He rushed about between London, Cambridge and Newstead, shooting gambling, swimming, alternately drinking deep and trying to starve himself into elegance,* greenroom hunting, traveling with disguised companions, patronizing the dancing master, Grimaldi the clown, and taking lessons in pugilism."

But even his guardian, Lord Carlisle, fell into the error of believing him worse than he really was, so that when he took his seat in the house of Lords he had no one to introduce him. In fact Byron was beginning to shew by his conduct two great faults of character, pride and a love of singularity, or rather than nothing, notoriety. He never attempted concealment of his vices or follies, and was inclined even to parade and excuse them.

In his *assumed* character of misanthrope men were in the mass no better than he, in fact worse, for the greater number added to their sins the still greater one of hypocrisy. Now Byron was no *real* misanthrope. No man with his quick and generous feelings and his love for the good and the beautiful things of life could be a genuine misanthrope. It was but a character he assumed. It gave him success; and to be successful, to be a *lion* of any kind and the cynosure of all eyes was what Byron dearly loved.

It was with some disgust at the growing coldness of respectable society, and at his friends standing aloof, that he left England with Hobhouse in July, 1809. They touched at Lisbon, Cadiz, Gibraltar, Malta, and Previsa in Albania, whence

---

* He had a horror of obesity, and was continually trying remedies to prevent it.

they toured it throughout the Turkish provinces to Athens. Here he remained for a considerable time, studying the monuments, making excursions to other parts of Greece, collecting materials for his poem of *Childe Harold*, the first two cantos of which were completed at Smyrna the next Spring.

After two years he returned to England and to Newstead, but not in time to see his mother die. His strange behaviour in not going to the grave with the procession but putting on a pair of gloves to box with a servant-boy makes one think that for the moment grief must have unhinged his mind. The truth is that some of his extraordinary eccentricities must have proceeded from some nervous weakness or other abnormal condition of his exceedingly emotional and intense nature. Five months after he made his maiden speech in the House. This was on the 27th Feb. 1812, and related to the penalties to be imposed on the Luddites. He was a liberal in his political opinions, and spoke afterwards in favour of Catholic Emancipation, but his speeches were evidently set compositions, and although clever enough in their way, show that he was not likely to acquire fame as a legislator.

The first two cantos of *Childe Harold* had been given to Mr. Murray to publish, and had for some months been undergoing revision. They appeared on the 29th Feb. 1812, just two days after his maiden speech. The success and sale of the book was unprecedented, rivalled only by Burns' first volume, and the *Lay of the Last Minstrel*. Seven editions ran through in four weeks. "I awoke," Byron said, "one morning and found myself famous."

For two years the noble author was the most popular poet in England, "the great romancer of his day, the darling of society." He was the talk of every London drawing-room; when he appeared in any public place there was a rush of people to look at him. He continued to work the vein of public taste that he had struck, and poured forth in succession several pieces similar in plot, sentiment and imagery, as the *Waltz*, the *Giaour*, *Bride of Abydos*, *Lara*, *Siege of Corinth*, *Parisina*, which last is of a higher order than the others. " They all exhibit a command of words, a sense of melody, a flow of rhythm and rhyme which mastered Moore and even Scott on their own ground. But they are potentially endless reproductions of one phase of an ill-regulated mind, the picture of the same vengeful man who knows no friend but his dog, and reads on the tombs of the great " only the nothing and the glory of a name "—the wandering outlaw of his own dark mind, who has not loved the world nor the world him. All this *decies repetita* grows into a weariness and vexation, Mr. Carlyle harshly compares it to the screaming of a meatjack."*

It was in this period, 1813-1816, that he became familiar with the phases of London life. He became both a social and a literary lion, and when he appeared at any assembly, or fête, or festival there would often be great jostling and craning of necks to get a sight of him. His manner was agreeable and engaging, with a species of *hauteur* not unbecoming in a lord and poet ; his conversation, according to his company, could be full of vivacity or sentiment, and his beautiful face, upon which was set the stamp of intellectual power and an emotional nature, attracted all. Women especially were drawn toward him. As a consequence, the doors of London drawing rooms were opened wide to welcome him. For several months he was the rage. He was familiar in the various green-rooms, and many a pretty actress ogled him. He invaded the world of the exquisites and daily shook hands with Beau Brummell. The lords and ladies at Court smiled upon him, and the " first gentleman in Europe " received him and complimented him so highly as to leave no doubt on his mind that *he* instead of Southey might have had the hundred marks and the butt of wine.

* Nichol's Life, p. 76.

But there were other and better as well as more lasting friendships. He made the acquaintance of Sir H. Davy, the Edgeworths, Sir Jas. Mackintosh, Colman and Kean, Grattan and Curran, and Madame de Stael. Scott and he met in London, in the spring of 1815, principally at Murray's. Scott, who had expected an eccentric fellow with an uneven and sourish temper, was agreeably disappointed.

Scott was not only a great poet but a man of sound sense and fine discernment, and his opinion of a brother poet is worth condensing :

"Courteous and even kind in manner, with no very fixed principles in religion and politics, the pleasure and the opportunity it gave him of wit and satire being no doubt at the bottom of this free-thinking habit. A patrician at heart, but generous of spirit and jovial in company, 'liking Moore and me because we were good-natured fellows, not caring for our dignity, but enjoying the *mot pour rire*.' Terribly sensitive as to his foot, melancholy, even gloomy at times, and suspicious of intended offence, but 'in a minute or two his mind, like a troubled spring, would work itself clear,' and he would again become genial and interesting."

They were ever after fast friends, frequently exchanging letters and gifts. Byron confessed and deplored his virulence towards Scott and others in the *Bards and Reviewers* and praised Scott's novels as the highest of their kind. Scott as generously acknowledged that the success of Byron had driven him from the field of poetry to the prose romance. And although there was a gulf between Byron and the *Lakists* as to their views of society and the true mission of poetry, which no amount of personal intercourse could bridge over, yet Byron at this time is found declaring admiration of Wordsworth's genius and reverence for his character, and even a good will towards Southey, which it seems Southey did not reciprocate.

All this belongs to the brighter side of Byron's nature, but there is unfortunately a darker side. Amours high and low in plenty, *liaisons* of all sorts and shades must be confessed. Some have since been proved innocent enough. Others were much exaggerated by scandal-mongers. But enough remains to prove to us that greatness of genius is too often found associated with looseness of morals. In Byron's case, too, he was his own worst enemy. He was careless of opinion. He was too communicative, even garrulous, about these delicate matters upon which prudent men are silent. He seldom seems to have put aside a pleasure for prudential reasons. It is true that his passions were seldom devoid of affectionate emotion, but they must be gratified, and at any cost. And cost was beginning to to be a matter for consideration. Newstead, heavily mortgaged on coming into his hands, gave him but £1,500 a year, and he was living at the rate of £4,000. In 1809 he writes to his mother : " Newstead and I stand or fall together." " I feel like a man of honour, I will not sell Newstead," and so on with the usual Byronic strength of phrase. Alas for his honour, or rather his knowledge of himself ; in 1812 he tried to sell but failed, in 1814 he did sell, and the unfortunate buyer, not being able to raise the whole amount, paid smart money to the tune of £25,000.

His friends, anxious to draw him from the vortex of dissipation and debt into which he was fast drifting, thought that both his fortune and his morals might be mended by a suitable marriage. His best friend, his half-sister, Augusta Leigh, always tolerant of his faults and careful of his interests, urged it upon him.

This constant pressure had at last its effect. " A wife," he confesses to Moore, " would be my salvation." " I want to see Venice and the Alps and the Parmesian cheese, and look at the coast of Greece from Italy. All this, however, depends on an

event which may or may not happen." He had already pro-
posed to a Miss Milbanke, daughter of Sir Ralph Milbanke, an
only child and an heiress. She was but 19, of considerable
beauty, and to Byron's first enthusiasm was " a *savante*, a
poetess, a paragon of only children, and perfection itself." His
proposal was not at first accepted, but two years after he re-
newed his suit, and was successful. The ill-starred and ill-
matched pair were married on the 2nd of Jan., 1815. Byron
never really loved her, but married mainly for a settlement.
She, no doubt, was fascinated by his fame and thought perhaps
to have the glory of bringing him back to the fold of respecta-
bility and religion. Both were disappointed. Byron did not
get control of her fortune, and she was quite unable to reform
him. His creditors, hearing he had married money, became im-
portunate in their demands. Some idea of the extraordinary
scene Newstead must have presented may be gotten from the
fact that during the year there were eight or nine executions on
the house and furniture. Their daughter Ada, afterwards
Lady Lovelace, was born on the 10th Dec., 1815. Five weeks
after Lady Byron left his house, ostensibly to visit her father's
home in Leicestershire, but never returned. The efforts of
friends to effect a reconciliation were unavailing, She remained
obstinate in her determination to live apart from her husband.

The matter will perhaps always remain a sort of domestic
mystery. She accused Byron of such gross offences and de-
grading acts towards herself as could be explained only by sup-
posing him mad. She distinctly implied that her life was in
danger. Of course, as the physicians said, Byron was no more
insane than he had ever been. The world is half full of such
mad men who, by loving and judicious treatment, may become
very passable husbands. It may well be doubted whether Lord
Byron would have made a good husband for any woman. But
there was some fault on her side. She was, perhaps, a model
of the proprieties, but her conscious virtue was sometimes too

intolerant of the irregularities from which Byron could not at once free himself, and which if provoked it was in his rebellious nature to parade. Beneath her gracious exterior there was an inveterate obstinacy which must have been especially unamiable and irritating to one of Byron's moody and volcanic temper. Her letters to Mrs. Leigh in reply to Moore's *Life of Byron* are certainly open to the charge of self-righteousness.

Byron, on the other hand, had no fault to find, and was, for a long time ready to be reconciled. "I never had," he says, "nor can have any reproach to make to her while with me. Where there is blame it belongs to myself, and if I cannot redeem it, I must bear it." The man who wrote this a skilful woman might surely have won.

Public rumour, of course, assigned a score of causes, each inconsistent with the others, and with common sense. Some are too silly, others too extravagant for the most credulous.

Then ensued that reaction against the once popular idol, that outburst of British virtue which Macaulay in his *Essay* has ridiculed, and which has furnished such merriment to the continental critics. The public took the wife's part. Byron was accused of all possible vices. He was likened to every monster of ancient or modern times. His most innocent actions were perverted. He was in danger of being insulted in Parliament and of being mobbed in the streets of London. "The news papers were filled with lampoons, the theatres shook with execrations. He was excluded from circles where he had been the observed of all observers. All those creeping things that riot in the decay of noble natures hastened to their repast ; and they were right, they did after their kind. It is not every day that the savage energy of aspiring demons is gratified by the agonies of such a spirit, and the degradation of such a name."* It mattered not that evidence as to the truth was wholly wanting ;

* Macaulay's Essay.

invention furnished it in plenty, and hundreds of virtuous and indignant people who knew nothing of the circumstances, believed and repeated stories of his excesses that were absolutely without foundation.

" On what grounds," he afterwards writes (1819), " the public formed their opinion I am not aware, but it was general, and it was decisive. It felt that if what was whispered and muttered and murmured was true, I was unfit for England ; if false, England was unfit for me." On the 25th April, 1816, Byron left England never to return. He left but one true heart behind him, his sister Augusta.

He started in a very luxurious, almost superb style, in a huge coach, and with four or five companions and attendants. Where the money came from is somewhat of a mystery. Newstead was not sold till 1818, and most of the purchase money (£90,000) went to pay off mortgages. He had begun by refusing money for his poetry, but when he found that to be lavish in his pleasures he must labour, he became exacting enough, and for the rest of his life drove hard bargains for his work and for his travelling expenses. He passed through the field of Waterloo (Canto II), up the Rhine to Basle, thence to the vicinity of Geneva, where he met Shelley. Here they lived in proximity during the summer, and made excursions together about the lake. Here was written *The Prisoner*, the third canto of *Childe Harold*, with much other work, and *Manfred* was begun, his great witch drama, supposed by some to reveal the secrets of his unfortunate and unhappy life. " But such reading between the lines would convict Sophocles, Schiller and Shelley of incest, Shakespeare of murder, Milton of blasphemy, Scott of forgery, and Marlowe and Goethe of compact with the Devil."* The Coliseum is its chief descriptive piece.

---

* Nicholl, Biography.

B

The Shelleys left for England in September. Next month Hobhouse and he set out for Italy, crossing the Simplon, and in November we find him at Venice, where Byron remained, with occasional trips to Rome, for three years. Here he plunged into the grossest excesses, associating with the lowest forms of vice that even Venice could afford.* From these gross amours he was rescued by his connection with the young Countess Guiccioli, a connection which the laxness of Italian manners palliated, and which her husband and brother seem to have permitted. His reckless living and debauchery, and his absurd regimen may have helped to shorten his life; they do not seem to have much impaired his productive powers, for he completed the fourth canto of Childe Harold, and besides other work, wrote *Beppo*, *Mazeppa*, and four cantos of *Don Juan*. He was called upon by few Englishmen, for his company was shunned by most tourists. But Shelley came to see him in August, 1818, and about a year after Tom Moore spent five or six days with him and the Countess, and obtained from him the materials for his celebrated *Memoirs*. Shortly after he was prostrated by a fever, and during his convalescence the Count appeared and took away his wife to Ravenna, whither Byron speedily followed. A separation took place between the Count and his wife, (he was sixty and she twenty), and Byron's intimacy with her and her brother was still maintained.

It was at Ravenna that most of his historical dramas were written. The verdict of Jeffrey and other critics of that time has never been reversed—for they are little else than a series of dull declamations. Byron had little dramatic talent; he could not go out of himself. In fact, he never wrote any of his works without some reference, direct or indirect, to himself.

In *Cain*, which under the form of a drama, is but a dialogue between the two halves of his mind, we find him grap-

---

* Shelley, who was a great worshipper of Byron's genius, condemns him for his debaucheries in very strong language.

pling with the religious doubt that had always existed in his mind. It is a protest of a rebellious nature against the decrees of a God who visited on their descendants the sins of Adam and Eve. It was published in December, 1821, about a month after he had left Ravenna and settled in Pisa with the Guicciolis. The poem raised a tempest in England among the clerics. In all (they said) of his works written in Italy there was an ethical looseness which was all the more seductive because conveyed in such vigorous verse and splendid imagery. Not content with thus defying public opinion and living a scandalous life, he was now attacking orthodoxy in her very citadel. The hubbub was fearful—even the critics took fright. Jeffrey, and Campbell, and Heber, even Moore, lamented its irreligious and sceptical tendency. Moore attributed it to Shelley's influence, The truth was that Shelley had no doubt; he was a complete unbeliever in Revelation. Byron *had* doubts, and *Cain* is their expression.

About the same time was published his *Vision of Judgment*, a parody of Southey's *Vision of Judgment*, which is a fulsome panegyric on George III., morally the best, but politically the worst of all the Guelphs. Southey in the preface had made some very severe remarks on *Don Juan*. Byron sent him a challenge, but a friend suppressed it. This poem, however, was his best revenge. Nichol says of it: "It is unmistakably the first of parodies, as the *Iliad* is the first of epics, or the *Pilgrim's Progress* the first of allegories. In execution it is almost perfect. From first to last every epithet hits the white; it is a flame with righteous wrath. No where in such space, save in some of the prose of Swift, is there in England so much scathing satire."

While at Pisa, Byron, Shelley and Leigh Hunt became partners (Byron supplying the money) in a newspaper called the *Liberal*, to be edited by Leigh Hunt in Italy, and published by John Hunt in London. The first number contained the

Vision of Judyment, for which no publisher could be found.* Only four or five numbers followed. Shelley was drowned the next summer. Hunt was a Radical and did not consider defe- rence due to Byron, although a Lord, and shewed it. On the other hand, Hunt was loose in his notions of money matters, and his wife and six children were no doubt trying. So they quarrelled. Hunt has left a mass of ill-natured gossip about Byron's weaknesses.

A little after this Byron, getting into some difficulty with the police, took up his residence near Genoa. To his intimacy with her family is due the Countess of Blessington's *Conversa- tions with Lord Byron*, which are still of considerable interest with regard to some minutiæ of the poet's personal appearance, habits, opinions, etc., at this time.

Byron's literary career was now drawing to a close. A few words concerning his last, and some think his greatest, work will be sufficient. He had been permitted by La Guiccioli to resume *Don Juan* in July, 1822. Cantos 6 to 12 were written at Pisa, 12 to 16 at Genoa, 1823. Perhaps no great work has evoked a greater amount of conflicting criticism. It was received in England with mingled execration and ap- plause. "This extraordinary work is, of course, excluded by its levities and audacities from any comparisons in which the moral element is taken into account, with such poems as the *Night Thoughts*, the *Task*, the *Seasons*, or the *Excursion ;* but looked at simply from an artistic point of view, and without reference to anything except the genius and power of writ- ing which it manifests, it will be difficult to resist its claim to be regarded, on the whole, as the greatest English poem that has appeared either in the present or the preceding century."†

---

* All three were contributors. It was to be an exponent of Liberalism, in poetry, morals and government. John Hunt was prosecuted and fined for publishing the *Vision* in the first number.

† Craik.

Neither in the *Childe Harold* nor in any of the earlier tales can be found more exquisite verse than is scattered through *Don Juan.* That there are in places excess of punning, buffoonery, violations of good taste, and even slang, cannot be denied, but there are also the most caustic and brilliant witticisms, the most sparkling fancy, the most tender and melodious passages. His command over so difficult a metre is almost wonderful, when the everchanging mood of the poem is considered. " From grave to gay, from lively to severe ; " from gloomiest melancholy to the maddest merriment. In it, too, are descriptive passages in Byron's best manner ; a few powerful and vigorous strokes, and the picture stands before us. Nearly always a human figure or personality is introduced into these descriptions who unbosoms to us his feelings, telling us his woes and his belief in the utter hypocrisy of all but himself.

He himself was the chief object in these pictures, whether Harold, Lara, Manfred, or Don Juan. Gloomy, misanthropical, despairing of good, prone to believe in the existence of evil, defiant of established social laws, believing them shams and mostly hypocrisies, proud and relentless of will, insensible either to the censures or to the applause of his fellow creatures, the same character is constantly before us. Much of this sadness and mental striving was feigned.* He was or had reason to be an unhappy man, but he soon found that by parading this unhappiness before the world he made a sensation and secured readers. His success induced him to pretend to much that he didn't feel, and it is often difficult to decide how much is genuine, and how much is mere affectation. One thing is certain that the gloomy egotism of his writings, the mystery of his unhappy domestic relations, the sudden change in popular

---

* In the 2nd Canto of *Childe Harold* he tells us he is insensible to fame or eulogy :
   " Ill may such contest now the spirit move,
     Which heeds nor keen reproof nor partial praise.
Yet a day or two before he published these lines he was childishly elated by the compliments paid to his maiden speech in the House of Lords.—Macaulay.

favour, his exile from England and immoralities abroad, and finally his self-sacrifice in the cause of Greek independence raised an interest in the poet-peer unprecedented in literary history, and have contributed very much to the popularity of his poetry. The power of the spell he once cast over the young and romantic has now nearly gone, and their idolatry has passed away. The one great evil of his life and works has been this, that they tended to leave the impression on youthful minds that there exists some necessary connection between intellectual greatness and moral depravity.

A dispassionate judgment can now be given. Posterity has reversed the verdict as to his superiority over Dryden, and Pope and Wordsworth. Much then admired has been rejected as worthless and even worse, but enough still remains to place him well within the front rank of English poets.

Byron, although aristocratic in taste and very tenacious of the privileges of his rank, was yet a hater of kings and dynasties. He was not the man to write and not act. He took part in the insurrections of 1820, and joined the secret society called the *Carbonari*, and spent money in arms and ammunition. The conspiracies were crushed for the time. Meanwhile the Greek war of liberation had begun, in April, 1821, and by the beginning of 1823, Greece was well nigh independent. Then the tide of success began to ebb, dissensions prevailed among the leaders. An invitation was given to Byron to lead and assist. Tired of his inaction at Genoa, of his periodical and its editor, even perhaps of his mistress, and desirous, as he always was, to shine, he left Guiccioli and Italy in July, 1823, with a couple of guns, arms and ammunition, a medicine chest, some horses and 50,000 Spanish dollars. Arriving at Cephalonia, he kept up a sort of royal state, had a body guard of Albanians, and intimated that if the Greeks wished a King, he would accept the office. He remained there nearly six months, waiting for the dissensions of the Greeks to cease and the promised fleet from the west to relieve Missolonghi, in which attempt the brave Marco Bozzaris had previously fallen. On the journey thither he made an imprudent plunge into the sea and contracted a fever that never wholly left him.

He arrived on the 5th Jan., 1824, and was received with great delight and enthusiasm. During the whole period he was engaged in the struggle, Byron exhibited the rarest qualities of courage, common sense and forbearance, repairing the walls, restraining license, calming dissensions, and acting as paymaster.

But his time was not for long. His constitution had become enfeebled by long continued excesses, and since he arrived in Greece, by exhausting labour. The ground about Missolonghi was a perfect bog, from which pestilential exhalations were constantly rising, and Byron's house was peculiarly ill situated by a muddy creek. He had been living on absurd diet from fear of becoming fat, and had altogether discarded animal food. Through the month of March he became stronger, and took a long ride on the 9th of April, but after becoming heated and drenched in a heavy shower, was obstinate in returning home by a boat. A rheumatic fever set in. Bleeding was then the regular treatment, but he would not consent to it till it was too late. On the 18th he was sinking and delirious, and thought himself at the head of his band of Suliotes. Among his last words were the names of Augusta and Ada. Next day, 19th April, 1824, his soul passed into eternity, and England had lost one of her greatest poets and Greece her noblest friend.

CHARACTERISTICS OF BYRON'S STYLE.

Vocabulary—Is extensive, largely Saxon, and monosyllabic, more especially in the *Prisoner of Chillon*. This accounts for the strength and vividness of much of his poetry, *e. g.*, *P. C.*, stanzas 9, 13, and *C. II.*, II., stanza 95, III., stanzas 1, 2. The use of certain archaisms was perhaps suggested by Percy's *Reliques* or Thomson's *Castle of Indolence*. It consists more in antiquated spelling than in the use of words which are obsolete. In Canto I. they occur most frequently, in Canto II. there are very few, and in Cantos III. and IV. hardly any at all. They are, as a rule, mentioned in the notes.

Dramatic Power.—In this Byron was wholly wanting. He could portray but one character. *Harold, the Giaour, Conrad, Lara,* and *Don Juan* are but varieties of the same man slightly altered by age, by education, or by environment. They are universally thought to be, and by Byron were no doubt desired to be, fit characterizations of himself : " A man proud, moody, cynical, with defiance on his brow and misery in his heart, a scorner of his kind, implacable in revenge, yet capable of deep and strong affection. His women, like his men, are all of one breed, women all softness and gentleness, loving to caress and be caressed, but capable of being transformed by passion into tigresses." The poet cannot withdraw himself from view as narrator, and allow his men and women to disclose their own character by their action and their words ; and the dialogue of his dramas is either a declamation or a soliloquy. He has, however, sought to imitate in some measure the action of the drama, and to relieve the monotony of descriptive narration and monologue by apostrophe, by interrogation, by exclamation, and by the use of demonstratives and pronouns of the first and second person.

See in illustration, *P. C.*, ll. 26, 39, and elsewhere ; *C. II.*, II., stanzas 73, 76, III., 1, *et seq.*, 19 and 22. This effect, too, is secured by his skilful

Transitions from one subject to another. In *C. II.* there is absolutely no unity of plot or design. Mere episodes of feeling, or bits of description which lead on to feeling, are connected only by the personality of the poet, who loves so much to expose them to public gaze. The reader may judge of their artistic effect for himself by noting the following :—The song of Tambourgi, between the subjects of Albania and Greece, preceding II., 73, stanzas 77-78, 81-82, 94-95, III., 16-17, 20-21, 45-46, 51-52. In the *P. C.*, which has more of the narrative style, and more interest and unity, there is less necessity for such devices.

Use of Contrast.—Contrast, in various ways, is one of the strongest characteristics of Byron's poetry. It would seem that his character, which somebody has described as a bundle of opposites, was reflected to some extent in this manner of writing. Sometimes it is seen in mere words, *C. II.*, II., ll. 694, 838-9, III., 265, 287, *P. C.*, 17 ; often in opposing pictures, *C. H.*, II., 797-8, III., 239, 250, and in the arrangement of subjects.

Alliteration.—This is elaborately employed by Byron, and seemingly with design. In many cases it is a fault, and but for the natural strength and condensation of his style would be a great weakness. It occurs so frequently that it cannot be missed. We refer to a few instances—*C. II.*, II., 746, 781, 788, 849, 864, *et seq.*, III., 215, 325, *P. C.*, 20, 21, 223.

Correspondence of Sound to Meaning.—*C. II.*, II., 79, III., 287, slowness and delay ; II., 798, III., 207, rapidity. Other cases have been mentioned in the notes.

Personification— Is too common to require special notice. As instances we have II., 742, 702 ; III., 424, 51, 193-4, 453.

Periphrases.—Byron is ingenious in expressions or epithets for common objects.   Note that for a bee and bee-hive, *C. II.*, II., 823-4, a cage, III., 133, a bow window, III., 199, a dance, III., 181, Arctic summer, *P. C.*, 85, the bird, *P. C.*, 284, the moon, II., 760.

Similes.—There are not many of any moment in Cantos I. and II. ; but they are frequent and more elaborate in III. and IV.   Examples—III., 129, 141, 289, 394, and III., 280, where there are several in succession : *P. C.*, 361-2, 293-4.

Metaphor.- This, the most common figure in Byron's, or indeed in most poetry, is naturally preferred to the simile by so energetic and condensed a writer.   Wherever the comparison is easy to be seen, metaphor is to be preferred, as it economises the attention.   Byron uses this figure so much that special mention of instances is not necessary.   Of the other less frequent figures we may note climax, III., 197 ; metonymy, III., 556 ; anastrophe, III., 293 ; and repetition, as in *P. C.*, 126, 240.   Other examples are mentioned in the notes, where deemed of sufficient importance.

Grammatical Peculiarities.—Byron was an exceedingly rapid writer, and spent little time in correcting and polishing his verse ; consequently we find some loose constructions.   The sense, rather than the form, is often allowed to guide the reader. Some of these are—using participles with no connection, *e. g.*, awaking, III., 5 ; untaught, III., 59 ; anacoluthon, II., 866, III., 429 ; ellipsis, III., 429 ; condensed expressions, II., 592, III., 322 ; zeugma, III., 322 ; anticipation, II., 783.

POSITION AND INFLUENCE OF BYRON'S POETRY.

Towards the middle of the 18th Century poetry had degenerated into a "a mere mechanic art," and the feeble successors and imitators of Pope could not hope to attain to his brilliant wit, his compact expression, and his wonderful power of reasoning in rhyme.

> "Manner was all in all, whate'er was writ,
> The substitute for genius, taste, and wit."

The revolt against a manner of writing which was in conformity not with dictates of nature and reason, but with absurd poetical canons respecting only the form and the fashion had for its great leader the poet Cowper. The first effective agent in awakening the new taste was, perhaps Percy's *Reliques*, 1765. The strength of the new movement was shown by the success attendant on the forgeries of McPherson and Chatterton, and was helped forward by Thomas Warton's *History of Poetry*, (1774). This work, one of our greatest literary histories, may be said to have founded a new school of criticism, which should depend for poetical principles on nature and not on the classical models of Greece and Rome. It was about this time, too, that our great peasant poet, Burns, appeared, (1786), whose verse, full of passion, if not of imagination, shewed that in the sister kingdom also there was a revolt against the artificial style, the languid manner, and "creamy smoothness" of the age gone by.

The causes of this literary revival have been variously stated, and it seems that according to the criticism and history of to-day no new work can appear in any department of thought or action, without being considered as the product of some general movement of the human mind, of which it is the exponent and result. Thus the great religious revival of the last century was but the reappearance of the old Puritan morality and ways of

thinking which had preceded the Restoration, and been sub-
merged by it, but had now again come to the surface to assert
their influence over religion and literature.   In politics that
influence was of little effect.   Of course it was found on the
side of William in 1688.

When the Parliament gained its victory over the Crown, set
up again the ancient landmarks of the constitution, and reformed the abuses of the last two Stuarts, it forgot to reform
itself.   It was in its unreformed condition out of touch and
harmony with the people, and not the ready reflex of the
national mind.   Thus it became possible for George III. to
manage it at his will, in consequence of which our finest colony
was lost, and Emancipation postponed half a century.   Thus it
was that the moral energy of Puritanism took a religious and
literary direction, inspired the great apostle of Methodism, and
flowed in rugged numbers from the pen of the Bard of Olney.

The Lakists, Wordsworth, Southey, and Coleridge, were successors of Cowper, as Byron has been said to be the successor of
Burns.   They all agreed in opposing freedom to formality, in
substituting new aims and methods for the old.   They broke
with the old school as Protestantism broke with the old Church,
but they separated again.   For the Lakists set up a new principle as to the subject matter of poetry.   Their leanings were
towards order, they celebrated the virtues of gentleness, of en-
during courage and of humility.   "The others were the
Radicals of the movement.   Dissatisfied with the existing order,
their sympathies were with strong will and passion and defiant
independence.   These found their master-types in Shelley and
Byron." *   It is in Byron's two greatest works, *Childe Harold*
and *Don Juan*, that we best see the influence of the revolutionary spirit.

---

* Nichol.

Byron, although a participator in the great literary commotion at the beginning of this century, was, strange to say, blind to the true meaning of the change that had come over the spirit of letters, and quite over valued the work of the artificial or classical school. He thought poorly of Chaucer and Spencer. He even thought of Churchill and Gifford as their superiors! He was no great admirer of Shakspeare; but Pope was the object of his devoted idolatry.

"Neither time, nor distance, nor grief, nor age, can ever diminish my veneration for him who is the great moral poet of all times, of all climes, of all feelings and of all stages of existence. Your whole generation is not worth one canto of the *Dunciad.*"

Yet, while he was thus extravagantly expressing his admiration, and while his imitations were complete failures, he was writing verse in his own manner which, if not so polished and smooth, had vastly greater energy and impressive power. Of Wordsworth he could hardly speak with patience; he condemns the *Lyrical Ballads* as miserably inadequate to his ability, and sets down a good part of the *Excursion* as twaddle.

"But Byron the critic and Byron the poet were two very different men. Though he said much of his contempt for mankind, his literary career indicated nothing of that lonely and unsocial pride which he affected. We cannot conceive him like Milton or Wordsworth, labouring on a poem in the full assurance that it would be unpopular and in full assurance that it would be immortal. He has said by the mouth of one of his heroes, that "he must serve who fain would sway." He was the creature of his age, and whenever he had lived he would have been the creature of his age. Under Charles I, Byron would have been more quaint than Donne. Under George I, the monotonous smoothness of Byron's versification and the terseness of his expression would have made Pope himself envious.

As it was he was the man of the last thirteen years of the eighteenth, and of the first twenty-three years of the nineteenth century. He belonged half to the old and half to the new school of poetry. His personal taste led him to the former ; his thirst for praise to the latter ; his talents were equally suited to both. His fame was a common ground on which the zealots on both sides, Gifford for example, and Shelley, might meet. He was the representative, not of either literary party, but of both at once and of their conflict, and of the victory by which that conflict was terminated. His poetry fills and measures the whole of that vast interval through which our literature has moved since the time of Johnson. It touches the *Essay on Man* at one extremity, and the *Excursion* at the other."—Macaulay.

On the Continent Byron's fame stands next to that of Shak-speare and Milton. For several years he was the most noted literary figure in Europe. His works have been translated into every European tongue, and his reputation has maintained its high rank without the fluctuations that have overcome the English mind. Goethe says, "the English may think of him as they please ; this is certain, they can show no living poet that is to be compared with him ;" and again, "the grandeur of Byron must certainly tend towards culture. We should take care not to be always looking for it in the decidedly pure and moral. Every thing that is great promotes cultivation as soon as we are aware of it." Taine speaking of the romantic movement, says : "One alone, Byron, attains the submit. He is so great and so English that from him alone we shall learn more truths of his country and his age than from all the rest together." Altogether the continental critics are wonderfully unanimous in assigning a very high place to Byron's poetry.

THE PRISONER OF CHILLON.

SONNET ON CHILLON.

ETERNAL Spirit of the chainless Mind!
    Brightest in dungeons, Liberty! thou art,
    For there thy habitation is the heart—
The heart which love of thee alone can bind;
And when thy sons to fetters are consigned—
    To fetters, and the damp vault's dayless gloom,
    Their country conquers with their martyrdom,
And Freedom's fame finds wings on every wind.
Chillon! thy prison is a holy place,
    And thy sad floor an altar—for 'twas trod,
Until his very steps have left a trace
    Worn, as if thy cold pavement were a sod,
By Bonnivard! May none those marks efface!
    For they appeal from tyranny to God.

I.

My hair is grey, but not with years,
    Nor grew it white
    In a single night,
As men's have grown from sudden fears:
My limbs are bowed, though not with toil,   5
    But rusted with a vile repose,
For they have been a dungeon's spoil,
    And mine has been the fate of those
To whom the goodly earth and air
Are banned, and barred—forbidden fare;   10

But this was for my father's faith
I suffered chains and courted death;
That father perished at the stake
For tenets he would not forsake;
And for the same his lineal race   15
In darkness found a dwelling-place;
We were seven—who now are one,
  Six in youth, and one in age,
Finished as they had begun,
  Proud of Persecution's rage;   20
One in fire, and two in field,
Their belief with blood have sealed,
Dying as their father died,
For the God their foes denied;
Three were in a dungeon cast,   25
Of whom this wreck is left the last.

II.

There are seven pillars of Gothic mould,
In Chillon's dungeons deep and old,
There are seven columns massy and gray,
Dim with a dull imprisoned ray,   30
A sunbeam which hath lost its way,
And through the crevice and the cleft
Of the thick wall is fallen and left;
Creeping o'er the floor so damp,
Like a marsh's meteor lamp: 35
And in each pillar there is a ring,
  And in each ring there is a chain;
That iron is a cankering thing,
  For in these limbs its teeth remain,
With marks that will not wear away,   40
Till I have done with this new day,
Which now is painful to these eyes,

Which have not seen the sun so rise
For years—I cannot count them o'er,
I lost their long and heavy score   45
When my last brother drooped and died,
And I lay living by his side.

III.

They chained us each to a column stone,
And we were three—yet, each alone ;
We could not move a single pace,   50
We could not see each other's face,
But with that pale and livid light
That made us strangers in our sight :
And thus together—yet apart,
Fettered in hand, but joined in heart;   55
'Twas still some solace, in the dearth
Of the pure elements of earth,
To hearken to each other's speech,
And each turn comforter to each
With some new hope or legend old,   60
Or song heroically bold ;
But even these at length grew cold.
Our voices took a dreary tone,   .
An echo of the dungeon stone,
A grating sound, not full and free   65
    As they of yore were wont to be ;
    It might be fancy, but to me
They never sounded like our own.

IV.

I was the eldest of the three ;
    And to uphold and cheer the rest   70
    I ought to do—and did my best—
    And each did well in his degree.
C

The youngest, whom my father loved,
Because our mother's brow was given
To him, with eyes as blue as heaven—   75
  For him my soul was sorely moved ;
And truly might it be distressed
To see such bird in such a nest ;
For he was beautiful as day—
  (When day was beautiful to me   80
  As to young eagles, being free)—
  A polar day which will not see
A sunset till its summer's gone,
  Its sleepless summer of long light,
The snow-clad offspring of the sun :   85
  And thus he was as pure and bright,
And in his natural spirit gay,
With tears for nought but others' ills,
And then they flowed like mountain rills,
Unless he could assuage the woe   90
Which he abhorred to view below.

v.

The other was as pure of mind,
But formed to combat with his kind ;
Strong in his frame, and of a mood
Which 'gainst the world in war had stood,   95
And perished in the foremost rank
  With joy :—but not in chains to pine :
His spirit withered with their clank,
  I saw it silently decline—
  And so perchance in sooth did mine :   100
But yet I forced it on to cheer
Those relics of a home so dear.
He was a hunter of the hills,

Had followed there the deer and wolf;
To him this dungeon was a gulf, 105
And fettered feet the worst of ills.

VI.

Lake Leman lies by Chillon's walls:
A thousand feet in depth below.
Its massy waters meet and flow;
Thus much the fathom-line was sent 110
From Chillon's snow-white battlement,
  Which round about the wave inthrals
A double dungeon wall and wave
Have made—and like a living grave.
Below the surface of the lake 115
The dark vault lies wherein we lay.
We heard it ripple night and day;
  Sounding o'er our heads it knocked;
And I have felt the winter's spray
Wash through the bars when winds were high 120
And wanton in the happy sky;
  And then the very rock hath rocked,
  And I have felt it shake, unshocked,
Because I could have smiled to see
The death that would have set me free. 125

VII.

I said my nearer brother pined,
I said his mighty heart declined,
He loathed and put away his food:
It was not that 'twas coarse and rude,
For we were used to hunter's fare, 130

And for the like had little care :
The milk drawn from the mountain goat
Was changed for water from the moat,
Our bread was such as captives' tears
Have moistened many a thousand years,   135
Since man first pent his fellow-men
Like brutes within an iron den ;
But what were these to us or him ?
These wasted not his heart or limb ;
My brother's soul was of that mould   140
Which in a palace had grown cold,
Had his free breathing been denied
The range of the steep mountain's side ;
But why delay the truth ?—he died.
I saw, and could not hold his head,   145
Nor reach his dying hand—nor dead—
Though hard I strove, but strove in vain,
To rend and gnash my bonds in twain.
He died—and they unlocked his chain,
And scooped for him a shallow grave   150
Even from the cold earth of our cave.
I begged them, as a boon, to lay
His corse in dust whereon the day
Might shine—it was a foolish thought,
But then within my brain it wrought,   155
That even in death his free-born breast
In such a dungeon could not rest.
I might have spared my idle prayer—
They coldly laughed—and laid him there :
The flat and turfless earth above   160
The being we so much did love ;
His empty chain above it leant,
Such murder's fitting monument !

VIII.

But he, the favourite and the flower,
Most cherished since his natal hour,   165
His mother's image in fair face,
The infant love of all his race,
His martyred father's dearest thought,
My latest care, for whom I sought
To hoard my life, that his might be   170
Less wretched now, and one day free;
He, too, who yet had held untired
A spirit natural or inspired—
He, too, was struck, and day by day
Was withered on the stalk away.   175
O God! it is a fearful thing
To see the human soul take wing
In any shape, in any mood:
I've seen it rushing forth in blood,
I've seen it on the breaking ocean   180
Strive with a swoln convulsive motion,
I've seen the sick and ghastly bed
Of Sin delirious with its dread:
But these were horrors—this was woe
Unmixed with such—but sure and slow.   185
He faded, and so calm and meek,
So softly worn, so sweetly weak,
So tearless, yet so tender, kind,
And grieved for those he left behind;
With all the while a cheek whose bloom   190
Was as a mockery of the tomb,
Whose tints are gently sunk away
As a departing rainbow's ray;
An eye of most transparent light,
That almost made the dungeon bright,   195
And not a word of murmur, not

q v. 74.

A groan o'er his untimely lot,—
A little talk of better days,
A little hope my own to raise,
For I was sunk in silence—lost   200
In this last loss, of all the most ;
And then the sighs he would suppress
Of fainting nature's feebleness,
More slowly drawn, grew less and less ;
I listened, but I could not hear ;   205 ·
I called, for I was wild with fear ;
I knew 'twas hopeless, but my dread
Would not be thus admonished ;
I called, and thought I heard a sound—
I burst my chain with one strong bound,   210
And rushed to him :—I found him not,
I only stirred in this black spot,
I only lived, *I* only drew
The accursed breath of dungeon-dew ;
The last, the sole, the dearest link   215
Between me and the eternal brink,
Which bound me to my failing race,
Was broken in this fatal place.
One on the earth, and one beneath—
My brothers—both had ceased to breathe :   220
I took that hand which lay so still,
Alas ! my own was full as chill ;
I had not strength to stir, or strive,
But felt that I was still alive—
A frantic feeling, when we know   225
That what we love shall ne'er be so.
      I know not why
      I could not die,
I had no earthly hope, but faith,
And that forbade a selfish death.   230

IX.

What next befell me then and there
  I know not well—I never knew—
First came the loss of light, and air,
  ' And then of darkness too :
I had no thought, no feeling—none—   235
Among the stones I stood a stone,
And was, scarce conscious what I wist,
As shrubless crags within the mist ;
For all was blank, and bleak, and gray.
It was not night, it was not day,   240
It was not even the dungeon-light,
So hateful to my heavy sight,
But vacancy absorbing space,
And fixedness, without a place ;
There were no stars, no earth, no time,   245
No check, no change, no good, no crime,
But silence, and a stirless breath
Which neither was of life nor death ;
A sea of stagnant idleness,
Blind, boundless, mute, and motionless !   250

X.

A light broke in upon my brain,—
  It was the carol of a bird ;
It ceased, and then it came again,
  The sweetest song ear ever heard,
And mine was thankful till my eyes   255
Ran over with the glad surprise,
And they that moment could not see
I was the mate of misery.
But then by dull degrees came back
My senses to their wonted track ;   260

I saw the dungeon walls and floor
Close slowly round me as before,
I saw the glimmer of the sun
Creeping as it before had done,
But through the crevice where it came,   265
That bird was perched, as fond and tame,
   And tamer than upon the tree ;
A lovely bird, with azure wings,
And song that said a thousand things,
   And seemed to say them all for me !   270
I never saw its like before,
I ne'er shall see its likeness more :
It seemed, like me, to want a mate,
But was not half so desolate,
And it was come to love me when   275
None lived to love me so again,
And cheering from my dungeon's brink,
And brought me back to feel and think.
I know not if it late were free,
   Or broke its cage to perch on mine,   280
But knowing well captivity,
   Sweet bird ! I could not wish for thine !
Or if it were, in winged guise,
A visitant from Paradise ; •
For—Heaven forgive that thought ! the while   285
Which made me both to weep and smile—
I sometimes deemed that it might be
My brother's soul come down to me.
But then at last away it flew,
And then 'twas mortal well I knew,   290
For he would never thus have flown,
And left me twice so doubly lone,
Lone as the corse within its shroud,

Lone as a solitary cloud,
   A single cloud on a sunny day,   295
While all the rest of heaven is clear,
A frown upon the atmosphere,
That hath no business to appear
   When skies are blue and earth is gay.

XI.

A kind of change came in my fate,   300
My keepers grew compassionate ;
I know not what had made them so,
They were inured to sights of woe,
But so it was :—my broken chain
With links unfastened did remain,   305
And it was liberty to stride
Along my cell from side to side,
And up and down, and then athwart,
And tread it over every part ;
And round the pillars one by one,   310
Returning where my walk begun,
Avoiding only, as I trod,
My brothers' graves without a sod ;
For if I thought with heedless tread
My step profaned their lowly bed,   315
My breath came gaspingly and thick,
And my crushed heart fell blind and sick.

XII.

I made a footing in the wall,
   It was not therefrom to escape,
For I had buried one and all   320
   Who loved me in a human shape ;
And the whole earth would henceforth be
A wider prison unto me :

No child, no sire, no kin had I,
No partner in my misery ;   325
I thought of this, and I was glad,
For thought of them had made me mad ;
But I was curious to ascend
To my barred windows, and to bend
Once more, upon the mountains high,   330
The quiet of a loving eye.

XIII.

I saw them, and they were the same,
They were not changed like me in frame ;
I saw their thousand years of snow
On high—their wide long lake below,   335
And the blue Rhone in fullest flow ;
I heard the torrents leap and gush
O'er channelled rock and broken bush ;
I saw the white-walled distant town,
And whiter sails go skimming down ;   340
And then there was a little isle,
Which in my very face did smile,
    The only one in view ;
A small green isle, it seemed no more,
Scarce broader than my dungeon floor,   345
But in it there were three tall trees,
And o'er it blew the mountain breeze,
And by it there were waters flowing,
And on it there were young flowers growing,
    Of gentle breath and hue.   350
The fish swam by the castle wall,
And they seeemed joyous each and all ;
The eagle rode the rising blast,
Methought he never flew so fast
As then to me he seemed to fly,   355

And then new tears came in my eye,
And I felt troubled—and would fain
I had not left my recent chain ;
And when I did descend again,
The darkness of my dim abode   360
Fell on me as a heavy load ;
It was as is a new-dug grave,
Closing o'er one we sought to save,—
And yet my glance, too much oppressed,
Had almost need of such a rest.   365

XIV.

It might be months, or years, or days,
     I kept no count I took no note,
I had no hope my eyes to raise,
     And clear them of their dreary mote ;
At last men came to set me free,   370
     I asked not why, and recked not where ;
It was at length the same to me,
Fettered or fetterless to be ;
     I learned to love despair.
And thus when they appeared at last,   375
And all my bonds aside were cast,
These heavy walls to me had grown
A hermitage—and all my own !
And half I felt as they were come
To tear me from a second home ;   380
With spiders I had friendship made,
And watched them in their sullen trade,
Had seen the mice by moonlight play,
And why should I feel less than they ?

We were all inmates of one place,   385
And I, the monarch of each race,
Had power to kill—yet, strange to tell !
In quiet we had learned to dwell ;
My very chains and I grew friends,
So much a long communion tends   390
To make us what we are :—even I
Regained my freedom with a sigh.

CHILDE HAROLD.

LXXIII.

Fair Greece ! sad relic of departed worth !
Immortal, though no more ; though fallen, great !
Who now shall lead thy scattered children forth,   695
And long accustomed bondage uncreate ?
Not such thy sons who whilome did await,
The hopeless warriors of a willing doom,
In bleak Thermopylæ's'sepulchral strait—
Oh ! who that gallant spirit shall resume,   700
Leap from Eurotas' banks, and call thee from the tomb ?

LXXIV.

Spirit of freedom ! when on Phyle's brow
Thou sat'st with Thrasybulus and his train,
Couldst thou forebode the dismal hour which now
Dims the green beauties of thine Attic plain ?   705
Not thirty tyrants now enforce the chain,
But every carle can lord it o'er thy land ;
Nor rise thy sons, but idly rail in vain,
Trembling beneath the scourge of Turkish hand ;
From birth till death enslaved ; in word, in deed, un-
     manned.   710

LXXV.

In all save form alone, how changed ! and who
That marks the fire still sparkling in each eye,.
Who would but deem their bosoms burned anew

With thy unquenchèd beam, lost Liberty!
And many dream withal the hour is nigh   715
That gives them back their father's heritage:
For foreign arms and aid they fondly sigh,
Nor solely dare encounter hostile rage,
Or tear their name defiled from Slavery's mournful page.

LXXVI.

Hereditary bondsmen! know ye not   720
Who would be free themselves must strike the blow?
By their right arms the conquest must be wrought?
Will Gaul or Muscovite redress ye? no!
True, they may lay your proud despoilers low,
But not for you will Freedom's altars flame.   725
Shades of the Helots! triumph o'er your foe!
Greece! change thy lords, thy state is still the same;
Thy glorious day is o'er, but not thy years of shame.

LXXVII.

The city won for Allah from the Giaour,
The Giaour from Othman's race again may wrest: 730
And the Serai's impenetrable tower
Receive the fiery Frank, her former guest;
Or Wahab's rebel brood, who dared divest
The prophet's tomb of all its pious spoil,
May wind their path of blood along the West;   735
But ne'er will freedom seek this fated soil,
But slave succeed to slave through years of endless toil.

LXXVIII.

Yet mark their mirth—ere lenten days begin,
That penance which their holy rites prepare
To shrive from man his weight of mortal sin,   740

By daily abstinence and nightly prayer:
But ere his sackcloth garb Repentance wear,
Some days of joyaunce are decreed to all,
To take of pleasaunce each his secret share,
In motley robe to dance at masking ball, 745
And join the mimic train of merry Carnival.

LXXIX.

And whose more rife with merriment than thine,
Oh Stamboul! once the empress of their reign?
Though turbans now pollute Sophia's shrine,
And Greece her very altars eyes in vain: 750
(Alas! her woes will still pervade my strain!)
Gay were her minstrels once, for free her throng,
All felt the common joy they now must feign,
Nor oft I've seen such sight, nor heard such song,
As wooed the eye, and thrilled the Bosphorus along. 755

LXXX.

Loud was the lightsome tumult on the shore,
Oft Music changed, but never ceased her tone,
And timely echoed back the measured oar,
And rippling waters made a pleasant moan :
The Queen of tides on high consenting shone, 760
And when a transient breeze swept o'er the wave,
'Twas, as if darting from her heavenly throne,
A brighter glance her form reflected gave,
Till sparkling billows seemed to light the banks they lave.

LXXXI.

Glanced many a light caique along the foam, 765
Danced on the shore the daughters of the land,
No thought had man or maid of rest or home,

While many a languid eye and thrilling hand
Exchanged the look few bosoms may withstand,
Or gently prest, returned the pressure still :   770
Oh Love ! young Love ! bound in thy rosy band,
Let sage or cynic prattle as he will.,
These hours, and only these, redeem Life's years of ill !

LXXXII.

But, midst the throng in merry masquerade,
Lurk there no hearts that throb with secret pain,   775
Even through the closest searment half betrayed ?
To such the gentle murmurs of the main
Seem to re-echo all they mourn in vain ;
To such the gladness of the gamesome crowd
Is source of wayward thought and stern disdain :   780
How do they loathe the laughter idly loud,
And long to change the robe of revel for the shroud !

LXXXIII.

This must he feel, the true-born son of Greece,
If Greece one true-born patriot still can boast :
Not such as prate of war, but skulk in peace,   785
The bondsman's peace, who sighs for all he lost,
Yet with smooth smile his tyrant can accost,
And wield the slavish sickle, not the sword :
Ah ! Greece ! they love thee least who owe thee most—
Their birth, their blood, and that sublime record   790
Of hero sires, who shame thy now degenerate horde !

LXXXIV.

When riseth Lacedemon's hardihood,
When Thebes Epaminondas rears again,
When Athens' children are with hearts endued,

When Grecian mothers shall give birth to men, 795
Then may'st thou be restored ; but not till then.
A thousand years scarce serve to form a state ;
An hour may lay it in the dust : and when
Can man its shattered splendour renovate,
Recall its virtues back, and vanquish Time and Fate ? 800

LXXXV.

And yet how lovely in thine age of woe,
Land of lost gods and godlike men, art thou !
Thy vales of evergreen, thy hills of snow,
Proclaim thee Nature's varied favourite now :
Thy fanes, thy temples to thy surface bow, 805
Commingling slowly with heroic earth,
Broke by the share of every rustic plough :
So perish monuments of mortal birth,
So perish all in turn, save well-recorded Worth ;

LXXXVI.

Save where some solitary column mourns 810
Above its prostrate brethren of the cave ;
Save where Tritonia's airy shrine adorns
Colonna's cliff, and gleams along the wave ;
Save o'er some warrior's half-forgotten grave,
Where the gray stones and unmolested grass 815
Ages, but not oblivion, feebly brave ;
While strangers only not regardless pass,
Lingering like me, perchance, to gaze, and sigh " Alas ! "

LXXXVII.

Yet are thy skies as blue, thy crags as wild ;
Sweet are thy groves, and verdant are thy fields, 820
Thine olive ripe as when Minerva smiled,
And still his honeyed wealth Hymettus yields ;
 D

There the blithe bee his fragrant fortress builds,
The freeborn wanderer of thy mountain-air ;
Apollo still thy long, long summer gilds,   825
Still in his beam Mendeli's marbles glare ;
Art, Glory, Freedom fail, but Nature still is fair.

LXXXVIII.

Where'er we tread, 'tis haunted, holy ground ;
No earth of thine is lost in vulgar mould,
But one vast realm of wonder spreads around,   830
And all the Muse's tales seem truly told,
Till the sense aches with gazing to behold
The scenes our earliest dreams have dwelt upon ;
Each hill and dale, each deepening glen and wold
Defies the power which crushed thy temples gone :   835
Age shakes Athena's tower, but spares gray Marathon.

LXXXIX.

The sun, the soil, but not the slave, the same ;
Unchanged in all except its foreign lord ;
Preserves alike its bounds and boundless fame
The Battle-field, where Persia's victim horde   840
First bowed beneath the brunt of Hellas' sword,
As on the morn to distant Glory dear,
When Marathon became a magic word ;
Which uttered, to the hearer's eye appear
The camp, the host, the fight, the conqueror's career.   845

XC.

The flying Mede, his shaftless broken bow ;
The fiery Greek, his red pursuing spear ;
Mountains above, Earth's, Ocean's plain below ;
Death in the front, Destruction in the rear !
Such was the scene—what now remaineth here ?   850

What sacred trophy marks the hallowed ground,
Recording Freedom's smile and Asia's tear ?
The rifled urn, the violated mound,
The dust thy courser's hoof, rude stranger ! spurns around.

XCI.

Yet to the remnants of thy splendour past   855
Shall pilgrims, pensive, but unwearied, throng ;
Long shall the voyager, with th' Ionian blast,
Hail the bright clime of battle and of song ;
Long shall thine annals and immortal tongue
Fill with thy fame the youth of many a shore ;   860
Boast of the aged ! lesson of the young !
Which sages venerate and bards adore,
As Pallas and the Muse unveil their awful lore.

XCII.

The parted bosom clings to wonted home,
If aught that's kindred cheer the welcome hearth ;   865
He that is lonely, hither let him roam,
And gaze complacent on congenial earth.
Greece is no lightsome land of social mirth :
But he whom Sadness sootheth may abide,
And scarce regret the region of his birth,   870
When wandering slow by Delphi's sacred side,
Or gazing o'er the plains where Greek and Persian died.

XCIII.

Let such approach this consecrated land,
And pass in peace along the magic waste ;
But spare its relics—let no busy hand   875
Deface the scenes, already how defaced !
Not for such purpose were these altars placed :
Revere the remnants nations once revered :

So may our country's name be undisgraced,
So may'st thou prosper where thy youth was reared,   880
By every honest joy of love and life endeared !

XCIV.

For thee, who thus in too protracted song
Hast soothed thine idlesse with inglorious lays,
Soon shall thy voice be lost amid the throng
Of louder minstrels in these later days :   885
To such resign the strife for fading bays—
Ill may such contest now the spirit move
Which heeds nor keen reproach nor partial praise,
Since cold each kinder heart that might approve,
And none are left to please when none are left to love. 890

XCV.

Thou too art gone, thou loved and lovely one !
Whom youth and youth's affections bound to me ;
Who did for me what none beside have done,
Nor shrank from one albeit unworthy thee.
What is my being ? thou hast ceased to be !   895
Nor staid to welcome here thy wanderer home,
Who mourns o'er hours which we no more shall see—
Would they had never been, or were to come !
Would he had ne'er returned to find fresh cause to roam !

XCVI.

Oh ! ever loving, lovely, and beloved !   900
How selfish Sorrow ponders on the past,
And clings to thoughts now better far removed !
But Time shall tear thy shadow from me last.
All thou couldst have of mine, stern Death ! thou hast ;
The parent, friend, and now the more than friend ;   905
Ne'er yet for one thine arrows flew so fast,

And grief with grief continuing still to blend,
Hath snatched the little joy that life had yet to lend.

XCVII.

Then must I plunge again into the crowd,
And follow all that Peace disdains to seek ?   910
Where Revel calls, and Laughter, vainly loud,
False to the heart, distorts the hollow cheek,
To leave the flagging spirit doubly weak ;
Still o'er the features, which perforce they cheer,
To feign the pleasure or conceal the pique ?   915
Smiles form the channel of a future tear,
Or raise the writhing lip with ill-dissembled sneer.

XCVIII.

What is the worst of woes that wait on age ?
What stamps the wrinkle deeper on the brow ?
To view each loved one blotted from life's page,   820
And be alone on earth, as I am now.
Before the Chastener humbly let me bow,
O'er hearts divided and o'er hopes destroyed :
Roll on, vain days ! full reckless may ye flow,
Since Time hath reft whate'er my soul enjoyed,   925
And with the ills of Eld mine earlier years alloyed.

I.

Is thy face like thy mother's, my fair child !
ADA ! sole daughter of my house and heart ?
When last I saw thy young blue eyes they smiled,
And then we parted,—not as now we part,
But with a hope.—   5
                  Awaking with a start,
The waters heave around me ; and on high
The winds lift up their voices : I depart,
Whither I know not ; but the hour's gone by,
When Albion's lessening shores could grieve or glad mine
    eye.   10

II.

Once more upon the waters ! yet once more !
And the waves bound beneath me as a steed
That knows his rider.   Welcome to the roar !
Swift be their guidance, wheresoe'er it lead !
Though the strained mast should quiver as a reed,   15
And the rent canvas fluttering strew the gale,
Still must I on ; for I am as a weed,
Flung from the rock, on Ocean's foam to sail
Where'er the surge may sweep, the tempest's breath prevail.

III.

In my youth's summer I did sing of One,   20
The wandering outlaw of his own dark mind ;
Again I seize the theme, then but begun,
And bear it with me, as the rushing wind

Bears the cloud onwards ; in that Tale I find
The furrows of long thought, and dried-up tears,   25
Which, ebbing, leave a sterile track behind,
O'er which all heavily the journeying years
Plod the last sands of life,—where not a flower appears.

IV.

Since my young days of passion—joy, or pain,
Perchance my heart and harp have lost a string,   30
And both may jar : it may be, that in vain
I would essay as I have sung to sing.
Yet, though a dreary strain, to this I cling ;
So that it wean me from the weary dream
Of selfish grief or gladness—so it fling   35
Forgetfulness around me—it shall seem
To me, though to none else, a not ungrateful theme.

V.

He, who grown aged in this world of woe,
In deeds, not years, piercing the depths of life,
So that no wonder waits him ; nor below   40
Can love or sorrow, fame, ambition, strife,
Cut to his heart again with the keen knife
Of silent, sharp endurance : he can tell
Why thought seeks refuge in lone caves, yet rife
With airy images, and shapes which dwell   45
Still unimpaired, though old, in the soul's haunted cell.

VI.

'Tis to create, and in creating live
A being more intense, that we endow
With form our fancy, gaining as we give
The life we image, even as I do now.   50

What am I? Nothing: but not so art thou,
Soul of my thought! with whom I traverse earth,
Invisible but gazing, as I glow
Mixed with thy spirit, blended with thy birth,
And feeling still with thee in my crushed feelings' dearth. 55

VII.

Yet must I think less wildly :—I *have* thought
Too long and darkly, till my brain became,
In its own eddy boiling and o'er wrought,
A whirling gulf of phantasy and flame :
And thus, untaught in youth my heart to tame,   60
My springs of life were poisoned.   'Tis too late !
Yet am I changed ; though still enough the same
In strength to bear what time can not abate,
And feed on bitter fruits without accusing Fate.

VIII.

Something too much of this :—but now 'tis past,   65
And the spell closes with its silent-seal.
Long absent HAROLD re-appears at last ;
He of the breast which fain no more would feel,
Wrung with the wounds which kill not, but ne'er heal ;
Yet Time, who changes all, had altered him   70
In soul and aspect as in age : years steal
Fire from the mind as vigour from the limb ;
And life's enchanted cup but sparkles near the brim.

IX.

His had been quaffed too quickly, and he found
The dregs were wormwood ; but he filled again,   75
And from a purer fount, on holier ground,
And deemed its spring perpetual ; but in vain !

Still round him clung invisibly a chain
Which galled for ever, fettering though unseen,
And heavy though it clanked not; worn with pain, 80
Which pined although it spoke not, and grew keen,
Entering with every step he took through many a scene.

X.

Secure in guarded coldness, he had mixed
Again in fancied safety with his kind,
And deemed his spirit now so firmly fixed 85
And sheathed with an invulnerable mind,
That, if no joy, no sorrow lurked behind;
And he, as one, might 'midst the many stand
Unheeded, searching through the crowd to find
Fit speculation; such as in strange land 90
He found in wonder-works of God and Nature's hand.

XI.

But who can view the ripened rose, nor seek
To wear it? who can curiously behold
The smoothness and the sheen of beauty's cheek,
Nor feel the heart can never all grow old? 95
Who can contemplate Fame through clouds unfold
The star which rises o'er her steep, nor climb?
Harold, once more within the vortex, rolled
On with the giddy circle, chasing Time,
Yet with a nobler aim than in his youth's fond prime. 100

XII.

But soon he knew himself the most unfit
Of men to herd with Man; with whom he held
Little in common; untaught to submit
His thoughts to others, though his soul was quelled
In youth by his own thoughts; still uncompelled, 105

He would not yield dominion of his mind
To spirits against whom his own rebelled ;
Proud though in desolation ; which could find
A life within itself, to breathe without mankind.

XIII.

Where rose the mountains, there to him were friends ; 110
Where rolled the ocean, thereon was his home ;
Where a blue sky, and glowing clime, extends,
He had the passion and the power to roam ;
The desert, forest, cavern, breaker's foam,
Were unto him companionship ; they spake   115
A mutual language, clearer than the tome
Of his land's tongue, which he would oft forsake
For Nature's pages glassed by sunbeams on the lake.

XIV.

Like the Chaldean, he could watch the stars,
Till he had peopled them with beings bright   120
As their own beams ; and earth, and earth-born jars,
And human frailties, were forgotten quite :
Could he have kept his spirit to that flight
He had been happy ; but this clay will sink
Its spark immortal, envying it the light   125
To which it mounts, as if to break the link
That keeps us from yon heaven which woos us to its brink.

XV.

But in Man's dwellings he became a thing
Restless and worn, and stern and wearisome,
Drooped as a wild-born falcon with clipt wing,   130
To whom the boundless air alone were home :
Then came his fit again, which to o'ercome,
As eagerly the barred-up bird will beat

His breast and beak against his wiry dome
Till the blood tinge his plumage, so the heat   135
Of his impeded soul would through his bosom eat.

XVI.

Self-exiled Harold wanders forth again,
With nought of hope left, but with less of gloom;
The very knowledge that he lived in vain,
That all was over on this side the tomb,   -   140
Had made Despair a smilingness assume,
Which, though 'twere wild,—as on the plundered wreck
When mariners would madly meet their doom
With draughts intemperate on the sinking deck,—
Did yet inspire a cheer, which he forbore to check. .   145

XVII.

Stop!—for thy tread is on an Empire's dust!
An Earthquake's spoil is sepulchred below!
Is the spot marked with no colossal bust?
Nor column trophied for triumphal show?
None; but the moral's truth tells simpler so,   150
As the ground was before, thus let it be;—
How that red rain hath made the harvest grow!
And is this all the world has gained by thee,
Thou first and last of fields! king-making Victory?

XVIII.

And Harold stands upon this place of skulls,   155
The grave of France, the deadly Waterloo!
How in an hour the power, which gave annuls
Its gifts, transferring fame as fleeting too!
In 'pride of place' here last the eagle flew,
Then tore with bloody talon the rent plain,   160

Pierced by the shaft of banded nations through ;
Ambition's life and labours all were vain ;
He wears the shattered links of the world's broken chain.

XIX.

Fit retribution ! Gaul may champ the bit
And foam in fetters ;—but is Earth more free ?   165
Did nations combat to make *One* submit ;
Or league to teach all kings true sovereignty ?
What ! shall reviving Thraldom again be
The patched-up idol of enlightened days ?
Shall we, who struck the Lion down, shall we   170
Pay the Wolf homage ? proffering lowly gaze
And servile knees to thrones ?   No ; *prove* before ye praise !

XX.

If not, o'er one fallen despot boast no more !
In vain fair cheeks were furrowed with hot tears
For Europe's flowers long rooted up before   175
The trampler of her vineyards ; in vain years
Of death, depopulation, bondage, fears,
Have all been borne, and broken by the accord
Of roused-up millions ; all that most endears
Glory, is when the myrtle wreathes a sword   180
Such as Harmodius drew on Athens' tyrant lord.

XXI.

There was a sound of revelry by night,
And Belgium's capital had gathered then
Her beauty and her Chivalry, and bright
The lamps shone o'er fair women and brave men ;   185
A thousand hearts beat happily ; and when
Music arose with its voluptuous swell,
Soft eyes looked love to eyes which spake again,

And all went merry as a marriage bell ;
But hush ! hark ! a deep sound strikes like a rising
    knell !   190

XXII.

Did ye not hear it ?—No ; 'twas but the wind,
Or the car rattling o'er the stony street ;
On with the dance ! let joy be unconfined ;
No sleep till morn, when Youth and Pleasure meet
To chase the glowing Hours with flying feet—   195
But hark !—that heavy sound breaks in once more,
As if the clouds its echo would repeat ;
And nearer, clearer, deadlier, than before !
Arm ! Arm ! it is—it is—the cannon's opening roar !

XXIII.

Within a windowed niche of that high hall   200
Sate Brunswick's fated chieftain ; he did hear
That sound the first amidst the festival,
And caught its tone with Death's prophetic ear ;
And when they smiled because he deemed it near,
His heart more truly knew that peal too well   205
Which stretched his father on a bloody bier,
And roused the vengeance blood alone could quell ;
He rushed into the field, and, foremost fighting, fell.

XXIV.

Ah ! then and there was hurrying to and fro,
And gathering tears, and tremblings of distress,   210
And cheeks all pale, which but an hour ago
Blushed at the praise of their own loveliness ;
And there were sudden partings, such as press
The life from out young hearts, and choking sighs

Which ne'er might be repeated ; who could guess   215
If ever more should meet those mutual eyes,
Since upon night so sweet such awful morn could rise !

XXV.

And there was mounting in hot haste : the steed,
The mustering squadron, and the clattering car,
Went pouring forward with impetuous speed,   220
And swiftly forming in·the ranks of war ;
And the deep thunder peal on peal afar ;
And near, the beat of the alarming drum
Roused up the soldier ere the morning star ;
While thronged the citizens with terror dumb,   225
Or whispering, with white lips—'The foe ! they come !
   they come ! '

XXVI.

And wild and high the ' Cameron's gathering ' rose !
The war-note of Lochiel, which Albyn's hills
Have heard, and heard, too, have her Saxon foes :—
How in the noon of night that pibroch thrills,   230
Savage and shrill ! But with·the breath which fills
Their mountain-pipe, so fill the mountaineers
With the fierce native daring which instils
The stirring memory of a thousand years,
And Evan's, Donald's fame rings in each clansman's
   ears !   235

XXVII.

And Ardennes waves above them her green leaves,
Dewy with nature's tear-drops as they pass,
Grieving, if aught inanimate e'er grieves,
Over the unreturning brave,—alas !
Ere evening to be trodden like the grass   240
Which now beneath them, but above shall grow

In its next verdure, when this fiery mass
Of living valour, rolling on the foe
And burning with high hope, shall moulder cold and low.

XXVIII.

Last noon beheld them full of lusty life,   245
Last eve in Beauty's circle proudly gay,
The midnight brought the signal-sound of strife,
The morn the marshalling in arms,—the day
Battle's magnificently stern array !
The thunder-clouds close o'er it, which when rent
The earth is covered thick with other clay,   251
 Which her own clay shall cover, heaped and pent,
Rider and horse,—friend, foe,—in one red burial blent !

XXIX.

Their praise is hymned by loftier harps than mine ;
Yet one I would select from that proud throng,   255
Partly because they blend me with his line,
And partly that I did his sire some wrong,
And partly that bright names will hallow song ;
And his was of the bravest, and when showered
The death-bolts deadliest the thinned files along, 260
 Even where the thickest of war's tempest lowered,
They reached no nobler breast than thine, young gallant
  Howard !

XXX.

There have been tears and breaking hearts for thee,
And mine were nothing had I such to give ;
But when I stood beneath the fresh green tree,   265
Which living waves where thou didst cease to live,
And saw around me the wide field revive
With fruits and fertile promise, and the Spring

Come forth her work of gladness to contrive,
With all her reckless birds upon the wing,   270
I turned from all she brought to those she could not bring.

XXXI.

I turned to thee, to thousands, of whom each
And one as all a ghastly gap did make
In his own kind and kindred, whom to teach
Forgetfulness were mercy for their sake;   275
The Archangel's trump, not Glory's, must awake
Those whom they thirst for; though the sound of Fame
May for a moment soothe, it cannot slake
The fever of vain longing, and the name
So honoured but assumes a stronger, bitterer claim.   280

XXXII.

They mourn, but smile at length; and, smiling, mourn :
The tree will wither long before it fall ;
The hull drives on, though mast and sail be torn ;
The roof-tree sinks, but moulders on the hall
In massy hoariness; the ruined wall   285
Stands when its wind-worn battlements are gone ;
The bars survive the captive they enthral ;
The day drags through, though storms keep out the sun ;
And thus the heart will break, yet brokenly live on :

XXXIII.

Even as a broken mirror, which the glass   290
In every fragment multiplies; and makes
A thousand images of one that was,
The same, and still the more, the more it breaks ;
And thus the heart will do which not forsakes,
Living in shattered guise ; and still, and cold,   295

And bloodless, with its sleepless sorrow aches,
Yet withers on till all without is old,
Shewing no visible sign, for such things are untold.

XXXIV.

There is a very life in our despair,
Vitality of poison,—a quick root   300
Which feeds these deadly branches; for it were
As nothing did we die; but Life will suit
Itself to Sorrow's most detested fruit,
Like to the apples on the Dead Sea's shore,
All ashes to the taste : Did man compute   305
Existence by enjoyment, and count o'er
Such hours 'gainst years of life,—say, would he name
threescore ?

XXXV.

The Psalmist numbered out the years of man :
They are enough ; and if thy tale be *true*,
Thou, who didst grudge him even that fleeting span, 310
More than enough, thou fatal Waterloo !
Millions of tongues record thee, and anew
Their children's lips shall echo them, and say—
' Here, where the sword united nations drew,
Our countrymen were warring on that day !'   315
And this is much, and all which will not pass away.

XXXVI.

There sunk the greatest, nor the worst of men,
Whose spirit, antithetically mixt,
One moment of the mightiest, and again
On little objects with like firmnesss fixt ;   320
Extreme in all things ! hadst thou been betwixt,
Thy throne had still been thine, or never been ;

E

* For daring made thy rise as fall : thou seek'st
  Even now to re-assume the imperial mien,
And shake again the world, the Thunderer of the scene ! 325

XXXVII.

Conqueror and captive of the earth art thou !
She trembles at thee still, and thy wild name
Was ne'er more bruited in men's minds than now
That thou art nothing, save the jest of Fame ;
Who wooed thee once, thy vassal, and became   330
The flatterer of thy fierceness, till thou wert
A god unto thyself : nor less the same
To the astounded kingdoms all inert,
Who deemed thee for a time whate'er thou didst assert.

XXXVIII.

Oh, more or less than man—in high or low,   335
Battling with nations, flying from the field ;
Now making monarchs' necks thy footstool, now   ;
More than thy meanest soldier taught to yield ;
An empire thou couldst crush, command, rebuild,
But govern not thy pettiest passion, nor,   340
However deeply in men's spirits skilled,
Look through thine own, nor curb the lust of war,
Nor learn that tempted Fate will leave the loftiest star.

XXXIX.

Yet well thy soul hath brooked the turning tide
With that untaught innate philosophy,   345
Which, be it wisdom, coldness, or deep pride,
Is gall and wormwood to an enemy.
When the whole host of hatred stood hard by,
To watch and mock thee shrinking, thou hast smiled
With a sedate and all-enduring eye ;—   350

When Fortune fled her spoiled and favourite child,
He stood unbowed beneath the ills upon him piled.

XL.

Sager than in thy fortunes ; for in them
Ambition steeled thee on too far to show
That just habitual scorn, which could contemn   355
Men and their thoughts ; 'twas wise to feel, not so
To wear it ever on thy lip and brow,
And spurn the instruments thou wert to use
Till they were turned unto thine overthrow :
'Tis but a worthless world to win or lose ;   360
So hath it proved to thee, and all such lot who choose.

XLI.

If, like a tower upon a headland rock,
Thou hadst been made to stand or fall alone,
Such scorn of man had helped to brave the shock ;
But men's thoughts were the steps which paved thy
 throne,   365 .
Their admiration thy best weapon shone ;
The part of Philip's son was thine, not then
(Unless aside thy purple had been thrown)
Like stern Diogenes to mock at men ;
For sceptred cynics earth were far too wide a den.   370

XLII.

But quiet to quick bosoms is a hell,
And *there* hath been thy bane ; there is a fire
And motion of the soul which will not dwell
In its own narrow being, but aspire
Beyond the fitting medium of desire ;   375
And, but once kindled, quenchless evermore,
Preys upon high adventure, nor can tire
Of aught but rest ; a fever at the core,
Fatal to him who bears, to all who ever bore.

XLIII.

This makes the madmen who have made men mad   380
By their contagion ; Conquerors and Kings,
Founders of sects and systems, to whom add
Sophists, Bards, Statesmen, all unquiet things
Which stir too strongly the soul's secret springs,
And are themselves the fools to those they fool ;   385
Envied, yet how unenviable ! what stings
Are theirs ! One breast laid open were a school
Which would unteach mankind the lust to shine or rule :

XLIV.

Their breath is agitation, and their life
A storm whereon they ride, to sink at last,   390
And yet so nursed and bigoted to strife,
That should their days, surviving perils past,
Melt to calm twilight, they feel overcast
With sorrow and supineness, and so die ;
Even as a flame unfed, which runs to waste   395
With its own flickering, or a sword laid by,
Which eats into itself, and rusts ingloriously.

XLV.

He who ascends to mountain-tops, shall find
The loftiest peaks most wrapt in clouds and snow ;
He who surpasses or subdues mankind,   400
Must look down on the hate of those below.
Though high *above* the sun of glory glow,
And far *beneath* the earth and ocean spread,
Round him are icy rocks, and loudly blow
Contending tempests on his naked head,   405
And thus reward the toils which to those summits led.

XLVI.

Away with these! true Wisdom's world will be
Within its own creation, or in thine,
Maternal Nature! for who teems like thee,
Thus on the banks of thy majestic Rhine?   410
There Harold gazes on a work divine,
A blending of all beauties; streams and dells,
Fruit, foliage, crag, wood, corn-field, mountain, vine,
And chiefless castles breathing stern farewells
From gray but leafy walls, where Ruin greenly dwells.

XLVII.

And there they stand, as stands a lofty mind,   · 416
Worn, but unstooping to the baser crowd,
All tenantless, save to the crannying wind,
Or holding dark communion with the cloud.
There was a day when they were young and proud;
Banners on high, and battles passed below;   421
But they who fought are in a bloody shroud,
And those which waved are shredless dust ere now,
And the bleak battlements shall bear no future blow.

XLVIII.

Beneath these battlements, within those walls,   425
Power dwelt amidst her passions; in proud state
Each robber chief upheld his armed halls,
Doing his evil will, nor less elate
Than mightier heroes of a longer date.
What want these outlaws conquerors should have   430
But history's purchased page to call them great?
A wider space, an ornamented grave?
Their hopes were not less warm, their souls were full as
    brave.

XLIX.

In their baronial feuds and single fields,
What deeds of prowess unrecorded died !   435
And Love, which lent a blazon to their shields,
With emblems well devised by amorous pride,
Through all the mail of iron hearts would glide ;
But still their flame was fierceness, and drew on
Keen contest and destruction near allied,   440
And many a tower for some fair mischief won,
Saw the discoloured Rhine beneath its ruin run.

L.

But Thou, exulting and abounding river !
Making thy waves a blessing as they flow
Through banks whose beauty would endure for ever, 445
Could man but leave thy bright creation so,
Nor its fair promise from the surface mow
With the sharp scythe of conflict,—then to see
Thy valley of sweet waters, were to know
Earth paved like Heaven ; and to seem such to me, 450
Even now what wants thy stream ? — that it should
    Lethe be.

LI.

A thousand battles have assailed thy banks,
But these and half their fame have passed away,
And Slaughter heaped on high his weltering ranks ;
Their very graves are gone, and what are they ?   455
Thy tide washed down the blood of yesterday,
And all was stainless, and on thy clear stream
Glassed, with its dancing light, the sunny ray ;
But o'er the blackened memory's blighting dream
Thy waves would vainly roll, all sweeping as they seem.

NOTES.

—o—

THE PRISONER OF CHILLON.

This poem was written at an inn in the little village of Ouchy, near Lausanne, where Byron and Shelley were detained for two days in June, 1816. The sonnet prefixed to the poem was written by Byron after he became aware of the true history of the prisoner of Chillon.

François de Bonnivard (1496-1570) was a Roman Catholic, and Prior of St. Victor, a considerable benefice close to Geneva. He assisted the Genevese to free themselves from the tyranny of the Duke of Savoy, and was for this reason, and not for his religious faith, secretly seized in 1530 and cast into the castle of Chillon, (he had previously been confined for two years, 1519-1521, at Grolée) where he remained till 1536. After Geneva had won its independence, the castle was taken by the Bernese, and Bonnivard was released. He became an honored resident of Geneva, gave his library to the town, and taught toleration in religious matters to its people, and is recorded in their annals as a learned, devout and even great man.

1. **Hair.**—Note the skill with which the poet begins his story with the personal appearance of the prisoner, and with the most striking point in it, viz., the premature grayness. Why has he let the prisoner tell his own story? Why not, "His hair was gray, etc."

Note in this stanza (and indeed in the others) the choice of specific terms, the great number of monosyllables ; and that at least eighty per cent. of the words are Anglo-Saxon. Is such choice characteristic of poetry in general, or of narrative and descriptive poetry in particular?

4. "Ludovico Sforza and others—The same is asserted of Marie Antoinette, wife of Louis XVI, though not in quite so short a period. Grief is said to have the same effect : to such, and not to fear, the change in hers was to be attributed." B. So Falstaff says, "Thy father's beard is turned white with the news."—*Henry iv.* ii. 4.

Grew and **Grown.**—Generally give the idea of gradual change, and so are opposed to the notion in *sudden fears*. Shaks. above says, *'tis turned*, and not *'tis grown*. Is *have* correct? Account for its use.

Fears.—Would *fear* be better, apart from the rhyme?   Why?

5. **My Limbs are Bowed.**—The poet seizes upon the next most prominent sign of premature old age.

6. If *but* has its usual adversative force here, the antithesis is not properly expressed. Why? Note the alliteration, of which Byron is very fond. The line is a very suggestive one.   The word *repose* is well chosen, calling up the picture of the prisoner lying on the damp dungeon floor, lack of food and exercise telling their tale upon his body, his soul consumed with sorrow, even as the rusting iron which held him to the pillar.

9. **Earth and air.**—What is meant?   Discuss the effect of printing "earth" with a capital, and of substituting "from" for "to."

10. **Banned and barred.**—*Banned* is in Spenser and Shaks. "cursed;" with Milton and later writers, "interdicted;" so *banned* and *barred* might seem tautologous, but "barred" adds a more specific idea, besides helping to keep up the picture of the dungeon. *Ban* originally meant to "proclaim," as "banns of marriage," and is commonly used of persons.

Forbidden fare.—Speaking of earth and air, *i. e.*, freedom, as necessary sustenance for mind and body. Give the derivation and different meanings of "fare."

11. If *this* refers to ll. 7-10, then l. 12 seems unnecessary; if it refers to l. 12, *it* would be better.

12. **Father's faith.**—See introductory note.   Why did the prisoner wish for death?

13. **That father.**—Defend if you can the use of this phrase instead of the ordinary one, "my father."   •

Punished at the stake.—What is meant?   Give any similar euphemism.

14. **Tenets.**—Religious principles.   Lat. "tenet," he holds.   For similar instances of Latin words adopted and naturalized as English nouns see *H. S. Gr.* v. 41.

15. **Lineal race.**—A weak periphrasis for "sons."   Who are descendants not lineal?

16. What is the periphrasis for "dungeon?"—Can you defend it?

17. Force of *are*? The patriotic and martyr brothers are a pure invention of the poet.

19. Paraphrase the line. Would "began" be better than "had begun?"

20. Proud, not of persecution, but of the faith that was the cause of it.

21-22. Explain fully, the meaning of "fire," "field," "blood."

Have sealed.—That is, their blood was the evidence of their faith, as a seal is the evidence of a maker's consent to a deed to which it is attached. Is the tense correct? Why?

24. In this line Byron sacrifices truth and even probability to his desire for a good, strong phrase. To take the line literally would remove the action of the poem to times when Christianity was still contending against paganism. Can you discover in the poem itself anything to indicate the age in which the events occurred?

25-26. Is *in* correctly used?

27. **Dungeon**, in l. 25, softens somewhat the abrupt beginning of stanza ii.

"Seven."—There were really 8. Why are the numbers 3 and 7 so often found in folklore and poetry?

Pillars.—Is there any difference between them and the columns of l. 29.

Of Gothic mould.—"Gothic Style," is a term applied (at first contemptuously, by the Renaissance architects) to most of the ambitious architecture in Western Europe, from the middle of the 12th to the 16th century; its peculiar features are pointed arches, groined vaults, and clustered columns. The pillars (or columns) may be distinctively Gothic, yet vary much. The early Norman shafts were mostly plain, massive circles, squares or octagons; later, fluted and otherwise decorated, and terminating in a capital, ornamented with foliage, or fruit, or figures.

28. **Chillon.**—A castle and fortress in the Canton of Vaud, built in 1238, about a mile and a half from Montreux, at the east end of Lake Leman, on an isolated rock four rods from the shore, and now used for military stores. "It is airy and spacious, consisting of two aisles almost like the crypt of a church, and lighted by several windows, through which the sun's light passes by reflection from the surface of the lake up to the roof, transmitting partly the blue color of the water."—*Murray*.

29. **Massy.**—Would *massive* do as well? Why not? Byron seems fond of this word, see l. 109, and *Ch. H.* i. 58, etc. Note the musical sound of ll. 27-30, due to the alliterations, the employment of liquids in the accented syllables, and to the ending with the open vowels (o, a).

Dim.—Not so in reality, see note on l. 28. *With.* Does the phrase, "with—ray," limit "dim," *with* being equal to "on account of," or is it co-ordinate with 'dim' and explanatory of it, limiting "columns?"

32. "And (which going) through," etc. Would it be an improvement to make the pause at *fallen* and have none after *left*? *Crevice.*—Another form of *crevasse*.

35. **Meteor lamp.**—The *Ignis fatuus* or Will o' the Wisp.

That iron.—Comp. "That father," of l. 13.

Cankering, the same word as *cancer*.

39 **These limbs.**—Note the dramatic touch here and elsewhere (this wreck, l. 26), (these eyes, l. 42). The narration is in the *first person ;* the narrator assumes the character of the actor and *points* to his shrunk limbs and wasted form. "Teeth," develop the figure.

41. Till death. "This new day." Justify the phrase.

42. Why *painful*?

43-44. These lines seem to read harshly. "These eyes " is not a harmonious phrase. "Mine," for "these," and "that" for the second "which," would be smoother. But is the sound here imitative of the sentiment ?"

Sunrise seems well chosen as the most attractive and striking object to one long unused to the light of day.

45. **Score.**—Literally a notch, from A. S. *sceran*, to cut. Show the connection of its different meanings, also of the kindred words, *share*, *shear*, *shire*, *shore*, *shred*.

The student should go over this word picture of the dungeon, noting the parts mentioned, the seven columns, the damp floor, the dim light, the rings and the chains, etc., and ask himself, "Does it, as a whole, present to the mind a clear and definite picture which, if I had the skill, I could put upon canvas?" If so, the stanza, as descriptive, is a good one. Byron, as we may note in the pathetic and beautiful ending of this very stanza, knew right well that more interest attaches to *persons* than to *things ;* and so he seldom gives us much pure description of locality as mere *place*, but seeks to strengthen and color the pictures by the human interests, feelings and associations connected therewith.

48. **Column stone.**—A rather peculiar expression for "column's base."

52. **But with.**—Parse these words.

Livid.—What is the literal meaning ?

53. Compare Milton **P. L. i. 61**, speaking of hell.

> " A dungeon horrible, on all sides round
> As one great furnace flamed ; yet from these flames
> No light, but rather darkness visible,
> Served only to discover sights of woe."

54-55. Point out the figures.—"Fetters" and "gyves" for the *feet*. Give the corresponding terms for the *hands*.

57. This line constitutes a sort of double metonymy. "Pure elements of earth," means the sky, sun, air, earth, etc., and these are the constituents of *freedom*. What were ' the four elements ? '

58. Would *listen* be an equally good word ? Why not ?

59. Is *turn* transitive or intransitive here ?

61. Is the boldness in the brothers, who in this situation could sing songs, or in the heroes whose deeds were the burden of their songs ?

63. Hales quotes an instance from Franklin's expedition to show that the voices of Arctic explorers change in this way.

64. **Stone.**—In a collective sense.

66. The phrase "of yore" very happily introduces and contrasts the idea of long confinement and the joyous freedom of youth.

Wont.—Pronounce, and distinguish in use from *wonted*.

67. **Fancy.**—Force of here ? Distinguish from *imagination* and *thought*.

69. Distinguish *eldest* and *oldest*.

70. What notion does "cheer" add, that "uphold" has not ?

71. What is peculiar in the use of *ought* here ?

72. **Did well.**—Explain the meaning.

In his degree.—In proportion to his age and experience of suffering.

73-75. **The youngest to him.**—An example of what is called *anacoluthon*, or want of sequence in the grammatical construction.

Loved.—As Jacob loved Joseph and Benjamin for their mother's sake.

76. Recalls the compassion of Reuben and Judah for Joseph in the pit, and also Judah's plea before Joseph for Benjamin, one of the most touching things in our or any literature.

77. **Distressed.**—Some editions read *distrest*. In older writers *t* for *ed* in preterites was common. When does *ed* take the *t* sound with us ? See *H. S. Grammar*, viii. 85. Archdeacon Hare advocated a return to this spelling on the score of appearance, and adduces in favor of it, a stanza of *Genevieve*.

> Her bosom heaved, she *stept* aside,
> As conscious of my look she *stept* ;
> Then suddenly, with timorous eye
> She fled to me and *wept*.

78. **Such bird**.—Note the poetic license, successfully used. Before what singular nouns is *such* regularly used without *a* or *an*?

81. Does "being free" modify *me* or *eagles*?

Is there a confusion of images in the passage?

80-81. The parenthesis awkwardly separates "day" from its appositive "polar day."

82-84. Seem to add little to the picture of the youth. The term "polar day" at first shocks us by introducing the notion of cold and discomfort, notions not willingly associated with that of beauty—Hence there is an incongruity in the picture. The resemblance, as the next line shows, is in the purity and brightness of both.

83. The "summer" of the polar day strikes us as an odd phrase till we consider that at the pole the day is six months long.

84-85. A beautiful couplet, melodious and true to nature. Note the alliteration, the sibilant and liquid letters, the movement from close to open vowels, and the imitative long vowels in the last two words of l. 84.

88. What two qualities does this line suggest?

89. Note the truly Byronic hyperbole and condensation. What is the correlative to *then*?

90-91. It would almost seem as if the stanza would end better without this couplet. Derive *assuage* and *abhorred*. Is the latter word properly used here? **Below**.—Explain what is meant.

92. What is the force of *as*?

93. Shew the adversative force of *but*.

94. "Strong of frame," is an old English idiom. Why would *of* not do here.

95. **"Had stood and perished,"**—What mood?

Discuss the effect of substituting *a* for *the* in this line.

96. **Foremost**.—Would *first* do equally well. Why is foremost called a double superlative? See *H. S. Gr.* vii. 27.

97. The repetition of *but* is awkward, whether it be taken as co-ordinate to l. 92, thus, "but not (formed) in chains to pine, or as making the infinitive phrase adversative to that in l. 92, "to combat but not to pine."

98. Show the special significance and propriety of the words "pine," "wither" and "decline."

"Clank." Give kindred words imitative of sounds.

Would *spirits* do equally well here?

99. What is the force of *silently*?

101. **Forced it on**—Comparing his spirit to a drooping soldier.

Relics.—Who and why so termed? What is peculiar in the use of the word here? Distinguish from *relict*.

105. Note how 105 contrasts with 103, and 106 with 104.

Note Byron's love of specific and avoidance of general terms; thus "deer and wolf," rather than "wild animals or game;" "fettered feet," than "imprisonment."

107. **Leman.**—L. Geneva is a crescent about 50 miles in length by 8 n its greatest width. Its waters are deeply blue and 1200 feet above the sea. Mt. Blanc can be seen 60 miles away from the western shore, and Jura from the southern. The greatest depth is not far from what B. states. Voltaire, Rousseau, Gœthe, Byron and many others mention it in their writings.

109. **Meet and flow.**—May refer to the entrance of the Rhone at the eastern end of L. Leman on the left, and in the vicinity of the castle.

110. B. says in his note, "800 ft. French measure."

111. **Battlement.**—A parapet or breastwork, loopholed or notched at the top for attack and defence.

Snow-white.—By contrast with the lake, or in reality?

117. **Ripple.**—Includes the notion of gentle sound. Looking at the ending of the stanza, it would seem better to omit this line. In the same way, line 121 seems out of harmony with the general gloom of the picture, unless the poet's idea is to contrast the freedom and light of the outer air with the gloom and sad plight of the prisoners.

121. What two ways of parsing and explaining *wanton* here? Which do you prefer and why?

122-123. "Rock," the noun, and "rock," the verb, have different derivations. The play upon words in these two lines is out of place; especially in a poem of this character.

Unshocked. Unshaken. What is the usual meaning?

Note that B. *artfully* makes the narrator appeal only to *hearing* and *feeling*, (117, 119, 122-3). In l. 124 "to see" is used; partly perhaps for rhyme with "free," which seems necessary to the fine thought and contrast of l. 125.

126. **Nearer.**—In what way?

129. Classify the dependent clause and tell its relation.

Rude.—Refers to the manner of taking rather than to the quality of the food.

131. Does this mean "We had little inclination for the pleasures of the table," or "It troubled us little that our food was coarse and rude?"

134-135. An effective and pathetic way of saying the bread was dry and hard.

Some editions read captive's. Which is better?

139. **These.**—Matters of food and drink.

140-141. These two lines seem a weak way (for Byron) of saying, "Even in a palace my brother would have died if his free breathing, etc." Contrast with the periphrasis in 134-135.

Range.—Give the grammatical relation.

145. The omission of the object of the verb "saw," leaving the imagination of the reader to supply it, is exceedingly effective. Our greater poets frequently employ this method of strengthening or suggesting a picture. Milton is especially strong in this presentation by omission or suggestion.

146. **Dead.**—Supply the ellipsis.

149. **He died.**—Discuss the effect of this repetition from l. 144.

They.—His keepers or gaolers. Note that throughout the poem, B. seldom mentions third parties, thus concentrating the whole interest on the Prisoner and his brethren.

150. **Scooped.**—Not much used by poets, but as employed here in connection with "shallow" it seems a very fitting word.

152. **Boon.**—Originally a prayer or request.

153. **Corse.**—Distinguish *corse, corps, corpse.*

154. What was the thought, and why foolish?

155. **Then.**—What is the force?

Wrought.—Formed from *worked*, which by metathesis becomes *wroked*. Compare with this line *Christabel.*

> "And to be wroth with one we love,
>   Doth *work* like madness in the brain."

157. Perhaps alluding to an old superstition that under certain circumstances the spirit appears or wanders about until decent burial is accorded the body.

160. **Earth.**—Nom. absol.—Develop the full meaning conveyed by the use of the phrases "flat" and "turfless."

162-163. We scarcely notice the inappropriate word "leant" in the general beauty of the closing couplet.

Empty chain.—Criticise this expression.

164. **Favorite and flower.**—Why? See ll. 73 et seq.

Natal hour.—Why better than to say "birth?"

167. Paraphrase.

169. **Latest.**—Is this the proper word?

Hoard.—Criticise the use of this word and suggest a more appropriate one.

172-173. See ll. 86 et seq., and ll. 60 et seq.

174. **Was struck.**—Note the omission of the agent (death). See remark on l. 145.

Name the appositive subjects of this verb.

175. **Was withered**—What would be the effect of omitting *was?*

178. What "shapes" of death are mentioned? Name the mood accompanying each. Name also the figures in ll. 175-184.

184. **These.**—Would "those" be better? Why? "Horror" is shuddering fear; "woe," deep grief.

Sure. Grief of course can kill, but was this the case here?

185. "The gentle decay and gradual extinction of this young life is the most tender and beautiful part of the poem."—JEFFREY.

186. **Faded.**—See ll. 164 and 175.

Note the admirable order of ideas and choice of words so well descriptive of this gradual "decline" in consumption—faded—worn, weak—tearless, tender—hectic of the cheeks—transparent eye—a little talk—a little hope—the deep sighs suppressed ;—all well known accompaniments of that fell disease.

189. "There is much delicacy in this plural. By such a fanciful multiplying of the survivors, the elder brother prevents self-intrusion ; himself and his loneliness are, as it were, kept out of sight and forgotten."—HALES.

190-193. Paraphrase.

194. **Light.**—Brightness.

195. One of Byron's venturesome hyperboles.

200. **Lost.**—Buried in despairing grief ; a play upon words in " lost in loss."

The most.—What is the usual phrase ?

204. " The sighs he would suppress—more slowly drawn." Explain.

B. does not *say* that breathing had ceased ; how does he imply it ?

A good example of effective omission.

205. Show that the statements (apparently contradictory) of ll. 205, 209, are perfectly natural.

207-208. Paraphrase.

211. **I found him not.**—Explain.

214. **Breath.**—From the walls exuded a moisture which made the air damp and deadly ; hence the use of " accursed."

215-216. **The dearest link—brink.**—Explain.

220. Discuss the effect of placing the dash after " both."

223. **Strive.**—Against what ?

225. **Frantic.**—B.'s love of alliteration seems to have led him to use this ill chosen word. " Frantic," from Gr. *phrenitis*, mental disorder, suggests some physical exhibition or passion, pain, or grief, not torpitude and quiescence.

226. **So.**—Show the pronominal force of this adverb, **H. S. Gr.**, vi. 33.

229-230. **Faith.**—In what ? Why is suicide a selfish death ?

231-232. He is supposed to have swooned and been delirious.

According to the critics, Stanza IX. best displays B.'s power over language and his force of style.

" In the P. of C. the influence of Scott is yet acting, and that of Coleridge and Wordsworth may be also seen, a fact due perhaps to the presence of Shelley, who was an intense Wordsworthian. B. accused Wordsworth of unintelligibility, and Coleridge of unmeaning metaphysics, yet for all his derision, no doubt felt their greatness."—HALES.

There is certainly nothing of Scott's method of treatment in Stanza IX. He nowhere deals at such length with the analysis of the feelings, or with the state of the mind (subjectivity).

235. What senses are implied by the language as lost ? Where ? The poet must not be taken too literally in l. 235, for see line 237, " scarce conscious what I knew."

236. Recalls Niobe's grief, and her transformation to stone.

238. Shew the points of this comparison :

What proofs does the poet give of the suspension of sense and motion ? Are these points (no light, no dark, gray, a stone, a crag, no stars, no earth, etc.) well taken ? Does consciousness still exist, and if so, of what?

243. **Vacancy.**—Which absorbed (and destroyed all notions of) space, a conception of which requires definite and coherent thought.

246. What is meant by "no check," "no crime ? "

250. **Blind, Mute.**—Transferred epithets.

251. Recalled from his torpor by a bird's song, as the Ancient Mariner rom his by the fish at play. He is again a human and cognizant being, and his sympathy with the living world is re-awakened.

259-260. Paraphrase and show the expressiveness of *dull*.

Wonted.—A double form from *won*, to dwell, thus wonned, wont, wonted. Distinguish "wont" and "wonted" in use, and "wont" and "won't" in pronunciation.

266-267. **Crevice.**—See line 32. "Was perched through the crevice," is a rather awkward expression.

274. Force of *so* in this line, and in line 276 ?

277. Parse *cheering*.

285. **The while.**—Parse. Why does Byron ask Heaven to forgive the thought ?

Visitant.—Is there any distinction between this and "visitor ? "

Is *Paradise* a perfect rhyme with "guise ? "

293. The comparison to a corse in a shroud seems fitting enough in the circumstances ; the resemblance to a cloud is not so clear ; certainly the association of two such images is not good.

295. Cf. Wordsworth. *Daffodils.*

> "I wandered lonely as a cloud
> That floats on high o'er vales and hills."

298. A decidedly prosaic line.

311. **Returning.**—What is the grammatical relation ?

321. What is the force of the phrase "in a human shape ? "

327. **Them.**—Whom ? **Had.**—Mood ?

331. Hales says, "A thoroughly Wordsworthian line." And so we may say of the next stanza. Few better pictures of pure description are

F

to be found. It shows Byron's power in that line when he chose. Note, too, all well chosen to indicate *life* and *freedom*, in contrast with the Prisoner's lot.

336. The Rhone has its origin in the glaciers ; it brings down much sediment and it is not blue till it leaves the lake.

339. **Town.**—Perhaps Vevay.

341. **Little isle.**—"Between the entrances of the Rhone, and Villeneuve, not far from Chillon, is a very small island, the only one I could perceive within the lake's circumference. It contains a few trees (I think not above three)."—B.

346-349. What is the effect of the repetitions ?

350. What are the gentler hues ?

351. Compare Coleridge's *Anc. Mar.*, 272-91, and Wordsworth's Song at the feast of Brougham Castle, 141-6,—perhaps even showing unconscious imitation.

353-354. Why the eagle rather than any other bird ?

Methought.—For origin see **H. S. Gr.** VIII., 167.

364. **Opprest.**—Tasking both eyes and mind by the unaccustomed scene.

368. The downcast eye is a sign of despair. Compare Fletcher :

> "Folded arms and fixed eyes,
>   A sigh that piercing mortifies,
>   A look that's fastened to the ground."

369. What was the dreary note ?

371. **Where.**—Supply the words it modifies.

372. **At length.**—At last it became the same, etc.

377-378. Recalls Lovelace's famous lines :

> "Stone walls do not a prison make,
>   Nor iron bars a cage ;
>   Minds innocent and quiet take
>   That for an hermitage."

380. Some editions have "sacred" for "second."

381-390. **Spiders.**—From "spin," (spinner, spinder). The student will not have to go far to find examples of spiders and mice furnishing occupation, and consequently solace to state prisoners.

382. **Sullen.**—Silent. Latin—*solus*, alone.

Trade.—Originally (from "tread") a beaten path, hence, a way of life.

384. In what did this feeling consist ?

389. Does B. forget that they had been burst and not reimpose l (305) ? or was the last a reason for their becoming friends like the spiders and the mice, to while away the time ?

390-391. Paraphrase fully.

The ending of the poem is unsatisfactory to the majority of readers, beautiful and tender though it may be throughout. A gloomy and jaundiced view of human nature and of the future is too often characteristic of Byron.

NOTES TO CHILDE HAROLD.

——o——

The first canto of the poem treats of Harold's wanderings, meditations and observations in Portugal and Spain. The second has mainly Greece for its theme. The earlier stanzas announce the subject, then follow the passage through the Straits into the Mediterranean, some stanzas on the ship itself, on the moon-lit night at sea, and the thoughts and feelings it engenders. The course is up the Adriatic to the shores of Illyria and Albania, by way of which Greece is approached. The long digression concerning Albania ends with the war song of the half-savage and half-Greek Suliotes living in the valley of the Acheron. In Stanza 73 the subject of Greece is resumed, although without much reference to the *course* of the journey. The change is somewhat abrupt, but the stanzas following are thought to be among the finest of the poem.

693. **Sad relic.**—From about the end of the 15th century (1460) up to Byron's time of writing, Greece had been under the dominion of the Turks, and all that ignorance, tyranny and greed could suggest was practised on the much-enduring Greeks till 1820, when a rebellion broke out, which, aided by volunteers, money and sympathy from the Christian nations, resulted in independence in 1829. At first a president was elected, but in 1832 Otho of Bavaria was chosen as king. See Byron's life for his part in the struggle for independence.

694. A good example of Byron's love of contrast by opposed notions.

695. Scattered children.—Denationalized. The true Greek is in the majority in the Peloponnesus, in Aetolia, Acarnania, Thessaly, and most of the islands, but there is a very large admixture of Albanians in Attica, Bœotia, Phocis and Argolis.

696. Uncreate.—Byron seems to coin this word.

697. Whilome.—An old dative. Cf. *Seldom*.

Await.—Is this verb correctly used here.

699. Bleak, Sepulchral.—*Bleak* is a fit enough epithet for the Pass, which is exposed to the N. and N.W winds. "Sepulchral" of course applies to Leonidas and the 300 Spartans who volunteered as a "forlorn hope," and perished in holding the pass against the Persians.

700. Resume.—Give the derivation and meaning, and exemplify its ordinary use.

701. Eurotas' banks.—The river on which ancient Sparta was built. Scarcely a trace of the city is left, but a small temple over the supposed tomb of Leonidas.

702. Phyle's brow.—A fort commanding the pass of the same name leading from Bœotia into Attica, where Thrasybulus collected his band to expel the 30 tyrants. Note the fine effect of the personification ; how much stronger to say "Spirit of freedom" than "freedom" simply.

"From Fort Phyle, of which large remains still exist, the plain of Athens, Mt. Pentelicus, Mt. Hymettus, the Aegean and the Acropolis burst upon the eye at once ; in my opinion a more glorious prospect than even Cintra or Istamboul."—*B*.

707. Carle.—A rustic or low fellow. Cf. "churl," from *ceorl* ; "carl" is intentionally contrasted with "tyrants," who were men of some position or rank.

710. In word unmanned.—It is not like brave men to rail and not fight.

711. Save form alone.—It must not be supposed from these upbraiding lines that B. despaired of the re-awakening of the Spirit of Liberty. His own life and letters prove the contrary.

713-714.—Who would but deem.—Who is there that would not deem that ?

Unquenched.—Does this apply to liberty in general (=unquenchable) or to the Greeks?

715. Many dream.—A dream realized in 1829, and indulged in long before by such patriots as Coray and Riga. Byron has left us a translation

of Riga's famous war song, "Sons of the Greeks, Arise," (1796) as litera
as possible, and imitating the metre.

717-718. Fondly.—In its old meaning "foolishly;" still so in the
north of England.

Solely.—Alone and unaided.

720-721. Hereditary bondsmen, etc.—These lines have passed into
a proverb, and were a favourite quotation of Dan. O'Connell's.

726. Shades of the Helots.—The wrongs of the Helots are well
avenged by the descendants of their tyrants, the Spartans, being in like
abject slavery.

727. Change.—Change if you will your Turkish masters for Russian or
French ; *you* will still be slaves.

729. City.—Constantinople, won by the Turks in 1453 under Moham-
med II. from the Giaours, *i.e.*, infidels, but especially Christians.

Allah.—The Arabic name of the Supreme Being.

730. The Turks call themselves Osmanli, from Osman, or Othman, the
founder of the Ottoman Empire (1258-1326).

731-732. Serai.—The Seraglio of the Sultan is his palace in the Golden
Horn, enclosed by walls three miles in circuit. The term "Sublime
Porte," often used by the Turkish Government, comes from its chief entrance. Strangers are admitted to all parts but the Harem, hence not
strictly *impenetrable.*

Tower.—"Byron uses this word vaguely for any conspicuous building,
as Athena's tower for the Parthenon, l. 836."—TOZER.

Frank.—Used in Turkey very generally for Western Europeans. The
French Language became common on account of the capture of Constantinople by the French and Venetians, under Baldwin Count of Flanders, on
the 4th Crusade, which never reached Palestine at all. Their occupation
lasted over 50 years. Of course the Seraglio was not then built.

733-735. Rebel brood.—The Wahabis, founded by Wahab, born in
the Highlands of Arabia about 1700. He and his followers inculcated a
purifying of Islamism generally. The Koran was unread, the five daily
prayers unsaid, Mecca was forgotten, tithes, ablutions and pilgrimages were
never kept. Wahab's first convert was a young chief, Saud, who drew
the sword for the new Puritan Islam. Saud's son carried on the conquest,
and his grandson in 1803 took Mecca, and next year Medina, rifling the
Prophet's tomb of all the treasures collected there *(pious spoil).* The
Sultan sent Mehemet Ali, pasha of Egypt, against them in 1811. Their

progress was arrested by other and later expeditions, but Wahabiism is still a formidable and dangerous power in the uplands of Arabia.

Pious spoil.—From nations conquered by Mahomet in the name of God. "There is but one God (Allah), and Mahomet is his prophet."

Wind and **along.**—"Suggest the slow and devious course of an advancing army."—T.

736. Byron's own conduct helped to defeat this prophecy.

738-740. **Lenten days.**—The Greek church is very severe in the matter of fasts, the great Easter fast (Lent) being 48 days, Christmas 39 days, and others making up nearly three-fourths of the year.

Shrive.—To remove. Cf. Shrove Tuesday, the day before the beginning of Lent (Ash Wednesday). "Shrive" is generally used of the person in the sense of "hear confession and absolve."

743-744. Note the archaic forms.

746. **Carnival.**—From the It., *carno-vale*, good bye to flesh-meat. The period of festivity immediately preceding Lent, among the nations of Southern Europe. The last day is Shrove, or Pancake Tuesday, with the English, the *Fastnacht* of the Germans. As fasts are little observed by Protestants no Carnival is held by them. The headquarters of the Carnival, with all its license, buffoonery, masking and masquerading, (*secret, mimic, and motley*) is Rome. Goethe has delightfully sketched it in his Italian Journey. Thousands else have described it, but not so well. Note in this stanza the personification of Repentance and Carnival, and the contrast and alliteration of the last two lines.

747-749. During Ramadan, the 9th month of the Mohammedan year, a strict fast is enjoined from dawn to sunset, but during the night some necessaries are allowed by the Koran, and this' permission is construed with great freedom.

Stamboul, or Istamboul, the Turkish name of Constantinople, said to be a contraction of Ε'ις τὴν πόλιν (On to the city !)

Empress.—Once the capital of the Greek Empire.

Sophia's shrine.—This magnificent cathedral, built by Justinian, A.D. 532, at a cost of sixty millions of dollars, has been turned into a Turkish mosque.

754-755. Recalls the use of *such* before a singular noun, in *Pris. of Chil.*, 78.

"To see *such bird* in such a nest."

Thrilled.—Quivered ; so in l. 768.

Bosphorus.—Ox-ford, or Cow-ford, from the legend of Io crossing it in the form of a cow.

758-759. **Timely.**—In time, *i.e.*, "the music" kept time and the oars kept time.

Pleasant moan.—What figure?

760. **Queen of Tides.—Consenting.** The moon, propitious and smiling.

"The moist star upon whose influence Neptune's empire stands."
—*Hamlet.*

762-764. It seemed as if her form (on account of being) reflected gave a brighter glance, darting, etc. Byron in his love of terseness sometimes overstrains the power of his participles.

Lave.—Is the tense correct?

765. **Caique.**—A skiff or light boat peculiar to Constantinople. What effect do you think has the inversion of the first three lines?

768-770. **Languid eyes.**—Casting languishing looks.

Cf. "Eyes love-languid thro' half tears."
—TENNYSON *Love and Duty.*

Note the peculiarity in the relation of *eye and hand* to the following predicates.

771-773. These three lines are a favourite quotation.

Bound, etc.—Expand this into an adverbial clause, and give its relation.

Cynic.—Derive, and show the connection.

Prattle.—Used to signify the childishness of such moralizing. What is the force of the affix?

Redeem.—What is the meaning here?

776. **Searment.**—Better a cerement : a waxed cloth (L. *cera*, wax,) used for a shroud ; here any garment folded closely about the form, after the manner of Eastern women.

777-778. **Main.**—The full phrase is "main sea." So "Main flood."—*Mer. Ven.*, iv, 1, 72.

All they mourn.—Their lost freedom.

780. **Wayward.**—This word is often incorrectly used as "fickle," "capricious ;" its proper meaning is "perverse," "obstinate in one's own way."

781. **Idly loud.**—Does this mean "loud with no meaning," or that idleness and loud laughter naturally go together?

788. Note the alliteration and sarcasm in "wield the sickle."

790. **Record.**—As to the accentuation cf. Chaucer. *C. T.* 7631.

> " And dronkenness is eke a foul record
> Of any man and namely of a lord."—T.

792-793. Men like the hardy Spartan, or like Epaminondas, the hero of Leuctra and Mantineia. Note the change in meaning that *hardihood* has undergone. What two meanings is it possible to attach to line 793?

794-795. The implied absence of "hearts" (courage) and men must be brought out by the stress of voice.

797-798. Note the harshness and difficulty of utterance of l. 797, and the ease and rapidity of the next. Why is this done and how is it effected?

800. **Recall back.**—Criticise ; and explain the meaning of vanquishing Time and Fate.

Note in the foregoing stanza the strength arising from the cumulation of the first four lines, the terseness of the phrases and the energy of emphasis, the many alliterations ; it furnishes a fair sample of Byron's mannerisms.

801-804. Greece is a land of charming contrasts in its climate and products. Every student of physical geography will know this comes from the nearness of every part to the sea, its comparatively low latitude, and its very diversified surface of plain and hill and mountain. " On Parnassus the snow is never entirely melted, notwitstanding the intense heat of the summer."—B.

805. Distinguish *temples* and *fanes*.

809. **Well recorded.**—He means which records prove to be worth ; occasionally, we know, the well-recording is the main part of the worth.

811. **Cave.**—Referring perhaps to the marble quarries of Mt. Pentelicus, whence most of the marble for public buildings at Athens came.

812-813. **Tritonia.**—Minerva (Athene), who was said to be daughter of the nymph of lake Tritonia in Libya.

Colonna's cliff.—Cape Sunium, the southern promontory of Attica, long called Colonna, from the columns, still standing, of a temple to Minerva.

Gray stones.—Certain colors seem associated with certain qualities ; thus white with purity, blue with fidelity, green with envy, etc. Here the "gray," or that neutral color produced by stress of sun and weather, suggests desolateness. Cf. Tennyson.

"On thy cold *gray* stones."—*P. Sea.*

816. Paraphrase this line. Note that in the number and length of the clauses beginning with "save" we almost forget the main clause, "so perish all." In the same way the exceptive clause, "but not oblivion," is meant to be of more importance than "brave the ages."

817-818. **Only not.**—All but regardless.

821. Pallas Athene, the Greek goddess corresponding to the Roman Minerva, was the protectress of Athens, and introduced the olive into Attica.

822. **Hymettus.**—Still as of old famed for its bees ; a mountain on the S. E. boundary of the plain of Athens.

824. **Free-born.**—What is the implied antithesis?

Mountain-air.—Better without the hyphen.

825-826. **Apollo.**—Phoebus the sun god. Mendeli is a corruption of Pentelicus. The quarries are on the mountain side, twelve miles away to the N. E., and their white veins may still be seen even at that distance. What island in the Ægean was noted for its marble?

828. A line often quoted.

829. **Is lost in vulgar mould.**—Not lost by being common earth, but hallowed by associations and memories which make it the wonder and pride of all who love liberty and learning.

831. **Muse's.**—There were nine muses, but the singular is used for the plural.

833. In B.'s time a boy's education began (and sometimes ended) with the study of the classics.

Wold.—Another form of *weald*. Primarily a wood, here probably open country.

836. **Athena's tower.**—The Parthenon (temple of Athena) was in the Acropolis of Athens, and contained the most noble specimens of Greek sculpture, designed by Phidias and executed by him or under his superintendence. It was in good condition till 1687, when in the war between Venice and Turkey a great part was laid in ruins. About the time of Byron's visit, Lord Elgin, then Ambassador to Turkey, bought a great number of the statues still remaining and brought them to England ; and in 1816 they were sold to the Government and deposited in the British Museum under the name of the Elgin Marbles.

Gray.—Why is this epithet selected?

837-838. Paraphrase, and explain the reference in "foreign lord."

839-843. The Battle field (Marathon) preserves its bounds as it had them on the morn. The inversion is rather harsh, and the correlation of "alike —— as" is not satisfactory.

Brunt.—Derive, and give the usual meaning. Cf. "The hottest of the fight."

Distant.—Is this a transferred epithet? "The plain of Marathon was offered to me for sale at about £900. Alas! was the dust of Miltiades worth no more?"—B.

844-845. Which uttered.—Parse and expand into a clause. Defend the order of the nouns in l. 845.

846-847. "Bow" and "spear," taken as the distinctive national weapons of Mede and Greek. Note the expressiveness of the epithets in these two lines, and how much they add to the mental picture.

848. Marathon is enclosed on three sides by the rocky arms of Mts. Parnes and Pentelicus, the fourth is bounded by the sea. Cf. in *The Isles of Greece.*

> " The mountains look on Marathon,
>   And Marathon looks on the sea."

849. Why not Destruction in the front and Death in the rear? Cf. *The Bard.*

> " Amazement in his van, with flight combined,
>   And sorrow's faded form, and solitude behind."

851. Derive "trophy" and "hallowed."

852-854. Explain "Freedom's Smile," "Asia's tear," "rifled urn."

Violated mound.—"The principal barrow (the reputed tumulus of the two hundred Athenians who fell) has recently been opened by Fauvel; few or no relics, as vases, etc., were found by the excavator."—B.

Rude.—Why so called?

857. Ionian blast.—Crossing the Ionian Sea from the west. Is *blast* an appropriate word?

863. Pallas (meaning the goddess of wisdom) to the sages, the Muse to the bards.

865. Kindred.—To one's temper or feelings.

868. Byron frequently speaks in this vein of Greece. See the Second Stanza of *The Giaour*, when he compares her appearance to the face of a corpse.

> " 'Tis Greece, but living Greece no more."

869. **Sadness sootheth.**—An inharmonious phrase, and ill-suited to the line. B. is supposed to be referring to himself in this stanza.

871. **Delphi's sacred side.**—The oracle of Delphi, with its famous fountain, Castalia, was at the foot of the southern slope of Mt. Parnassus.

Magic waste.—Show the force and appropriateness of these words.

875. Many have loudly condemned the act of the British Government in regard to the Elgin Marbles. See note on l. 836. No doubt the question has two sides to it ; there is no doubt that Byron's indignation was strengthened by the bad treatment (as he conceived) of the British public.

See his *Curse of Minerva*,

> " 'Scaped from the ravage of the Turk and Goth,
> Thy country sends a spoiler worse than both."

879-880. **So may'st**, etc.—In this way, *i. e.*, acting in accordance with my advice, mayst thou, etc.

Thou.—Who is meant ?

882-885. **For thee.**—The form of this line was perhaps suggested by that in Gray's *Elegy*—

> " For thee, who, mindful of th' unhonored dead."—T.

Idlesse.—Archaic for "idleness."

Soon shall.—Discuss the effect of substituting " will" for " shall."

890. The concluding stanzas were written at Newstead Abbey, after his return to England in July, 1811. The allusion is to the death of two or three of his intimate friends, and of his mother, who died very shortly after his return.

891. The subject of the stanza is only a matter of conjecture.

The identity of Childe Harold with Byron himself is apparent from the last four lines.

Are "did" and "shrank" correct forms ?

Albeit.—Derive, and write out in full the following clause.

898-899. How different the *hopeful* Spirit of Tennyson's noble lines :

> " 'Tis better to have loved and lost,
> Than never to have loved at all."

902. Supply the words necessary to show the grammatical construction.

903. At last time will relieve me of sorrow's dark shadow, as I shall rejoin them in the next world.

905. **Parent.**—See note on l. 890.

Friend.—Perhaps his friend Eddlestone, an old Cambridge comrade, who died shortly after Byron's return.

More than friend.—It is doubtful who is referred to ; perhaps the "thou" of l. 891, perhaps the "Thyrza" of his occasional pieces, whom Moore thought an imaginary person, but others his cousin. For the grammatical construction of the phrase see *H. S. Gr.* v., 75.

910. **Peace.**—Peace of mind.

912. **Distort.**—A well chosen word.

To leave.—Supply "only." Expand into a clause. See *H. S. Gr.* xv., 13.

Still.—Continually.

917. Distinguish "feign" and "dissemble."

918-919. What is his answer to these two lines ?

922. Can you see any incongruity in this line with the rest of the Stanza Contrast the sunny spirit of Wordsworth, rebounding and recovering (as is natural and right) from grief.

> "Then sing ye birds, sing, sing a joyous song,
> And let the young lambs bound.
> What though the radiance that was once so bright
> Be now for ever taken from my sight."

926. **Eld.**—Archaic and poetical.

CANTO III.

The quotation prefixed by Byron to this Canto, " that application might force you to think of other things ; there is in truth no remedy but that and time," is from a letter of Frederick the Great of Prussia, to the great Mathematician, D'Alembert. The sadness and tumultuous state of feeling induced by his domestic unhappiness, and the publicly expressed disapproval of his conduct weighed heavily on a man of Byron's highstrung and sensitive nature. This is reflected in the differences between Cantos III. and IV., and the two of six years before. The changes are more abrupt, the style more vigorous and impassioned, the mechanism of the verse less careful and regular. For a consideration of these differences see Critical Introduction.

2. **Ada.**—B.'s daughter Ada was born in December, 1815 : he and his wife separated in January, 1816, and in the following April he left England never to return. She married Lord Lovelace in 1835, and died in 1852.

The poet recurs in thought to the time when he was leaving England, conceiving himself as asleep, and on shipboard crossing the Channel.

6. **Awaking.**—What is the relation? Criticize the construction of the sentence.

11. Note the transition in the second stanza to indicate the poet's attempt to throw off the gloom and sadness; in I. the waters heave and the winds wail; in II. the waters bound and roar, and the wind is a tempest rending the canvas.

12-13. **As a steed that knows, etc.**—Why is this qualification put in? What difference in meaning if omitted?

His rider.—Why is "*his*" more effective than "its" would be?

17. **On.**—Notice the bold employment of "on" as a verb; cf. "glad" in stanza I. Perhaps Byron is next to Shakespeare in his frequent employment of one part of speech for another.

As a weed.—A seaweed floating hither and thither as wind and tide may carry it, is a fine picture of a man in Byron's plight—homeless, friendless, and driven from his native shores by his own proud spirit and the world's contumely.

20. **Youth's summer.**—He was now but 30 years of age; his poetical powers were strengthening rather than declining; as Cantos III. and IV. are confessedly superior to Cantos I. and II.

One.—Childe Harold.

21. **Outlaw of his own dark mind.**—This may mean flying from his evil conscience, *i.e.*, to get rid of his sense of guilt and shame, or may simply mean exiled from society.

23. **Bear it with me.**—What was the theme? Does he mean "continue the theme," or ruminate upon it?

25. An elaborate metaphor, likening the furrows that thought and grief grave upon the face to the sandy and infertile bed of the torrent. Point out clearly the points of resemblance. The passage (ll. 24-8) may be freely paraphrased thus:—"In that Tale I find deep streams of thought and welling fountains of sympathy with the oppressed. Those streams are now dry, those fountains are now exhausted, and in the sterile sands of life which the torrent of youthful passion has left behind, not one flower of thought or feeling can evermore appear."

Byron from his compactness of expression and pregnant meaning, furnishes excellent material for paraphrasing.

26. **Ebbing**.—Suggesting a *tide* of passion so natural to youth.

29. **Joy or pain**.—The two kinds of passion.

30. As my heart has lost some chord of sympathy, so my verse may be wanting in some notes of harmony.

32. **Essay**.—Another form of *assay*. In what sense is the latter now used? To sing as I have.

33. **Strain**.—Derive, and show the connection of the different meanings.

34. **So that**.—For the nature of the following clause, see *H. S. Gr.* XIV., 21, *g.*

Wean me from the dream.—See the motto he prefixes to the Canto. Refer to passages in his life justifying "dream of gladness." May "dream," have the same meaning in "dream of grief" and "dream of gladness?"

36. Justify the use of *shall* instead of *will*.

38. What peculiarity in the use of *who* here?

40. **Waits**.—Awaits to surprise. Note the different force of *so that* from l. 34.

'Below.—In this world below.

43. **Of silent sharp endurance**.—Not referring to the possessor, but descriptive of the knife as silent, keen, and lasting.

44. Why in lone caves? Bring out the adversative force of *yet* by expanding *lone, yet rife*, into two clauses.

46. **Haunted cell**.—Chambers of the brain, peopled by the creatures of thought and fancy. In Canto II., Stanza 6, he has told us (in his reflections on a skull) some of its tenants :

> "Yes, this was once Ambition's airy hall,
> The dome of Thought, the palace of the Soul ;
> Behold through each lack-lustre, eyeless hole,
> The gay recess of Wisdom and of Wit,
> And Passion's host, that never brooked control ;
> Can all saint, sage, or sophist, ever writ
> People this lonely tower, this tenement refit ?"

47-50. May be paraphrased thus : In giving to the creations of fancy, the form and attributes of life, we thereby live a life of intenser feeling and deeper thought. Thus the life we image forth is the source of new life and interest to us. Even so it is to me now.

"Lord Byron we think formerly complained of those who identified him with his hero : in this last part, however, (Canto III.) it is really impracticable to distinguish them. The author and his hero travel and reflect together, there is the same tone of misanthropy, sadness, and scorn, which we were formerly willing to regard as the assumed costume of the Childe."—*Jeffrey*.

51-55. May be freely paraphrased thus : "I and my blighted life are nothing ; not so thou O my Ideal (soul of my thought) of the free and noble and blessed thing that life should be. Seeing but unseen, with Thee I traverse the earth, whilst my whole being interfused ,with thy spirit and nature (birth) glows at the wrongs I have endured, and in Thee alone can find that support and sympathy, elsewhere denied me."

53. "Invisible but gazing" may be taken as limiting "whom."

54. The two phrases seem tautologous.

55. This line may be expanded thus : "And I can from Thee (my Ideal) rekindle and revive the embers of thought and feeling crushed out and extinguished by misfortune and obloquy."

56-59. See line 21.

59. **Phantasy and flame.**—Hendiadys for "flaming fancies." "*Phantasy*" is but the earlier form of "fancy." Derive, and give other words from the same root.

60-61. What would you adduce from his parentage and rearing and domestic troubles to account for such a state of mind ?

61. **'Tis too late.**—For what ?

62. **Am I changed.**—In what way ?

63. **Time can not abate.**—Is this true ?

65. **Something too much of this.**—Sc. "I have said." The phrase is doubtless, a remembrance from *Hamlet* III., 2, 79.

Note that Byron dismisses himself and his incurable griefs, but immediately introduces Harold, who goes on in the same vein.

66. **Spell.**—A form of words which, when recited, was supposed to have magical power.

The line means "my chant of doom is ended." I have placed upon it the *seal* (the witness of my promise) of silence, Cf. the common phrase : "His lips were sealed."

67. **At last.**—In his preface to Cantos I. and II., Byron says, "Had I proceeded with the poem, this character (of the Childe) would have deepened as he drew to the close, for the outline I once meant to fill up for him was, with some exceptions, the sketch of a modern Timon, perhaps a poetical Zeluco."

68. Of the breast.—Discuss the substitution of " with " for " of."

71. In soul and aspect.—With reference to change of "soul" through increase of years, many examples might be cited to show that age does not always tame it; but want of correspondence between "age" and "aspect" is so seldom seen that the phrase " had altered him in aspect as in age," is almost a truism. In the phrase " Age has greatly altered him," the mind reverts instantly to the *appearance*.

73. What does the *cup* represent ? Why said to be *"enchanted ?'* What does the *brim* represent ? What is the metaphor in *sparkle ?*

Is *but* correctly placed.

74-76. Quaffed.—Show the appropriateness of this word.

Wormwood.—Expand the metaphor.

Purer fount, etc.—Refers to his travels in Greece, recorded in Canto II.

80. Worn with pain, etc.—Perhaps refers to his physical malformation.

" The chain caused pain in the wearing, which silently wasted him and became acute, penetrating more and more as he moved forward, sc. because it was caused by a fetter round the ankles."—*Tozer*. Many attempts were made to cure or lessen his deformity.

80. Pined.—Caused him to pine ; transitive.

82. There is something like a climax in the last five lines, but it would end more strongly if the full stop were after "took." "Through many a scene" seems weak : would "through every scene" be an emendation ?

83-84. Guarded.—"Studied" is the common epithet.

Mixed again.—Probably refers to his return after his Grecian travels with Hobhouse ; stanza XI, perhaps to the time preceding and shortly after his marriage ; stanza XII, to his final departure.

85-91. And thought this spirit so fixed and guarded by this invulnerable mood (of coldness) that even if no joy were got from life, no sorrow lurked behind, and that he, unobserved, but observant, might find in the unheeding world about him as fit food for speculation as the wondrous works of Nature had before furnished him in foreign lands.

93. Curiously.—With close inspection.

95. And not feel that there are some desires and longings which never die through age ; " all "=altogether.

96. Fame is the goddess ; the star is the prize of wealth or title she holds to view ; the steep is the difficulty and labor between men and the prize ;

the alternate unfolding and closing of the clouds represent their alternate hopes and fears.

98-100. Show the appropriateness of "vortex" and "giddy."

Chasing time.—Cf. stanza 22 :

> " To chase the glowing Hours with flying feet."

Explain how " Harold chasing Time " and " Time chasing Harold " may both be good metaphors.

102. **To herd.**—Expressing contempt and disgust.

103-105. Explain and paraphrase "untaught———thoughts." Stanza VIII. to XII. will furnish a useful although difficult exercise in paraphrasing.

108-109. Which spirit (his) could find a life within itself (Stanza VI.), so as to breathe.

110. Mountain scenery seems to have been a passion with Byron.—Shakespeare and Burns deal largely in meadows, and glades, and streams, but little in mountains ; while Wordsworth, Shelley, and especially Byron, were enthusiastic about them. Byron speaks of watching the Malvern hills when a boy " with a sensation I cannot describe." In the *Island*, speaking of the mountain memories of his youth, he says :

> " The infant rapture still survived the boy ;
> And Loch-na-gair with Ida looked o'er Troy,
> Mixed Celtic memories with the Phrygian mount,
> And Highland linns with Castalie's clear fount."

111. Cf. his familiar lines beginning : " And I have loved thee, Ocean."

113. **Power.**—Seems to mean " impelling motive."

115. **Mutual language.**—In a language understood by both ; this meaning implies a strong (not to say violent) personification. We ought not to push the figure so far as the conception of dialogue. These things (mountain, ocean, sky, etc.), spoke to him in a dumb language, it is true, but none the less they inspired him with thoughts, and gave him glowing images, which he in articulate language gave back again to them in his verse.

116-118. **Clearer, etc.**—Paraphrase fully. Expand the metaphors in *pages* and *glassed*.

Cf. Keeble. *Christian Year :*

> " One *page* of Nature's beauteous book."

And Manfred, addressing the Witch of the Alps, II., 2 :

> " Beautiful Spirit, in thy clear brow
> Wherein is *glassed* serenity of soul."

G

119. **Chaldean.**—A caste of the Babylonians, the teachers and priests of the people, who also studied astronomy and astrology, kept the records of the Kingdom and possessed all the scientific knowledge then going. Astrology, like astronomy, was the knowledge of the stars, but became restricted to their supposed influence on the birth and fortunes of men.

120. **Bright.**—The verse pause after "bright," separating it from its closely connected phrase "as their own beams," tends to emphasize it.— Is there such a break between as to justify this separation by the final pause? As to Byron's carelessness in metre see *Introduction*.

114. **Clay will sink, etc.**—Paraphrase from *The Wisdom of Solomon*. 8. 15:

> "For the corruptible body presseth down the soul,
> And the earthly tabernacle weigheth down the mind
> That museth upon many things."—*Tozer*.

Explain clearly what is meant by "spark immortal," "light," "link."

126. **As if.**—Supply the ellipsis fully.

127. **Its brink.**—In what sense is the phrase "heaven's brink" a proper one?

128. **Thing.**—Expressive of what feelings?

129. **Wearisome.**—Full of (some) weariness. Just as in Puritan times a *painful* sermon was one on which pains had been expended.—*Hiley*.

130. **Drooped.**—In spirit or flight of soul as etc. The falcons are high flying birds, striving to rise above their quarry, on which they descend.

132. **Fit.**—Rebellion against the shams and conventionalities of society.

135-136. **So the heat, etc.**—He was consumed by an inward and repressed fire of indignation. Note the *anacoluthon* in regard to "which to overcome." Is the mood of *tinge* correct?

139-145. The connection is:

"This very knowledge that all intercourse with his fellowmen was mere vanity and vexation of spirit, had made him, although despairing, put on a smiling appearance, which inspired an inward content which he forbore to check."

In spite of this, however, Harold goes on as before, seeing little good but much evil in everyone and everything, and is as moody and dark of mind as any one can well be.

142. Is *were* correct? Write out the *as* clause in full.

As on....deck.—Has Byron seized the most salient points of the picture?

146. **Stop.**—" Siste viator, heroa calcas ! "

The student must remember that the year of writing was 1816, when the interest in the great struggle with Napoleon was still alive in men's minds. This fact justifies the abrupt introduction.

147. **Earthquake's spoil.**—Develop the meaning fully.

149. **Trophied column.**—There is one now, erected since Byron's time. " Trophied," literally "adorned with trophies," but here meaning " memorial."

150. **Moral's truth.**—What is the moral that is more manifest with no memorial?

154. Explain why " first " and why " last."

King-making Victory.—Some think this refers to the Holy Alliance of the sovereigns of Russia, Austria, and Prussia, and most of the other European rulers, to preserve their crowns and dynasties, first published in February, 1816. But more generally it refers to the security of the crowned heads and the crushing out of the dreaded revolutionary spirit after the victory of Waterloo. Perhaps it may refer merely to the restoration of Louis XVIII.

155. **Place of skulls.**—No doubt an allusion to Golgotha.

157. **Power which gave.**—Destiny, which gives and takes away, and transfers fame from one to another.

159. **Pride of place.**—A term in falconry, meaning the highest pitch of flight. Cf. *Macbeth*, 2, 4, 12 :

" A falcon towering in her pride of place."—*B.*

Eagle.—Who is meant and why so called?

160. Representing the closing scenes of the battle as a death agony.

163. Bring out the force of the metaphor by paraphrasing.

164. **Fit retribution !**—Seemingly an exclamation of surprise that the tyranny of One (Napoleon) should be destroyed only to be replaced by the many (the various Kings of the Holy Alliance).

169. **Patch'd up idol.**—The idol of Tyranny thrown down and broken, only to be raised again and reconstructed in this new form (Holy Alliance).

171. **Wolf.**—" It is not inconsistent with Byron's sympathy with the revolutionary Carbonari of Italy—the secret society whose object was to destroy all kingly governments—to imagine that *Wolf* may even mean Guelph."—*Hiley.*

Byron seems to have admired Napoleon's talents, and this admiration, with a person of such a temperament, would help largely towards an approval of his policy and principles. To Kings in general, and to the Guelphs in particular, he was a bitter enemy, if we may judge from his writings.

172. **Prove.**—Prove that Waterloo was fit retribution before you praise.

174. **If not.**—Supply the ellipsis.

In vain.—Because liberty is still far distant.

Flowers rooted up.—" A highly poetical expression for the desolation caused by war. In Landseer's fine painting, " Time of war," one of the most effective touches is the introduction of the flowers in the midst of the carnage and ruin."—*T.*

178. **Broken.**—In vain (as regards Freedom) have death, etc., been brought to an end (broken) by the Alliance (accord) against Napoleon.

179. **Most endears.**—What justifies war with its evils is the freedom won by it.

Myrtle wreathes a sword.—A quotation from the Greek song composed in honor of Harmodius and Aristogiton, who in 514 B.C., assassinated Hipparchus, one of the Tyrants of Athens, at the festival of Minerva (Panathenæa). Myrtle branches were carried as expressive of Love and Peace, and the daggers used were concealed in them. Cf. "Sword in Myrtles drest," Keble's *Christian Year*, 3rd Sunday in Lent.

182. The change to the description of the Ball is in Byron's usual abrupt way.—Jeffrey's criticism is well in point here.—" There can be no more remarkable proof of the greatness of Lord Byron's genius than the spirit and interest he has contrived to communicate to his picture of the oft-drawn and difficult scene of the breaking up from Brussels before the great battle. All our bards great and small, from Scott and Southey down to hundreds without names, have adventured upon this theme and failed in the management of it. It required some courage therefore to venture on such a theme, a theme, too, alien in its general conception to the prevailing tone of Byron's poetry. See however with what easy strength he enters upon it, and with how much grace he gradually finds his way back to his own peculiar vein of sentiment and diction."

182. **Sound of revelry.**—The Duchess of Richmond's ball on the evening of the 15th of June, 1815. Quatre Bras was fought next day, and Waterloo two days later.

189. **Marriage bell.**—Note the intended contrast with "Knell."

190. Byron for poetical purposes represents the news of the coming of the French as a *surprise*. It was not so, however, to the Duke. He had received the news some hours before, but dressed leisurely and went to the ball. At midnight the general officers were summoned, a little later the younger ones were quietly called away.

Rising. The first stroke ; commencing.

194-195. These much quoted and beautifully suggestive lines remind us of Gray's lines in the *Bard* :

> " In gallant trim the gilded vessel sails,
> Youth on the prow and Pleasure at the helm."

Chase the hours.—Give in other language the full meaning of this line, and cf. note on l. 98.

196. Note the slowness and heaviness of this line as compared with the ease ahd lightness of 105.

198. Note the climax.

199. Byron has merely antedated the effect. During the three following days the cannonading could be distinctly heard in Brussels, giving rise of course to all sorts of unfounded fears and reports.

201. **Fated chieftain.**—William Frederick, duke of Brunswick, killed at Quatre-Bras.

203. **Caught its tone.**—Recognized it as the booming of cannon. He had been forbidden by Napoleon to succeed to the duchy of his father, killed at Auerstadt, October 14th, 1806. He led 700 Hussars, called the Black Brunswickers from wearing mourning for his father.

Death's prophetic ear.—An allusion to the superstition still common in remote districts, that a warning comes to those about to die. So among the Highlanders a spectre of one's self (wraith) appeared before death, and among the Lowlanders a tingling in the ears (death-bell) announced the death of a friend. Almost every soldier can tell of warnings or presentiments that he has heard of.

205-206. Paraphrase fully, and note any peculiarities in the form of the expression.

207. **Quell.**—Exemplify the more common meaning and use of this word.

211. **All.**—Adv. not of extent but of intensity ; stronger than "quite."

215. **Ne'er might be repeated.**—Why? What two meanings may "might" have here? Is "guess" properly used?

216. **Mutual.**—Expand into a clause; distinguish "mutual" and "common."

Note that the poet *artfully carries* us back to l. 188 by the periphrasis of l. 216, and that he has selected *the eyes* as conveying most delicately and tellingly the passion of love. Byron himself had beautiful eyes.

218-226. Has the poet chosen the most salient points and the best for his picture of such a scene as this must have been ?

Clattering car.—May refer to waggons laden with war material.

Alarming.—Calling to arms.—" Alarm " and "alarum " are both from Italian *all'arme, i.e.,* " all to arms ! "

Morning star.—Is sometimes above the horizon three hours before sunrise.

227. **Cameron's Gathering.**—A piece of music known by this name or " Lochiel's March."

228. **Lochiel.**—Macaulay's and Campbell's Lochiel was Sir Evan Cameron, of Lochiel, called Black Evan (Evan-dhu), a determined Royalist, the last to submit to Cromwell, the first among the Highlanders to declare for Charles II. He has been called the Ulysses of the Highlands. He fought at " Killiecrankie," and died in 1719. His grandson Donald ("the gentle Lochiel ") was with Charles Edward in the '45, retired to France after Culloden, and died there in 1748. The great grandson, Donald, was in the Grenadier Guards and fought at Waterloo.

Albyn.—Scotland. Albion is England.

230. **Pibroch.**—The music of the bagpipe—the national instrument of Scotland. Sir W. Scott tells us that a good judge of bagpipe music, can point out in a well-composed pibroch, the parts imitative of the march, the fight, the pursuit, etc. Instances of its effects upon Highland regiments are related that almost strain our credulity.

231. **With.**—One would expect *as* to correspond with *so* in the next line.

233. Is *which* subject or object of instils ?

236. " The wood of Soignies is supposed to be a remnant of the forest of Ardennes, immortal in Shakespeare's *As You Like It.*"—*B*. In ancient times the name Ardennes was applied to all the country between the Rhine and the Sambre. It consists of low hills, scarcely any over 2000 feet, or plateaux inclining to the North and North East. Even now large portions are covered with considerable forests of oak and beech.

243. **Rolling.**—Like lava down the volcano's side.

250. **Thunder clouds.**—The smoke of battle which closes down like a curtain, lifts upon a wholly changed and terrible scene. It is said there was a thunder-storm on the day of Waterloo, but there is probably no reference to it here.

Which when rent.—A Latinism. Give the natural expression.

253. **Blent**—blended.—Point out the beauties in stanzas 27, 28, giving a reason in each case why you consider it so.

253. **Loftier harps.**—Perhaps he refers to Scott.

255. **One.**—Major Howard, son of the Earl of Carlisle, who was Byron's guardian.

Blend me with his line.—There was some family connection.

257. **Some wrong.**—Probably refers to some ill-natured lines in *English Bards and Scotch Reviewers.*

262. Howard is pronounced as a monosyllable. Elsewhere he pronounces Charles as a dissyllable.

266. **Living.**—Note the antithesis.

268. **Contrive.**—Implies a scheme or plan.

270. **Reckless.**—Devoid of care. Is it a suitable word?

271. **Those.**—Who are meant?

273. **One as all.**—One equally with another, or "one like all." A very awkward expression.

275. **For their sake.**—Does "their" refer to the dead or to the relatives?

276. Explain the allusions in Archangel's and Glory's trump.

277-280. At first the glory of the death somewhat soothes the grief, but afterwards when the bereaved find this is also vanity, the grief returns keener than ever.

280. In this stanza note that the poet is returning to the oft repeated misanthropic vein. Byron seldom gives sufficient force to the maxim that Time is a mighty healer.

284. **Roof tree,**—The beam or pillar supporting the roof.

285. **Hoariness.**—From the mould upon it.

286. **Battlements.**—See *Prisoner of Chillon*, III. Note.

287. **Enthral.**—Distinguish "enslave," and "enthral."

289. **Brokenly.**—In the phrases "these few *broken* remarks." "Words *brokenly* spoken" the meaning is "disjointedly," "ramblingly;" but here the word means "although broken."

Discuss the appropriateness of the various metaphors used in this stanza to illustrate his idea that an outward mechanical life may go on though the true life of inner enjoyment and beauty has perished.

290. "The simile of the broken mirror carries out and amplifies the idea contained in 'brokenly.' The broken heart feels its sorrow with greater intensity, and recalls the image of the lost object of affection in a great variety of ways, just as every fragment of the broken mirror has the same power of reflection as the mirror itself when unbroken." —*Tozer.*

292. Give the analysis of ll. 290-293, supplying the necessary ellipses. Note the unusual form "which not forsakes."

295. Living on in its broken condition.—Byron is now back again into his usual misanthropical and pessimistic mood. There is a change of image (and a little abrupt) in these next lines.

296. **Bloodless.**—Must mean "without affection."

297. Externally the coldness and hardness of age ; internally a grief still nursed. Would you apply Burns' line still further in Byron's case and say "nursed to keep it warm?"

299-300. "As a poisonous sap may keep alive a tree, so despair may furnish life to us." Discuss the truth of such a statement.

Byron has the same idea in the *Dream*, Stanza VIII., speaking of the Wanderer (supposed to be himself) :

> "He fed on poisons, but they had no power,
> But were a kind of nutriment."

Quick.—Compare "the quick and the dead."

302. **As nothing did we die.**—Death would be release and relief. The *Childe*, doesn't, like *Hamlet*, speculate on the *after* possibility of torment.

304. The simile appears a little lacking. He must mean that a "sort of life" may be maintained upon "Sorrow's fruit," a tasteless and imperfect life, indeed, but still a life. Just so the apples of Sodom may sustain life, although they are ashes to the taste.

Thevenot says : "There are apple trees on the sides of the Dead Sea which bear fruit lovely to the eye, but within full of ashes. Witman says the same of the oranges there."—*Brewer.* They are really a species of gall-nut. Byron omits reference to their appearance, as typifying the life of the Wanderer, because he wishes to intimate its *gloominess* as to prospect, and its want of satisfying as to real enjoyment.

308-311. See *Psalms* xc, 10.—"The Psalmist's estimate is high enough, and more than enough, if thy record O fatal Waterloo of the allotted span of life be taken as the true one."

Some consider "tale" to mean number, as in "the tale of bricks" in *Exodus.* "And if the number of thy slain be the true number, that allotted span (70) is more than it ought to be."

Of course the student will know that the *average* length of human life is not the half of 70 ; and also that so early after the great fight, the most exaggerated reports of the number killed would be current.

314. **United nations.**—Name them.

316. **This is much.**—For what does "this" stand ? Parse "all."

317. The Stanzas following, on Napoleon, are distinctly more favorable than the *Ode to Napoleon*, written in 1814, just after his exile to Elba.

318. **Spirit.**—There is either an anacoluthon here, or a harsh ellipsis of a verb.

Antithetically.—"Apt for all things, but excellent only in war ; adoring chance, force, success, splendour and noise, more than true glory."—*De Tocqueville.* Cf. Young. *Night Thoughts.*

"From different natures marvellously mixt."

320. **Been betwixt.**—Bring out the meaning by paraphrasing fully this and the next line.

323. **As fall.**—Supply·the ellipsis and justify the statements.

325. **Thunderer of the scene.**—Imitating the phrase, "hero of the scene," and probably alluding to Jove, the chief of the Gods, who wielded the thunderbolt as his peculiar weapon. Just so Napoleon was chief of Kings, and his peculiar weapons were his cannons.

327. **Trembles still.**—"Napoleon's hat and grey surtout placed on the end of a stick on the coast of Brest, made all Europe run to arms."—*Chateaubriand,* quoted by Tozer.

Wild.—What is the force of the epithet ?

329. Classify and give the relation of the clause "that thou art nothing."

333. **Inert.**—Because they were astounded, and deemed thee, etc.

Astounded. Give derivation, kindred forms, and a native equivalent.

335. Parse briefly in this stanza "less," "making," "more," "skilled," "learn."

337. See *Joshua,* 10, 24, for an instance of the custom in which the metaphor originated.

Compare with what follows B.'s fine and much quoted lines in *The Age of Bronze,* Stanza III. :

> "Yes ! where is he the champion and the child
> Of all that's great or little, wise or wild ?
> Whose game was empires, and whose stakes were thrones ;
> Whose table, earth—whose dice were human bones."

340. **Pettiest passion.**—Napoleon's littleness, meanness, and jealousy of other successful military leaders are well known. The active principle in his character was an enormous selfishness, and a callousness of heart which shrank from no cruelty or injustice. As instances of the above we may mention the death of Moreau, the divorce of Josephine, the murder (it was nothing less) of the duke d'Enghien, the squabbling with Hudson, the Governor at St. Helena, the *deliberate* falsifications of history in his memoirs.

341. **Skilled in men's spirits.**—In selecting men fitted by their courage and talents for his work. . . Few had a greater discerning power in

this way than Napoleon. Among his 16 or 18 Marshals, some were from the best blood of France, others from the lowest grade of society. The influence of his example in his own person and practice in promoting *merit*, wherever found, was tremendous in binding to him the hearts of his soldiers. Therefore it has been said that Napoleon himself, an autocrat that would brook no restraint in military or civil matters, made by his life and example a *democratic* impress on the nations of Europe.

344. Brooked.—Certainly not with the patience and uncomplaining fortitude naturally to be expected from so great a man.

349. Hast smiled.—Distinguish in meaning between this tense and "didst smile."

353. Sager.—Write out the clause in full.

354. To shew.—Connect with "steeled thee on" and not with "too far."

358. Spurn.—Napoleon has been described as wholly without natural affection for his kind. He might use the highest or the lowest as his instruments, but when no longer needed he flung them aside.

365-366. Their belief in his invincibility made him invincible for a time.

367. Philip's son.—Alexander, King of Macedon.

The argument of Stanza XLI., seems to be this : Thy part was not the cynic's, to snarl and mock at the weakness and meanness of men, but rather the part of Alexander to look on them with habitual and silent scorn. We may pity and tolerate a cynic in private life, but the whole earth must not be made a den for the sceptred cynic to rage and rule in.

Then.—While emperor.

369. Diogenes.—The celebrated cynic philosopher of Sinope. See the classical dictionary for an account of his alleged interview with Alexander the Great, and for other stories told of him.

370. Quick.—Restless.

There.—Show the pronominal force by substituting a phrase.

373. Motion.—Cf. ll. 131 *et seq.* ; although differently applied this is Ambition.

375. Fitting medium.—He may refer to Aristotle's Golden Mean, in which he places all the virtues ; or perhaps he used " medium " as equivalent to "space" or "scope."

378. Fever at core,—In apposition with " fire and motion," ll. 372-373.

381. Contagion.—Distinguish from infection ; which is better here ?

383. Sophists.—A name applied to the leading public teachers in Ancient Greece during the 5th and 4th centuries B.C. They are represented by the comic poets as ostentatious impostors, flattering the rich and duping the young. Although Solon, Pythagoras, Socrates, Plato, and Aristotle, have been designated Sophists, yet the word conveyed to many minds the idea of intellectual ability united to a certain moral obliquity. Byron uses it in this sense for those who have led the world astray in the realm of thought.

385. Begin by duping and end by being duped.

391. So trained and bigotedly fond of strife.

393. **Overcast.**—Explain the figure.

397. Like that of Hudibras :

" Which ate into itself for lack
Of somebody to hew and hack "

Note the metaphors of the "wave," "twilight," "sky," "flame," the "sword." Byron's has such a wealth of comparisons, and they succeed each other with such rapidity (sometimes abruptness) that the effect is apt to be confusing.

398. **Mountain tops.**—Grandeur of thought or action.

399. **Peaks.**—Summits of ambition, power and place.

Clouds and snow.—The occupants or possessors are henceforth isolated and solitary in their grandeur.

400-406. The mountaineer sees high above him the shining sun, so the sun of glory still dazzles and attracts *him.* The mountaineer sees earth and sea outspread before him, so he too has the world at his feet. The mountaineer sees about him and near him only icy rocks and clouds, and everlasting snow. So he, too, is a solitary being, cut off from sympathy and communion with his fellows. The cold breath of envy and detraction blows upon him, and the tempests of prejudice and passion continually assail him. These are the only rewards for him who achieves grandeur of thought or action.

Note the confusion of figures. The comparison is first to the peaks and then to the mountaineer upon them.

407. **Enough of this.**—The true wisdom lies in studying the great Book of Nature, or in making a new world of one's own mind :

" My mind to me a kingdom is."

414. **Stern.**—With stern aspect, transferred epithet.

415. **Greenly.**—Referring to the parasitic growth that starts up on decaying or mouldering walls.

418. **Crannying.**—Penetrating the crannies—a venturesome use of the word.

423. **Shredless.**—Bring out the force by a paraphrase.

426. Power dwelt.—A very fine and perfect image: the Passions are the retinue, accompaniment, and consequence of Power.

427-428. Alluding to feudal times, when

> "The good old rule
> Sufficed them.; the simple plan
> That they should take who have the power,
> And they should keep who can."—*Rob Roy's Grave.*

430-433. Paraphrase fully, and point out the ambiguity in 430.

436. Love's blazon.—In the tournaments the devices on their shields often had some relation to their lady-love.

437. Emblems.—Perhaps love-gages, or pledges of love, given to the Knights by their ladies, and worn by them as distinctions in the lists. Cf. *Lady of the Lake*, 4, 27 :

> "It shall wave
> Like plumage on thy helmet brave."

439. Still.—Their flame of love ever took the form of fierceness.

440. Fair mischief.—Mischief, the cause of which was a contest for some fair one . . ; or perhaps (but not so good) "for some mischievous fair one."

442. Discoloured.—Note the suggestiveness of the epithet.

446. So.—Expand into a a clause.

448. Scythe.—The "scythe" gives us the idea of *sweeping* and *general* destruction ; as it is the weapon assigned to Father Time, the idea of *lastingness* is also suggested. Line 447 is but the Scriptural figure that "all flesh is but grass." The poet thus ingeniously contrasts the shortness and uncertainty of human life, and the everlasting conflict and carnage going on, with the gladness bestowed by this noble stream, which would if undisturbed go on in its shining beauty forever.

450. Lethe.—Among the ancient Greeks and Romans a river of the lower world. He who bathed in its waters forgot all his previous life.

Byron's meaning seems to be :

Thy beauties, O Rhine, make us forget all other beauties of nature ; but even thy loveliness cannot shut out the memory of the terrible scenes thy banks have witnessed . . If thy waters, like Lethe could obliterate the past, then thy banks would be a perfect heaven of delight.

454. Weltering.—Wallowing or rolling in something foul or liquid.

456. Blood of yesterday.—Referring to Waterloo.

458. Glassed.—Was reflected.

459.460. Thy waves may wash away the stains of blood and battle; but nothing can ever make us forget the awful desolation and carnage thy shores have witnessed.

SELECTIONS

FROM

ADDISON'S ESSAYS

WITH

ANNOTATIONS AND LIFE OF THE AUTHOR.

LIFE OF ADDISON.

Joseph Addison was born on the first day of May, 1672, and was the eldest son of Lancelot Addison, himself an important personage of that time, having been a royal chaplain, a D.D. of Oxford, and an author of some repute. He successively became Archdeacon of Salisbury and Dean of Lichfield, and perhaps would have been made a bishop after the revolution, if his ultra royalism had not displeased William III, and Tillotson.

Young Addison, a gentle and studious lad, was sent to the Charterhouse School, and at fifteen to Queen's College, Oxford, and thence to Magdalen College, where he resided ten years. He had been transferred to this College on account of his classical attainments, which were already considerable, but more especially on account of his taste and skill in Latin versification, which was then considered the proper aim and ornament of a classical education. He was distinguished by his shy and retiring manners, but his reputation for scholarship stood very high. He was not unpopular among his companions, and was in favor with the heads of the college and so was elected to a fellowship in 1699. A few years before he had made his first essay in English verse in some complimentary lines to Dryden. Dryden, whom the Revolution had deprived of court favour and patronage, was much gratified at the young scholar's praise.

An interchange of civilities and good offices took place. Addison was probably introduced by Dryden to Congreve and was certainly presented by Congreve to Charles Montague, then Chancellor of the Exchequer, and leader of the Whig party in the House of Commons.

It had been Addison's first intention to enter the Church, and such was his father's wish. He had good reason to expect preferment. His father's eminence, his own well recognized scholarship and the influence of such a wealthy college as Magdalen might have led him to expect in the future even a bishopric. The Revolution had thrown the chief power in the state into the House of Commons. The leaders of the dominant party in that branch of the legislature had the power to make the future of any rising young man. The press had become free, and to gain the ear of the Commons was now the certain road to success. The floor of the house or the public prints was now the arena in which political victory must be won. Hence literary and oratorical ability were eagerly sought for and encouraged. Montague, himself no mean versifier, was a judicious and liberal patron of literature, and in this was ably assisted by the most learned and virtuous politician of the time, Lord Chancellor Somers. These, having no office just ready to offer Addison, secured for him a pension of £300 a year. This with his fellowship, made it possible for him to travel through France, Italy and Switzerland, during the years 1699-1703. In the meantime, however, King William had died, the Whig ministry had resigned, and his pension had stopped. He himself averred that he got but a single payment of it.

Addison found himself in such straitened circumstances that he was compelled for a year to accept a tutorship to a young English traveller, with whom he travelled over a great part of Switzerland and Germany.

Toward the end of 1703 he returned to England and was cordially received by his Whig friends, and was elected a member of the celebrated Kit Cat Club. For several months, however, his prospects were gloomy enough. His pecuniary difficulties were pressing him hard, and there was no chance of employment unless there should be a change in the political world.

That change, however, came sooner than he expected. The Tory party at that time was divided on the question of the war. The country gentlemen and the clergy were averse to interfering in continental affairs. But the chiefs of the party, those who had most influence with the Queen and the House, saw that the interests of England demanded a vigorous war policy, and were accordingly willing and anxious to get the support of the Whigs to sustain them in power, and were thus making overtures to such men as Somers and Sunderland, Cowper and Halifax. The chief Tory leaders who were in this way inclined towards coalition were Marlborough and Godolphin. In August, 1704, the battle of Blenheim gave great joy to the Whig party and the ministry, and it was necessary to celebrate in verse a victory which lifted the English name again into respect after the disasters of William's campaigns. Godolphin, although more versed in negotiating loans or in the pedigrees of racers and game-cocks, than in matters of learning and literature, was nevertheless scandalized at the exceeding badness of these compositions.* He applied to Montague—Montague mentioned Addison, and the next morning, "his garret, up three pair of stairs, over a small shop in the Haymarket," was visited by a messenger from Godolphin. Addison gladly undertook the task and in due time appeared the *Campaign*, which had a remarkable success with the public, and procured for him a Commissionership† at two hundred a year, with promises for the future. The poem is as good as could be expected from one made to order, and the versification is correct and smooth.

The promotion of Addison was rapid. In 1705 the Whigs were more successful at the polls; the Coalition was openly

---

* Macaulay, has quoted the following specimen.
 "'Think of two thousand gentlemen at least,
 And each man mounted on his capering beast;
 Into the Danube they were pushed by shoals."

† It was a Commissionership made vacant by the death of *John Locke*, the famous author of the *Essay on the Human Understanding*.

H

avowed, Somers and Montague entered the Cabinet, and Addison became an Under Secretary of State. In 1707 he went as Montague's Secretary on the mission to George, Elector of Hanover. In 1708 he entered parliament, afterwards being member for Malmesbury till his death. The Whigs were successful at this election and obtained complete control of the Government. Somers became Lord-President, Wharton Lord-Lieutenant, and Addison Chief Secretary for Ireland. This post was worth about £2000 a year, and another minor one attached to it made his income not less than £2500.

That his rise should have been so rapid is a little wonderful, seeing he came of no great or wealthy family, and that his nervousness and diffidence as a speaker in the House were such that after his first failure he never opened his lips in debate. One reason given is that the ability to write was then more in demand than the ability to speak. The newspaper was not then the great collector of news, the record and moulder of public opinion that it has since become. The Parliamentary debates were not reported. The great dailies were not established for half a century after this. As a consequence the pamphlet, the broadside, and the newsletter were in constant request ; and the literary ability of men like Addison or Swift was then sure of reward. But perhaps another and powerful reason was the character of the man. Seldom are there found united in the same person so many pleasing and amiable qualities. The envy that his talents and success would have excited in the case of other men, was in him completely disarmed by his modesty and bashfulness. At a time when politics were distinguished by meanness and duplicity it was a pleasure to find a politician who had some regard for truth and social decency, and whose manners were those of a Christian and a gentleman. He was a charming conversationist. Whether in serious or lively converse he was *facile princeps*. All his intimates united in praise of his courtesy and colloquial powers. The brilliant Mary Montague said " that she had known all the wits, and that Addison was the best company in the world. The malignant Pope was forced to own that there was a charm in Addison which could be found nowhere else. Swift, when burning against the Whigs, could not but confess to Stella that after all he had never known any associate so agreeable as Addison. Steele an excellent judge of lively conversation, said that the conversation of Addison was at once the most polite and the most mirthful that could be imagined ; Young, an excellent judge of serious conversation, said that when Addison was at his ease he went on in a noble strain of thought and language so as to chain the attention of every hearer." We can mention only two faults, both excusable under the circumstances and redeemed a hundred times by his goodness of heart and his uniform sweetness of temper, his sprightly wit, his keén sense of humour and the ridiculous, always charitably exercised, and his complete freedom from rancor and party spite. He was a little too fond of the company and adulation of inferior men, who elevated him to the position of an oracle, and he was a little too fond of the bottle. But we must remember that in the time of Anne, deep drinking needed no apology ; it was a custom with all in the fashionable world, and to be carried home dead drunk at four o'clock in the morning was not considered to be a detraction from any gentleman's character.

His years of official service are almost a literary blank. Some pamphlets now forgotten, his opera of *Rosamond*, which contained some indifferent lyrical poetry, may be noted ; also some contributions to *The Tatler* during the last few months of his tenure of office. But a change was impending which was to give him leisure for work of more lasting value than his political services. The trial of Addison's old school-friend, Sacheverell, the victory of Mrs Masham over the Duchess, the sympathy of the Queen with the Pretender, above all the general weariness of the war, all contributed to place the Tories in power, in the summer of 1710, where they remained for four years. Those four years were mainly spent by Addison in writing those essays which have made his name famous where-ever English is spoken. The Whigs had been completely routed at the elections, and an entire change of Ministry took place. These reverses bore with especial hardness upon Addison. He was deprived of his secretaryship and with difficulty retained his small Irish holding. Only a little before he had resigned his fellowship, and he himself speaks of having lost money in the West Indies. Yet his emoluments must have been considerable, for early next year we find him buying an estate near Rugby and paying for it ten thousand pounds. The only other explanation possible must be his thrifty and economical habits, or a supposed legacy left him by his younger brother, who was for a time governor of Madras.

Addison had still another solace amid the general ruin of the Whigs; the leading members of that party were pursued with especial malignity, he was almost the only exception. The most violent and unfair means were used to oust other Whigs from their boroughs; he alone was allowed to be returned by acclamation. During the election he edited a political journal, called the *Whig Examiner*, which contained some of the bitterest things that he was capable of writing. Yet he was so much esteemed by the Tories, so generally beloved for his kindliness of heart, and admired for his abilities, that he successfully solicited for Ambrose Phillips and Richard Steele the retention of their places under the government.

Steele had been a schoolfellow of Addison's at the Charter-house, continued on intimate terms with him afterwards, and was attached to the same political party. He seems to have inherited from his Irish mother the impulsive ardour, the high animal spirits, the bright fancy and the quick wit, very com-monly thought to be characteristic of the Irish race. He left

Merton College without taking his degree, and became a captain in the Horse Guards. Although disinherited for this imprudence he was still gay and thoughtless, sinning and repenting only to sin again In 1701 we find him writing a religious treatise* as a self-imposed penance ; in 1702 he had taken to writing comedies† to enliven his character—probably all the while deep in debt and tipsy every night. He married two moderate fortunes, yet owing to drink and play, to fine turn-outs and other extravagances, he was often harassing his friends for money, and in fear of the sheriff's officer.

In 1706 Steele was appointed Gazetteer by Sunderland, probably at Addison's request, and in this capacity must have had access to earlier and more authentic information than that in the ordinary news-letter. This advantage he turned to account in the new periodical which appeared in April 1709 and was called by him *The Tatler*. It was to appear three times a week, on Tuesdays, Thursdays, and Saturdays, under the pseudonym of Isaac Bickerstaff, Astrologer, which Swift in the previous year had already made famous.

It was to contain a short essay, some foreign news, court talk, and the fashions, theatrical gossip, literary and religious criticism, and reports from the various coffee-houses. " Steele was not " ill-qualified to conduct the work which he had planned. His "public intelligence he drew from the best sources. He had " read much more than the dissipated men of that time were in " the habit of reading. He had a small share of book-learning, " but a vast acquaintance with the world. He had lived with " gownsmen, with troopers, with gentlemen ushers of the Court, " with men and women of fashion ; with authors and wits, with " the inmates of the sponging houses, and with the frequenters " of all the clubs and coffee-houses in the town. His style was

* *The Christian Hero*, dedicated to Lord Cutts.

† *Grief à la mode* 1702, *The Tender Husband* 1703; his best was the *Conscious Lovers*, 1722. Of course his fame rests upon his essays, which are inferior only to Addison's.

" easy and not incorrect; and though his wit and humour were
" of no high order, his gay animal spirits imparted to his com-
"positions an air of vivacity which ordinary readers could
" hardly distinguish from comic genius."*

Addison was ignorant of the venture and was in Dublin at
the time, but soon began to contribute, at first in notes and
sketches, which Steele filled up, but later on during the last
months of his tenure of office, in more finished, complete and
serious papers. He is thought to have had a hand in some
sixty or seventy of the two hundred and seventy-one papers
contained in *The Tatler*.

During the same time *The Tatler* had undergone a considerable change. It had been giving up politics and general news
ever since Steele had lost his place of Gazetteer.* It had
latterly become a mere series of essays or papers on books,
morals, manners, customs &c. Addison, now at leisure and
living in London, was pre-eminently qualified for such work.
So it was resolved to begin a new work on an improved plan,
to be issued every day except Sundays. The undertaking seemed
to many a bold one, but Steele was confident of the versatility
and fertility of Addison's genius. Thus on the 2nd of January,
1711, appeared the last number of *The Tatler*, and on the first
of the following March the first number of *The Spectator*.†

The results amply justified Steele's faith. No similar work
ever had such success. The first regular issue was 2000 copies,
which soon rose to 4000. For certain papers 20,000 copies
were required, and when the first volume of these essays was
bound up 10,000 copies was quite insufficient to supply the first

---

* Macaulay.

* He was allowed to retain his place in the Stamp Office, on the promise of good
behaviour (i.e to abate the vehemence of his Whiggism). Addison kept him up to
that point for two years.

† The student must not forget that although *The Tatler* was the most popular periodical as yet known in England, Addison's contributions constituted the best part of it;
many of Steele's are interesting, a few admirable, but all of Addison's.

demand. It should be remembered that the English of that day
were not as now a reading people, the population was scarcely
a fifth of what it now is, books were comparatively scarce and
dear, the farmers, the shop keepers, and even the gentry, were
deplorably ignorant and inappreciative of literary men or the
works they wrote. Except among the aristocracy, in some
large provincial towns and in the City of London itself, few
buyers would be found. If we take these things into consideration we may fairly conclude that, reckoned by the sales alone,
The Spectator was one of the greatest literary successes of modern times.

It was not till the middle of 1712 that this extraordinary
popularity had diminished in any marked degree. On the 6th
December the last number of the seventh volume was issued,
No. 555, in which Steele, over his own name, as in the concluding number of the *Tatler*, two years previous, pays a high
tribute to Addison's abilities, and acknowledges in feeling
terms how greatly he has been indebted to Addison's taste and
judgment. It is somewhat difficult to decide upon the relative
merits of Steele and Addison. Some think that in original
humor and sketches of eccentric character, in the delineations
of the various phases of London life, Steele was at least Addison's equal. Even in these, however, Addison's were more
naturally and elegantly written, and in the department of
literature, Steele had neither the learning nor the critical
acumen to make his criticism of much worth. Altogether
beyond the power of Steele were those reflections of a moral,
religious and philanthropical nature which enrich so many of
the Saturday night papers. The philosophy is not, perhaps,
very deep, the speculations are, in many cases, superficial, but
there is always an elevated tone of moral purity, a devout trust
in the truths of religion, enlivened, it may be, with gentle, even
sportive, humour, and adorned with the gayest wit and the

sweetest flowers of fancy, and never descending to ribaldry or skeptical scoffing.

In March, 1713, Steele set on foot the *Guardian*, which ran to 175 numbers. Of these Addison wrote but one in the first volume, but in the second and concluding volumes about 50, being a more frequent contributor than Steele. This was the last writing they did in conjunction. The *Englishman*, issued three times a week, was even a worse failure than the *Guardian*. On Friday, June 18th, 1714, the last volume of the *Spectator* was begun. It was issued three times a week, and contained nothing of Steele's, as the *Englishman* had contained nothing of Addison's. It terminated with the eightieth number on Dec. 20th. Addison's papers constitute about one-third, chiefly at the beginning of the series. They are more uniformly serious in their nature, less sprightly in their vein than the earlier, but some of the finest may be found there, *e.g.*, *The Mountain of Miseries* and the *Reflections by Moonlight*.

Why Addison gave less assistance in the later periodicals may have been that he was preparing his tragedy of *Cato* for publication. A great part had been written at the time of his return from Italy, and his diffidence and modesty alone had kept it back. With many misgivings, he at last yielded to the importunity of his friends, and permitted it to be brought out at Drury Lane, April, 1713. Its success was phenomenal. The managers had spared no magnificence in scenery and dresses. The prologue was written by Pope, the principal character was played by Booth.

Every exertion was made by his political friends to pack the house, and there was a great crowd of Whig men of letters and fashion from the coffee-houses, Whig lawyers from the Inns of Court, Whig commoners and Whig lords from parliament. On the other hand the Tories were well inclined towards Addison. He was thought by them to be a gentleman of such

wit and virtue, of such brilliant talents and unexceptionable
modesty, that his name should be kept free from the stains and
bitterness of party warfare.   They affected to find in the ambition of Julius Caesar a parallel to the ambition of the great military captain who had just been hurled from power, and the
Tory *Examiner* vied with the Whig *Guardian* in expressing
delight and admiration.   Such a union of sentiment among
such rancorous partisans is of itself a glowing tribute to the
sweetness and purity of the author's character.   The piece had
no willing detractors ; the curtain went down amid thunders of
applause.   The play ran for thirty-five nights without interruption to overflowing houses, was sent down to Oxford, and
there among the gownsmen excited as much admiration and
eulogy as it had in the metropolis.

  Macaulay characterizes the tragedy as follows :

  " About the merits of the piece which had so extraordinary
" an effect, the public, we suppose, has made up its mind.   To
" compare it with the masterpieces of the Attic stage, with the
" great English dramas of the time of Elizabeth, or even with
" the productions of Schiller's manhood would be absurd indeed.
" Yet it contains excellent dialogue and declamations, and among
" plays fashioned on the French model, must be allowed to rank
" high ; not indeed with *Athalie* or *Saul ;* but we think not
" below *Cinna,* and certainly above any other English tragedy
" of the same school, above many of the plays of Corneille,
" above many of the plays of Voltaire and Alfieri, and above
" some plays of Racine.   Be this as it may, we have little
" doubt that *Cato* did as much as the *Tatlers, Spectators* and
" *Freeholders* united to raise Addison's fame among his contem-
" poraries."

  Frigid declamation, although delivered in the finest of solemn
tones, enriched with the noblest moral sentiments, and graced
with the smoothest of diction, is a poor substitute for true

dramatic power and passion, but this was an age in which dramatic power and passion were well nigh extinct. The dazzling success of *Cato* was mainly due to the interest and influence of the politicians. As a stage piece it is to all intents and purposes dead, and by no ability in its acting or' brilliancy in its setting can it be again galvanized into life.*

The career of Addison as a man of letters was now almost finished. He was elevated to a kind of literary primacy, and perhaps no primate was ever less tyrannous or more lenient to the sins of his fellows than the gentle satirist. Even literary envy seems to have been disarmed by such pre-eminence and such modesty. With but two exceptions, Addison remained on the best of terms with the chief literary men of his day. Pope, now a young man of about twenty-five, was one of these, Addison had again expressed his admiration of Pope's genius, as shewn in the *Essay on Criticism* and the *Rape of the Lock*. There was but one criticism unfavorable to *Cato*; Pope, because he hated the author (John Dennis), wrote an exceedingly foolish and spiteful pamphlet in its defence. Addison very naturally disclaimed any connection with it, and expressed his disapproval of it as being unworthy of a scholar and a gentleman.

---

* It is worth noticing how many things in *Cato* keep their ground as habitual quotations:
"Big with the fate of Cato and of Rome."
"'Tis not in mortals to command success,
But we'll do more Sempronius; we'll deserve it."
"Blesses his stars and thinks it luxury."
"I think the Romans call it Stoicism."
"My voice is still for war."
"The woman who deliberates is lost." And the eternal
"Plato thou reasonest well," etc.
which avenges perhaps on the public their neglect of the play--Thackeray's note.
He might have added:
"A day, an hour of virtuous liberty
Is worth a whole eternity in bondage." And
"When vice prevails and impious men bear sway,
The post of honor is a private station."
Not inapt to Addison's situation and political surroundings.

For this Pope never forgave him.   His petty and malignant
nature viewed every subsequent act of Addison's as intended to
injure him.   Pope asked his advice about a change he contem-
plated in the *Rape of the Lock*, and was persuaded that it was
insidiously given.   Tickell's version of the first book of the
Iliad appeared a little before his, and although the preface
intimated a discontinuance of the remainder, and acknowledged
Pope's superiority, yet Pope accused Addison of the villainy of
translating it and publishing it in Tickell's name simply and
solely to ruin the sale of his translation, upon which he was
then at work.   It was but an illustration of the venom and
faithlessness in anything good that lay deeply ingrained in the
nature of the man, who, crooked and perverse himself, could
not imagine in any one else a course of conduct honourable and
fair.   That evil imagination produced these " brilliant and
energetic lines, which everybody knows by heart, or ought to
know by heart."*   Most will acknowledge that judged by his
writings, and the accounts of contemporary writings, the character attributed to Addison was eminently false and wide of the
mark.   Whatever truth there might be in the lines :

> " Like Cato gives his little Senate laws,
>   And sits attentive to his own applause."

it could not be said with any semblance of justice that he was
wont to

> " Damn with faint praise, assent with civil leer,
>   And without sneering teach the rest to sneer."

or that he was always

> " Willing to wound, and yet afraid to strike."

---

* Atticus, in the *Epistle to Dr. Arbuthnot*.   It is sad to think of how much poetry
of the very highest kind malevolence and ill-humour have been the source.   Note Pope
in the 18th century venting his spleen on every living being ; Byron, a hundred years
later, defying public opinion, declaiming *ad nauseam* against the hollowness and
hypocrisy of the world.   Let us charitably remember, however, Pope's bodily ailments
and care for his poor old mother, Byron's love for his sister, and his misfortunes of
parentage and deformity.   It is but right to say that there are other and more
lenient views of Pope's conduct in this famous quarrel, views which place Addison in a
far less enviable light.

He need have had no fear in striking, but with such incomparable powers of ridicule as he possessed, and with such a vulnerable opponent as Pope would have been, he refrained from retort of any kind, and took a noble revenge by warmly praising Pope's *Iliad*, and advising every lover of letters to buy a copy.

The death of Anne in August made a great change in Addison's fortunes. He was at once appointed to office by the new (Whig) Government, occupying for a while his old post under the Lord Lieutenant, and after a little, early in 1715, was made one of the Lords at the Board of Trade. From September of that year till the middle of the next (June 1716), he edited a paper called the *Freeholder*, which is the best of his political writings, much more temperate and thoughtful, and not less vivacious than his *Examiner*. In August, 1716, he made the greatest mistake of his life, marrying the Countess Dowager, of Warwick, a widow of fifteen years' standing. The courtship was short, the marriage proved unhappy. She could boast of nothing but her ancient family, was violent in temper, and so proud that in entering into the alliance she conceived herself as conferring rather than receiving an honor. Some have thought that Addison sought refuge from his domestic bickerings and discomforts in drink, but this has been strenuously denied.* From whatever cause arising we know that his health was at this time in a very precarious condition, and that he was wholly unfit to assume the duties of a still higher position, being subject at times to distressing attacks of asthma.

The dissensions in the ministry came to a crisis in April, 1717, Townsend, Walpole, and Cowper retiring, Stanhope and

---

* It is said that till his health failed him he was glad to escape from the Countess Dowager and her magnificent dining room (at Holland House) to some tavern where he could enjoy a laugh, a talk about Virgil and Boileau, and a bottle of claret with the friends of his happier days.

Sunderland forming a new cabinet.* Addison was offered a secretaryship of state, and, owing it is said to his wife's importunity reluctantly accepted. It was soon plain that he was wholly unsuited to this post. He had not the executive energy and grasp to master the many details of such an office. It was impossible that a man who could scarcely open his lips in debate, could successfully meet an opposition headed by a man like Walpole. He held his appointment but eleven months. Ill health was assigned as the reason for his resignation, and he was pensioned off with fifteen hundred a year.

His only other serious quarrel occurred not long after this. Steele, who had not been so fortunate as Addison, thought his old friend neglected him, and resented very much his selection of Tickell for his private secretary. This was not true, for Addison had helped him after his expulsion from parliament by the Tories, had assisted him in procuring his title and in more substantial benefits. While Steele was in his irritable mood, the celebrated bill for limiting the number of peers was brought in. Steele attacked the bill vehemently in a paper called the *Plebeian.* Addison, as his duty to his party demanded, replied in the *Old Whig.* One rejoinder led to another. Steele with great bitterness attacked personally the members of the administration. Addison replied in terms of great severity, but did not violate the ordinary proprieties of language. The consequence was that the two friends, who had studied together as boys, who had worked together as literary co-mates, who had fought side by side and suffered in many a political battle, became estranged and never met again.

Steele had the last word in the controversy. Addison had little inclination and less ability to reply, for he was fast hastening to the grave. His old complaint, the asthma, had

---

* Sometimes called the *German* Ministry, depending, as it did, for its existence largely on Court favor.

returned with redoubled severity, and to this were now added symptoms of dropsy. He bore all with the most admirable resignation and fortitude, constituted Tickell his literary executor, and calmly prepared himself for death. This took place at Holland House on the 17th June, 1719. His deathbed was an example of that serenity and unfaltering faith in the goodness of God, which we might expect from the author of the *Spectator*. "I have sent for you," he said to his son-in-law, "to see in what peace a Christian can die." The dominant feelings in Addison's religion were his gratitude for the gifts that God had ever been giving him, a firm belief in the continuance of this goodness, and a cheerful piety founded on such a trust. That trust is most beautifully expressed in one of his best known paraphrases,* one of the 23rd Psalm :

> "Tho' in the paths of death I tread,
> With gloomy horrors overspread,
> My steadfast heart shall fear no ill,
> For Thou, O Lord, art with me still ;
> Thy friendly crook shall give me aid,
> And guide me thro' the dreadful shade."

Let us conclude this rapid sketch of his life with a few sentences from Macaulay, whose essay upon his life and works is one long and splendid panegyric :

"His body lay in state in the Jerusalem Chamber, and was borne thence to the Abbey at dead of night. The choir sang a funeral hymn. Bishop Atterbury, one of those Tories who had loved and honored the most accomplished of the Whigs, met the corpse and led the procession by torchlight round the shrine of St. Edward and the graves of the Plantagenets to the chapel of Henry the Seventh. On the north side of that chapel, in the

---

* In No. 441. Addison has left us a number of beautiful hymns and paraphrases which have been incorporated in the various hymnologies and are well worth the student's attention, for in this cast of thought and its appropriate diction he was fitted to excel.

vault of the House of Albemarle, the coffin of Addison lies
next to the coffin of Montague.   *   *   *   Many
tributes were paid to the memory of Addison; one alone is
now remembered.   Tickell bewailed his friend in an elegy
which would do honour to the greatest name in our literature,
and which unites the energy and magnificence of Dryden to the
tenderness and purity of Cowper.*   *   *   *   It is
strange that neither his noble and opulent widow, nor any of
his powerful and attached friends should have thought of placing
even a simple tablet inscribed with his name on the walls of
the Abbey.   At length, in our own time, his image, skilfully
graven, appeared in Poet's Corner.   It represents him, as we
can conceive him, clad in his dressing gown, stepping from his
parlor at Chelsea* into his trim little garden, with the Account
of the Everlasting Club, or the Loves of Hilpa and Shalum, just
finished for the next day's *Spectator* in his hand.   Such a mark
of national respect was due, above all, to the great satirist, who
alone knew how to use ridicule without abusing it, who, without
inflicting a wound, effected a great social reform, and who
reconciled wit and virtue, after a long and disastrous separation,
during which wit had been led astray by profligacy and virtue
by fanaticism."

---

* Previous to his marriage, Addison occupied a small house at Chelsea, once the
abode of Nell Gwynne.

LITERARY CHARACTER.

General Plan.—The idea of the *Spectator* was probably conceived by Addison, and is, perhaps, meant, in some measure, as
his own portrait. The *Spectator's* account of himself is given
in No. 1. A country gentleman's son, taciturn and studious
at the schools and university, travels in foreign parts, learning
many languages, visiting even Grand Cairo, "to take the
measure of a pyramid," finally returns to England and becomes
a frequenter of the theatres, coffee houses and all places of
public resort. Whenever he sees a concourse of people he
mixes with them, but never opens his lips except in his
own club. He espouses no party, observing strict neutrality
betwixt Whigs and Tories. He has friends, however, who are
partisans and talkers in addition to being spectators. The
Spectator's club consists of several gentlemen whose characters
were first sketched by Steele. Four of these, the templar, the
clergyman, the soldier (Captain Sentry), and the merchant (Sir
Andrew Freeport) are not very interesting. The other two,
roughly drawn by Steele, were retouched and happily coloured
by Addison till they stand before us as Sir Roger de Coverley
and Will Honeycomb. There is not much plot. The old
bachelor baronet (Sir Roger), whimsical and odd, simple as a
child, gentle as a woman, comes up to town, visits the theatres,
walks in the Abbey, takes trips on the water, is frightened by
the Mohocks, in fact entertains us, delights us with his true
gentlemanliness, his goodness and his rustic ways. The *Spectator* visits Coverley Hall in the summer, is charmed with all
he sees, makes the acquaintance of Will Wimble, Tom Touchey
and other local celebrities. The elderly rake, Will Honeycomb, who at sixty consoles himself with a farmer's daughter,
is amusing with his vanity and his assurance.

The club do not write the essays; the *Spectator* does all that. They furnish the material for his delightful papers, but, with the exception of a few letters, take no part in their elaboration. Addison has spent his strength upon the portrait of the country gentleman; the British merchant is treated with considerable fulness by both Addison and Steele. For the legal profession and the clerical, the templar and the clergyman furnish but scanty sources of information; Captain Sentry with Addison is little more than a name. Steele introduces him in several papers.

Subjects of the Essays.—These take in all phases of ordinary life and knowledge; no practical subjects are excluded except politics; social eccentricities, allegories, both grave and gay, humorous sketches of character, literary criticisms, philosophical speculations, dreams and visions, the theatres and witchcraft, the various follies and fashions of the metropolis, all these and a score of other topics furnish themes for this keen and kindly observer, and all are treated with such knowledge of the human heart and of the world, that we can return to some of them for the twentieth time.

Contributors.—Including the 8th volume, the *Spectator* contains 635 papers. Addison wrote 274; Steele, 240; John Hughes, 11, besides some letters and parts of papers; Eustace Budgell, 37; Henry Grove, 4. Other participants, but to a very small extent, were Pope, Parnell (author of the *Hermit*), Tickell, Swift, Henry Martyn, Isaac Watts and Ambrose Phillips (Namby Pamby). The papers of Addison are always distinguished by the signature of one of the letters of the word *Clio*.

The Moral Element.—"The great and only end of these speculations," says Addison in one of his *Spectators*, "is to banish vice and ignorance out of the territories of Great Britain." All his papers are strictly moral in their cast of

I

thought. That terrible age of profanity and profligacy which Charles II. brought was happily passing away when the *Tatler* appeared. Jeremy Collier had shamed the stage into something like decency. Yet the pernicious notion still lingered in many minds that there was some necessary connection between genius and vice, between domestic virtue and stupidity. This notion Steele and Addison helped largely to dispel. They showed Englishmen that humour might be rich, that wit might be keen, in company with the strictest regard for decency and religion. The English temper came to its true balance between the coldness and rigidity of Puritanism and the lewdness and passion of the Restoration. He scornfully rejects low bodily pleasures ; he attacks every fashion and folly which tends towards immorality, *e.g.*, low-necked dresses ; he paints for us the staid English housewife, grave and matronly, unaffected, without coquetry, devoted to her husband, and to the moral rearing of her family. See his remarks on the French in No. 45, and on flirtations and extravagant toilets in 317 and 323. Domestic virtue and purity are held to be the distinguishing aims for English men and women. These alone give solid and lasting happiness ; these alone make a nation prosperous at home and respected abroad. Such sentiments as these would do honour to any great writer in any age or country ; they especially confer honour upon Addison, writing as he did in an age and society corrupted by, and not yet purified from the taint of that moral poison which infected England during the Restoration period. It is the glory of Addison to have had a great share in bringing about this great change in public taste. Since his time few gross violations of decency occur either in pieces designed for the stage or in periodicals. He attained in no small degree the professed object of satire, to cure vice and folly by holding them up to ridicule.

Religious Treatment.—When Addison approaches this subject he is always penetrated by the proper spirit of gravity and reverence, but with him true religion is cheerful (494), and he laughs at Puritanic piety in the person of Sombrius (494). He was not affected by current writings of the English deists, who substituted a sort of natural religion for the truth of revelation. He is thoroughly orthodox in the matter of a future state (600), of the creation of the world (565), of the efficacy of prayer (207), of the atoning power of Christ's Sacrifice (459), and of growth in grace (111); as well on most other points where he is sufficiently definite to enable us to discover his exact views. Addison's is an *active* piety; he wants fixed days of devotion and meditation, forbids swearing, and elevates the practical part of religion, which he calls morality, (494), to a higher position than faith, "because a person may be qualified to do greater good to mankind by morality without faith, than by faith without morality." * As we might expect, he is opposed to persecution and disabilities of every kind, and although his peace-loving nature and his party allegiance restrained him, yet he would have welcomed more lenience to dissenters.

Emotional Feelings.—He had little depth of feeling; was not so successful as Steele in the pathetic, and was gifted with no passionate nature or imagination. De Quincy says: "Though Addison generally hated the impassioned and shrank from it as a fearful thing,† yet this was when it was confined with forms of life and fleshly realities (as in dramatic works), but not when combined with elder forms of eternal abstraction. Hence he did not read and did not like Shakespeare—the music here was too rapid and life-like—but he sympathized profoundly in the

---

* Addison's philosophy in religion, politics and social reform, was largely utilitarian. The reader must remember that the essays are superficial and discursive rather than deep and penetrating. Most of our deepest thinkers have had a contempt for him. But they forget the *object* and *times;* if he had thought too deeply he would not have been read.

† He considered it impolite, and unbecoming to an English gentleman of well governed feelings. Taine says, Addison well hits the *beau idéal* of the cold, correct and formal English character.

solemn cathedral-chanting of Milton." This incapacity for rapid changes of feeling in the same composition may be owing to his somewhat inert and lymphatic temperament.   Even Thackeray says: "I don't think he indulged very much in the vanity of grieving."   Johnson says his chief phase of feeling was "gay malevolence and satiric humour," made successful by his elegance of language, and his inimitable way of putting things.

Scholarship.—"It is already pretty well known that Addison had 'no very intimate acquaintance with the literature of his own country.   It is known also that he did not think such an acquaintance anywise essential to the character of an elegant scholar and *litterateur*.   Quite enough he found it and more than enough for the time he had to spare, if he could maintain a tolerable familiarity with the foremost Latin poets, and a very slender one indeed with the Grecian."   *De Quincy.**

---

* From the quotations given above, it will be conjectured that DeQuincy is hostile to Addison.   He it is who takes the strongest position in asserting his "malignant jealousy" of Pope, and Pope's comparative innocency.

PECULIARITIES OF STYLE.

Vocabulary.—He uses a large proportion of words of Latin origin, especially in his serious pieces, but is not on that account unidiomatic. He is only fairly copious on lighter topics, his command of epithets is good. " Choiceness and not profusion is at all times his characteristic ; yet we find him varying his expressions with the greatest ease on simple themes. Thus in his paper on the ' Lover,' upon the female passion for china-ware, he describes it with considerable variety, ' brittleware,' ' frail furniture,' ' perishable commodity,' ' All chinaware is of a weak and transitory nature,' ' the fragility of china is such as a reasonable being ought by no means to set his heart upon.' "* He frequently uses a strictly colloquial vocabulary, but he is very careful to avoid expressions harsh to the ear ; the melodious flow of his prose is due, according to Bain, to the fewness of abrupt consonants, " the rhythmical construction, or the alternation of long and short, emphatic and unemphatic sounds."

Character of Sentences.—The loose sentence is a prevailing feature throughout *The Spectator ;* clause after clause of explanation or addition is tacked on, by relatives or conjunctions. In his desire to be easy (on the reader we suppose) he studiously avoids the periodic sentence. Hence his style is flowing, easy to grasp (*simple*) and familiar, but he falls into the vices of this structure again and again, *e. g.,* the misplacement of clauses, phrases, and adverbs, causing *ambiguity* and *confusion* of thought. He occasionally makes use of the balanced sentence, and with good effect, as in No. 417, comparing Homer and Virgil, and in some others of his critical papers. It is a little

---

* Minto.

strange that he has not made more use of it, seeing that it is a form calculated to please the ear and make the meaning clearer.

Diffuseness.—This is a consequence of Addison's love for the expository and loose structure of sentence, and of a lack of clear ideas. It takes the forms of Tautology, Redundance, and Circumlocution, and is much found in our older writers. Hooker, Tillotson, Locke, and Addison furnish many examples. Here are a few from the last : " heightened and enlivened," "diffused and spread abroad," " perceive and know," " finite and limited," " perplexes and disturbs," " serious and contemplative natures," " so little and so inconsiderable." * This way of writing tends to feebleness, especially when the mood of the writer is one of contemplation and not one of passion. Economy of words should be studied by those who wish to attain *strength* and *clearness* of style.† Johnson says Addison's prose is "a model of the middle style, always equable, always easy, without glowing words or pointed sentences."

Sense of the Ludicrous. It is upon this and his grace of expression that Addison's fame is founded. His humor may not be so amiable as Thackeray describes it; the geniality may have come from Steele, and more malice may have lain in his nature than is commonly supposed, but there are at least three defences to be set up : (1) His satire arouses no angry passions or bitterness of party spirit; (2) It is never personal, but is directed against classes of fools and vices, and (3) he always employed it on the side of virtue and religion.

There are many other points connected with the *form* of Addison's writing, but these must be left to the notes for separate notice. We will close by quoting a few characteristic extracts :—

* Several of these are in a single paper, No. 565.

† Spencer, *Philosophy of Style*, where, however, the principle is made to dwarf most other considerations, and seems pushed too far.

He was the man of all that ever lived most hostile to what was even good in pedantry, to its tendencies towards the profound in erudition, towards minute precision and the non-popular; the champion of all that is easy, natural, and superficial.—*DeQuincey.*

Addison's personal appearance has not been very vividly recorded. Thackeray speaks of "his chiselled features, pure and cold." We know also that he was a fair man, of a full habit of body, soft and flabby from wine bibbing and want of exercise. He was so weakly a child that he was christened on the day of his birth, not being expected to live.—*Minto.*

Addison is *The Spectator.* About three-sevenths of the work are his; and it is no exaggeration to say, that his worst essay is as good as the best essay of any of his coadjutors. His best essays approach near to absolute perfection; nor is their excellence more wonderful than their variety. His invention never seems to flag, nor is he ever under the necessity of repeating himself or of wearing out a subject.—*Macaulay.*

It is pleasing to remember that the relation between Swift and Addison was, on the whole, satisfactory from first to last. The value of Swift's testimony, when nothing personal inflamed his vision or warped his judgment, can be doubted by nobody.—*Thackeray.**

Whoever wishes to attain an English style, familiar but not coarse, and elegant but not ostentatious, must give his days and nights to the volumes of Addison.—*Dr. Johnson.*

He does not rise to the source of the beautiful at once, like genuine artists, by force and lucidity of natural inspiration; he lingers in the middle regions amid precepts subject to taste and common sense. This is why Addison's criticism is so solid and so poor.—*Taine.*

---

* The student must remember the bitter, biting nature of Swift, and his Toryism.

ADDISON.

No. 21.]   *Saturday, March 24, 1711.*   [*Addison.*

——— *Locus est et pluribus Umbris.*—Hor.

1. I AM sometimes very much troubled, when I reflect upon the three great Professions of Divinity, Law, and Physick; how they are each of them over-burdened with Practitioners, and filled with Multitudes of Ingenious Gentlemen that starve one another.

2. We may divide the Clergy into Generals, Field-Officers, and Subalterns. Among the first we may reckon Bishops, Deans, and Arch-Deacons. Among the second are Doctors of Divinity, Prebendaries, and all that wear Scarfs. The rest are comprehended under the Subalterns. As for the first Class, our Constitution preserves it from any Redundancy of Incumbents, notwithstanding Competitors are numberless. Upon a strict Calculation, it is found that there has been a great Exceeding of late Years in the Second Division, several Brevets having been granted for the converting of Subalterns into Scarf-Officers; insomuch that within my Memory the price of Lutestring is raised above two Pence in a Yard. As for the Subalterns, they are not to be numbred. Should our Clergy once enter into the corrupt Practice of the Laity, by the splitting of their Freeholds, they would be able to carry most of the Elections in *England.*

3. The Body of the Law is no less encumbered with superfluous Members, that are like *Virgil's* Army, which he tells us was

so crouded, many of them had not Room to use their Weapons. This prodigious Society of Men may be divided into the Litigious and Peaceable. Under the first are comprehended all those who are carried down in Coach-fulls to *Westminster-Hall* every Morning in Term time. *Martial's* description of this Species of Lawyers is full of Humour :

Iras et verba locant.

Men that hire out their Words and Anger ; that are more or less passionate according as they are paid for it, and allow their Client a quantity of Wrath proportionable to the Fee which they receive from him. I must, however, observe to the Reader, that above three Parts of those whom I reckon among the Litigious, are such as are only quarrelsome in their Hearts, and have no Opportunity of showing their Passion at the Bar. Nevertheless, as they do not know what Strifes may arise, they appear at the Hall every Day, that they may show themselves in a Readiness to enter the Lists, whenever there shall be Occasion for them.

4. The Peaceable Lawyers are, in the first place, many of the Benchers of the severals Inns of Court, who seem to be the Dignitaries of the Law, and are endowed with those Qualifications of Mind that accomplish a Man rather for a Ruler, than a Pleader. These Men live peaceably in their Habitations, Eating once a Day, and Dancing once a Year, for the Honour of their Respective Societies.

5. Another numberless Branch of Peaceable Lawyers, are those young Men who being placed at the Inns of Court in order to study the Laws of their Country, frequent the Play-House more than *Westminster-Hall*, and are seen in all publick Assemblies, except in a Court of Justice. I shall say nothing of those Silent and Busie Multitudes that are employed within Doors in the drawing up of Writings and Conveyances ; nor of those

greater Numbers that palliate their want of Business with a Pretence to such Chamber-Practice.

6. If, in the third place, we look into the Profession of Physick, we shall find a most formidable Body of Men : The Sight of them is enough to make a Man serious, for we may lay it down as a Maxim, that when a Nation abounds in Physicians it grows thin of People. Sir *William Temple* is very much puzzled to find a reason why the Northern Hive, as he calls it, does not send out such prodigious Swarms, and over-run the World with *Goths* and *Vandals*, as it did formerly ; but had that Excellent Author observed that there were no students in Physick among the Subjects of *Thor* and *Woden*, and that this Science very much flourishes in the North at present, he might have found a better Solution for this Difficulty, than any of those he has made use of. This Body of Men in our own Country, may be described like the *British Army* in *Cæsar's* time : Some of them slay in Chariots and some on Foot. If the Infantry do less Execution than the Charioteers, it is because they cannot be carried so soon into all Quarters of the Town, and Dispatch so much Business in so short a Time. Besides this Body of Regular Troops, there are Stragglers, who, without being duly listed and enrolled, do infinite Mischief to those who are so unlucky as to fall into their Hands.

7. There are, besides the above-mentioned, innumerable Retainers to Physick, who, for want of other Patients, amuse themselves with the stifling of Cats in an Air Pump, cutting up Dogs alive, or impaling of Insects upon the point of a Needle for Microscopical Observations ; besides those that are employed in the gathering of Weeds and the Chase of Butterflies : Not to mention the Cockle-shell Merchants and Spider-Catchers.

8. When I consider how each of these Professions are crouded with Multitudes that seek their Livelihood in them, and how many Men of Merit there are in each of them, who may be

rather said to be of the Science than the Profession ; I very much wonder at the Humour of Parents, who will not rather choose to place their Sons in a way of Life where an honest Industry cannot but thrive, than in Stations where the greatest Probity, Learning and Good Sense may miscarry. How many men are Country-Curates, that might have made themselves Aldermen of *London* by a right Improvement of a Smaller Sum of Money than what is usually laid out on a learned Education ? A sober, frugal Person, of slender Parts and a slow Apprehension, might have thrived in Trade though he starves upon Physick; as a man would be well enough pleased to buy Silks of one, whom he would not venture to feel his Pulse. *Vagellius* is careful, studious, and obliging, but withal a little thick-skulled ; he has not a single Client, but might have had Abundance of Customers. The Misfortune is that Parents take a Liking to a particular Profession, and therefore desire their Sons may be of it. Whereas, in so great an Affair of Life, they should consider the Genius and Abilities of their Children more than their own Inclinations.

9. It is the great Advantage of a trading Nation, that there are very few in it so dull and heavy, who may not be placed in Stations of Life which may give them an Opportunity of making their Fortunes. A well regulated Commerce is not, like Law, Physick or Divinity to be overstocked with Hands ; but on the contrary, flourishes by Multitudes, and gives Employment to all its Professors. Fleets of Merchantmen are so many Squadrons of Floating Shops, that vend our Wares and Manufactures in all the Markets of the World, and find out Chapmen under both the Tropicks. C.

Sævit atrox Volscens, nec teli conspicit usquam
Auctorem nec quo se ardens immittere possit.—VIR.

1. There is nothing more betrays a base, ungenerous spirit, than the giving of secret stabs to a man's reputation. Lampoons and satires, that are written with wit and spirit, are like poisoned darts, which not only inflict a wound, but make it incurable. For this reason I am very much troubled when I see the talents of humour and ridicule in the possession of an ill natured man. There cannot be a greater gratification to a barbarous and inhuman wit, than to stir up sorrow in the heart of a private person, to raise uneasiness among near relations, and to expose whole families to derision, at the same time that he remains unseen and undiscovered. If besides the accomplishments of being witty and ill-natured, a man is vicious into the bargain, he is one of the most mischievous creatures that can enter into a civil society. His satire will then chiefly fall upon those who ought to be the most exempt from it. Virtue, merit, and everything that is praiseworthy, will be made the subject of ridicule and buffoonery. It is impossible to enumerate the evils which arise from these arrows that fly in the dark, and I know no other excuse that is or can be made for them, than that the wounds they give are only imaginary, and produce nothing more than a secret shame or sorrow in the mind of the suffering person. It must indeed be confessed, that a lampoon or a satire do not carry in them robbery or murder; but at the same time how many are there that would not rather lose a considerable sum of money, or even life itself, than be set up as a mark of infamy and derision? And in this case a man should consider, that an injury is not to be measured by the notions of him that gives, but of him that receives it.

2. Those who can put the best countenance upon the outrages of this nature which are offered them, are not without their secret anguish. I have often observed a passage in *Socrates's* behaviour at his death, in a light wherein none of the critics have considered it. That excellent man, entertaining his friends a little before he drank the bowl of poison with a discourse on the immortality of the soul, at his entering upon it says, that he does not believe any the most comic genius can censure him for talking upon such a subject at such a time. This passage, I think, evidently glances upon *Aristophanes,* who writ a comedy on purpose to ridicule the discourses of that divine philosopher. It has been observed by many writers, that *Socrates* was so little moved at this piece of buffoonery, that he was several times present at its being acted upon the stage, and never expressed the least resentment of it. But with submission, I think the remark I have here made shows us, that this unworthy treatment made an impression upon his mind, though he had been too wise to discover it.

3. When *Julius Cæsar* was lampooned by *Catullus,* he invited him to a supper, and treated him with such a generous civility, that he made the poet his friend ever after. Cardinal *Mazarin* gave the same kind of treatment to the learned *Quillet,* who had reflected upon his Eminence in a famous Latin poem. The Cardinal sent for him, and, after some kind expostulations upon what he had written, assured him of his esteem, and dismissed him with a promise of the next good abbey that should fall, which he accordingly conferred upon him in a few months after. This had so good an effect upon the author, that he dedicated the second edition of his book to the Cardinal, after having expunged the passages which had given him offence.

4. *Sextus Quintus* was not of so generous and forgiving a temper. Upon his being made pope, the statue of *Pasquin* was one night dressed in a very dirty shirt, with an excuse written

under it, that he was forced to wear foul linen, because his laundress was made a princess. This was a reflection upon the Pope's sister, who, before the promotion of her brother, was in those mean circumstances that *Pasquin* represented her. As this pasquinade made a great noise in *Rome*, the Pope offered a considerable sum of money to any person that should discover the author of it. The author, relying upon his Holiness's generosity, as also on some private overtures which he had received from him, made the discovery himself ; upon which the Pope gave him the reward he had promised, but at the same time, to disable the satirist for the future, ordered his tongue to be cut out, and both his hands to be chopped off. *Aretine* is too trite an instance. Every one knows that all the kings of Europe were his tributaries. Nay, there is a letter of his extant, in which he makes his boasts that he had laid the Sophi of *Persia* under contribution.

5. Though in the various examples which I have here drawn together, these several great men behaved themselves very differently towards the wits of the age who had reproached them, they all of them plainly showed that they were very sensible of their reproaches, and consequently that they received them as very great injuries. For my own part, I would never trust a man that I thought was capable of giving these secret wounds, and cannot but think that he would hurt the person, whose reputation he thus assaults, in his body or in his fortune, could he do it with the same security. There is indeed something very barbarous and inhuman in the ordinary scribblers of lampoons. An innocent young lady shall be exposed, for an unhappy feature. A father of a family turned to ridicule, for some domestic calamity. A wife be made uneasy all her life, for a misinterpreted word or action. Nay, a good, a temperate, and a just man, shall be put out of countenance, by the representation of those qualities that should do him honour. So pernicious

a thing is wit, when it is not tempered with virtue and humanity.

6. I have indeed heard of heedless, inconsiderate writers, that without any malice have sacrificed the reputation of their friends and acquaintance to a certain levity of temper, and a silly ambition of distinguishing themselves by a spirit of raillery and satire : as if it were not infinitely more honourable to be a good-natured man than a wit. Where there is this little petulant humour in an author, he is often very mischievous without designing to be so. For which reason I always lay it down as a rule, that an indiscreet man is more hurtful than an ill-natured one ; for as the former will only attack his enemies, and those he wishes ill to, the other injures indifferently both friends and foes. I cannot forbear, on this occasion, transcribing a fable out of *Sir Roger l'Estrange*, which accidentally lies before me. ' A company of waggish boys were watching of frogs at the side ' of a pond, and still as any of 'em put up their heads they'd be ' pelting them down again with stones. *Children* (says one of ' the frogs), *you never consider that though this may be play to* ' *you, 'tis death to us.*'

7. As this week is in a manner set apart and dedicated to serious thoughts, I shall indulge myself in such speculations as may not be altogether unsuitable to the season : and in the mean time, as the settling in our selves a charitable frame of mind is a work very proper for the time, I have in this paper endeavoured to expose that particular breach of charity which has been generally overlooked by divines, because they are but few who can be guilty of it.　　　　　　　　　　　　　　C.

No. 26.]   *Friday, March* 30, 1711.   [*Addison.*

Pallida mors æquo pulsat pede pauperum tabernas
Regumque turres, O beate Sexti,
Vitæ summa brevis spem nos vetat inchoare longam.
Jam te premet nox, fabulæque manes,
Et domus exilis Plutonia——.—HOR.

---

1. When I am in a serious humour, I very often walk by my-self in *Westminster* Abbey; where the gloominess of the place, and the use to which it is applied, with the solemnity of the building, and the condition of the people who lie in it, are apt to fill the mind with a kind of melancholy, or rather thought-fulness, that is not disagreeable. I yesterday passed a whole afternoon in the church-yard, the cloisters, and the church, amusing myself with the tomb-stones and inscriptions that I met with in those several regions of the dead. Most of them recorded nothing else of the buried person, but that he was born upon one day and died upon another: The whole history of his life, being comprehended in those two circumstances that are common to all mankind. I could not but look upon these registers of existence, whether of brass or marble, as a kind of satire upon the departed persons; who had left no other memorial of them, but that they were born and that they died. They put me in mind of several persons mentioned in the bat-tles of heroic poems, who have sounding names given them, for no other reason but that they may be killed, and are cele-brated for nothing but being knocked on the head.

Γλαῦχον τε, Μεδόντα τε, Θερσιλοχόν τε.—HOM.

Glaucumque, Medontaque, Thersilochumque.—VIRG.

2. The life of these men is finely described in Holy Writ by the path of an arrow which is immediately closed up and lost.

K

3. Upon my going into the church, I entertained myself with the digging of a grave ; and saw in every shovelful of it that was thrown up, the fragment of a bone or skull intermixed with a kind of fresh mouldering earth that some time or other had a place in the composition of an human body. Upon this I began to consider with myself, what innumerable multitudes of people lay confused together under the pavement of that ancient cathedral ; how men and women, friends and enemies, priests and soldiers, monks and prebendaries, were crumbled amongst one another, and blended together in the same common mass ; how beauty, strength, and youth, with old age, weakness and deformity, lay undistinguished in the same promiscuous heap of matter.

4. After having thus surveyed this great magazine of mortality, as it were in the lump, I examined it more particularly by the accounts which I found on several of the monuments which are raised in every quarter of that ancient fabric. Some of them were covered with such extravagant epitaphs, that, if it were possible for the dead person to be acquainted with them, he would blush at the praises which his friends have bestowed upon him. There are others so excessively modest, that they deliver the character of the person departed in Greek or Hebrew, and by that means are not understood once in a twelve-month. In the poetical quarter, I found there were poets who had no monuments, and monuments which had no poets. I observed indeed that the present war had filled the church with many of these uninhabited monuments, which had been erected to the memory of persons whose bodies were perhaps buried in the plains of Blenheim or in the bosom of the ocean.

5. I could not but be very much delighted with several modern epitaphs, which are written with great elegance of expression and justness of thought, and therefore do honour to the living as well as to the dead. As a foreigner is very apt to conceive

an idea of the ignorance or politeness of a nation from the turn
of their public monuments and inscriptions, they should be sub-
mitted to the perusal of men of learning and genius before they
are put in execution. Sir Cloudesly Shovel's monument has
very often given me great offence. Instead of the brave rough
English admiral, which was the distinguishing character of that
plain gallant man, he is represented on his tomb by the figure
of a beau, dressed in a long periwig, and reposing himself upon
velvet cushions under a canopy of state. The inscription is
answerable to the monument ; for instead of celebrating the
many remarkable actions he had performed in the service of his
country, it acquaints us only with the manner of his death, in
which it was impossible for him to reap any honour. The Dutch,
whom we are apt to despise for want of genius, shew an infinitely greater taste of antiquity and politeness in their buildings
and works of this nature, than what we meet with in those of
our own country. The monuments of their admirals, which have
been erected at the public expense, represent them like themselves ; and are adorned with rostral crowns and naval ornaments, with beautiful festoons of seaweed, shells and coral.

6. But to return to our subject. I have left the repository of
our English kings for the contemplation of another day, when
I shall find my mind disposed for so serious an amusement. I
know that entertainments of this nature, are apt to raise dark
and dismal thoughts in timorous minds and gloomy imaginations ; but for my own part, though I am always serious, I do
not know what it is to be melancholy ; and can, therefore, take
a view of nature in her deep and solemn scenes, with the same
pleasure as in her most gay and delightful ones. By this means
I can improve myself with those objects, which others consider
with terror. When I look upon the tombs of the great, every
emotion of envy dies in me ; when I read the epitaphs of the
beautiful, every inordinate desire goes out ; when I meet with

the grief of parents upon a tombstone, my heart melts with compassion; when I see the tomb of the parents themselves, I consider the vanity of grieving for those whom we must quickly follow. When I see kings lying by those who deposed them, when I consider rival wits placed side by side, or the holy men that divided the world with their contests and disputes, I reflect with sorrow and astonishment on the little competitions, factions and debates of mankind. When I read the several dates of the tombs, of some that died yesterday, and some six hundred years ago, I consider that great day when we shall all of us be contemporaries, and make our appearance together.

No. 47.]   *Tuesday, April* 24, 1711.   [*Addison.*

Ride si sapis ————. —Mart.

1. Mr. Hobbs, in his discourse of Human Nature, which, in my humble opinion, is much the best of all his works, after some very curious observations upon laughter, concludes thus: ' The passion of laughter is nothing else but sudden glory ' arising from some sudden conception of some eminency in our- ' selves by comparison with the infirmity of others, or with our ' own formerly: for men laugh at the follies of themselves ' past, when they come suddenly to remembrance, except they ' bring with them any present dishonor.

2. According to this author, therefore, when we hear a man laugh excessively, instead of saying he is very merry, we ought

to tell him he is very proud. And, indeed, if we look into the bottom of this matter, we shall meet many observations to confirm us in his opinion. Every one laughs at some body that is in an inferior state of folly to himself. It was formerly the custom in every great house in England to keep a tame fool dressed in petticoats, that the heir of the family might have an opportunity of joking upon him, and diverting himself with his absurdities. For the same reason idiots are still in request in most of the courts of Germany, where there is not a prince of any great magnificence, who has not two or three dressed, distinguished, undisputed fools in his retinue, whom the rest of the courtiers are always breaking their jests upon.

3. The Dutch, who are more famous for their industry and application, than for their wit and humour, hang up in several of their streets what they call the sign of the Gaper, that is, the head of an idiot dressed in a cap and bells, and gaping in a most immoderate manner : this is a standing jest at Amsterdam.

4. Thus every one diverts himself with some person or other that is below him in point of understanding, and triumphs in the superiority of his genius, whilst he has such objects of derision before his eyes. Mr. Dennis has very well expressed this in a couple of humorous lines, which are part of a translation of a satire in Monsieur Boileau.

Thus one fool lolls his tongue out at another,
And shakes his empty noddle at his brother.

5. Mr. Hobbs's reflection gives us the reason why the insignificant people above mentioned are stirrers up of laughter among men of a gross taste : but as the more understanding part of mankind do not find their risibility affected by such ordinary objects it may be worth the while to examine into the several provocatives of laughter in men of superior sense and knowledge.

6. In the first place I must observe, that there are a set of merry drolls whom the common people of all countries ad-

mire, and seem to love so well, that they could eat them according to the old proverb: I mean those circumforaneous wits whom every nation calls by the name of that dish of meat which it loves best. In Holland they are termed pickled herrings; in France, jean pottages; in Italy, maccaronies; and in Great Britain, jack puddings. These merry wags, from whatsoever food they receive their titles, that they may make their audiences laugh, always appear in a fool's coat, and commit such blunders and mistakes in every step they take, and every word they utter, as those who listen to them would be ashamed of.

7. But this little triumph of the understanding, under the disguise of laughter, is nowhere more visible than in that custom which prevails everywhere among us on the first day of the present month, when every body takes it in his head to make as many fools as he can. In proportion as there are more follies discovered, so there is more laughter raised on this day than on any other in the whole year. A neighbour of mine, who is a haberdasher by trade, and a very shallow, conceited fellow, makes his boasts that for these ten years successively he has not made less than an hundred April fools. My landlady had a falling out with him about a fortnight ago, for sending every one of her children upon some sleeveless errand, as she terms it. Her eldest son went to buy a half-penny worth of inkle at a shoemaker's; the eldest daughter was dispatched half a mile to see a monster: and in short the whole family of innocent children made April fools. Nay, my landlady herself did not escape him This empty fellow has laughed upon these conceits ever since.

8. This art of wit is well enough when confined to one day in a twelvemonth; but there is an ingenious tribe of men sprung up of late years, who are making April fools every day in the year. These gentlemen are commonly distinguished by the name of

biters ; a race of men that are perpetually employed in laughing at those mistakes which are of their own production.

9. Thus we see, in proportion as one man is more refined than another, he chooses his fool out of a lower or higher class of mankind ; or to speak in a more philosophical language, that secret elation and pride of heart, which is generally called laughter, arises in him from his comparing himself with an object below him, whether it so happens that it be a natural or an artificial fool. It is indeed very possible that the persons we laugh at may in the main of their characters be much wiser men than ourselves ; but if they would have us laugh at them, they must fall short of us in those respects which stir up this passion.

10. I am afraid I shall appear too abstracted in my speculations, if I shew that when a man of wit makes us laugh, it is by betraying some oddness or infirmity in his own character, or in the representation which he makes of others ; and that when we laugh at a brute or even an inaminate thing, it is at some action or incident that bears a remote analogy to any blunder or absurdity in reasonable creatures.

11. But to come into common life I shall pass by the consideration of those stage coxcombs that are able to shake a whole audience, and take notice of a particular sort of men who are such provokers of mirth in conversation, that it is impossible for a club or merry-making to subsist without them ; I mean those honest gentleman that are always exposed to the wit and raillery of their well-wishers and companions ; that are pelted by men, women, and children, friends and foes, and in a word, stand as butts in conversation for every one to shoot at that pleases. I know several of these butts who are men of wit and sense, though by some odd turn of humour, some unlucky cast in their person or behaviour, they have always the misfortune to make the company merry. The truth of it is, a man is not qualified for a butt, who has not a good deal of wit and vivacity,

even in the ridiculous side of his character. A stupid butt is only fit for the conversation of ordinary people. Men of wit require one that will give them play, and bestir himself in the absurd part of his behaviour. A butt with these accomplishments frequently gets the laugh of his side, and turns the ridicule upon him that attacks him. Sir John Falstaff was an hero of this species, and gives a good description of himself in his capacity of a butt, after the following manner; " Men of all sorts (says that merry knight) take a pride to gird at me. The brain of a man is not able to invent anything that tends to laughter more than I invent, or is invented on me. I am not only witty in myself but the cause that wit is in other men."

C.

No. 50.]   *Friday, April* 27, 1711.   [*Addison.*

Nunquam aliud Natura, aliud Sapientia dixit.

Juv.

1. When the four Indian Kings were in this country about a-twelvemonth ago, I often mixed with the rabble, and followed them a whole day together, being wonderfully struck with the sight of everything that is new or uncommon. I have, since their departure, employed a friend to make many inquires of their landlord the upholsterer, relating to their manners and conversation, as also concerning the remarks which they made in this country: for, next to the forming a right notion of such

strangers, I should be desirous of learning what ideas they have conceived of us.

2. The upholsterer finding my friend very inquisitive about these his lodgers, brought him some time since a little bundle of papers which he assured him were written by King Sa Ga Yean Qua Rash Tow, and, as he supposes, left behind by some mistake. These papers are now translated, and contain abundance of very odd observations, which I find this little fraternity of kings made during their stay in the Isle of Great Britain.. I shall present my reader with a short specimen of them in this paper, and may perhaps communicate more to him hereafter. In the article of *London* are the following words, which without doubt are meant of the church of St. Paul.

3. 'On the most rising part of the town there stands a huge
'house, big enough to contain the whole nation of which I am
'king. Our good brother E Tow O Koam, King of the Rivers, is
'of opinion it was made by the hands of that great God to whom
'it is consecrated. The kings of Granajah and of the Six Nations
'believe that it was created with the earth, and produced on
'the same day with the sun and moon. But for my own part,
'by the best information that I could get of this matter, I
'am apt to think that this prodigious pile was fashioned into
'the shape it now bears by several tools and instruments of
'which they have a wonderful variety in this country. It was
'probably at first a huge misshapen rock that grew upon the
'top of the hill, which the natives of the country (after having
'cut it into a kind of regular figure) bored and hollowed with
'incredible pains and industry, 'till they had wrought in it all
'those beautiful vaults and caverns into which it is divided at
'this day. As soon as this rock was thus curiously scooped to
'their liking, a prodigious number of hands must have been
'employed in chipping the outside of it, which is now as smooth
'as the surface of a pebble; and is in several places hewn out

'into pillars that stand like the trunks of so many trees bound
'about the top with garlands of leaves.   It is probable that
'when this great work was begun, which must have been many
'hundred years ago, there was some religion among this people ;
'for they give it the name of a temple, and have a tradition
'that it was designed for men to pay their devotions in.   And
'indeed, there are several reasons which make us think that
'the natives of this country had formerly among them some sort
'of worship ; for they set apart every seventh day as sacred :
'but upon my going into one of these holy houses on that day,
'I could not observe any circumstance of devotion in their be-
'haviour : there was indeed a man in black who was mounted
'above the rest, and seemed to utter something with a great
'deal of vehemence ; but as for those underneath him, instead
'of paying their worship to the deity of the place, they were
'most of them bowing and curtsying to one another, and a con-
'siderable number of them fast asleep.

4. ' The queen of the country appointed two men to attend
'us, that had enough of our language to make themselves
'understood in some few particulars.   But we soon perceived
'these two were great enemies to one another, and did not
'always agree in the same story.   We could make a shift to
'gather out of one of them, that this island was very much in-
'fested with a monstrous kind of animals, in the shape of men,
'called Whigs ; and he often told us, that he hoped we should
'meet with none of them in our way, for that if we did, they
'would be apt to knock us down for being kings.

5. ' Our other interpreter used to talk very much of a kind of
'animal called a Tory, that was as great a monster as the Whig,
'and would treat us as ill for being foreigners.   These two crea-
'tures, it seems, are born with a secret antipathy to one another,
'and engage when they meet as naturally as the elephant and
'the rhinoceros.   But as we saw none of either of these species,

' we are apt to think that our guides deceived us with misre-
' presentations and fictions, and amused us with an account of
' such monsters as are not really in their country.

6. 'These particulars we made a shift to pick out from the
' discourse of our interpreters ; which we put together as well as
' we could, being able to understand but here and there a word
' of what they said, and afterwards making up the meaning of
' it among ourselves. The men of the country are very cunning
' and ingenious in handicraft works ; but withal so very idle,
' that we often saw young lusty rawboned fellows carried up
' and down the streets in little covered rooms by a couple of
' porters, who are hired for that service. Their dress is like-
' wise very barbarous, for they almost strangle themselves about
' the neck, and bind their bodies with many ligatures, that we
' are apt to think are the occasion of several distempers among
' them which our country is entirely free from. Instead of those
' beautiful feathers with which we adorn our heads, they often
' buy up a monstrous bush of hair, which covers their heads,
' and falls down in a large fleece below the middle of their backs ;
' with which they walk up and down the streets and are as proud
' of it as if it were of their own growth.

7. 'We were invited to one of their public diversions, where
' we hoped to have seen the great men of their country running
' down a stag or pitching a bar, that we might have discovered
' who were the persons of the greatest abilities among them ;
' but instead of that, they conveyed us into a huge room lighted
' up with abundance of candles, where this lazy people sat still
' above three hours to see several feats of ingenuity performed
' by others, who it seems were paid for it.

8. ' As for the women of the country, not being able to talk
' with them, we could only make our remarks upon them at a
' distance. They let the hair of their heads grow to a great
' length ; but as the men make a great show with heads of hair

' that are not of their own, the women, who they say have very
' fine heads of hair, tie it up in a knot, and cover it from being
' seen.   The women look like angels, and would be more beauti-
' ful than the sun, were it not for little black spots that are apt
' to break out in their faces, and sometimes rise in very odd
' figures.   I have observed that those little blemishes wear off
' very soon ; but when they disappear in one part of the face,
' they are very apt to break out in another, insomuch that I
' have seen a spot upon the forehead in the afternoon, which was
' upon the chin in the morning."

9. The author then proceeds to shew the absurdity of breeches
and petticoats, with many other curious observations, which I
shall reserve for another occasion.   I cannot however conclude
this paper without taking notice that amidst these wild remarks
there now and then appears something very reasonable.   I cannot likewise forbear observing, that we are all guilty in some
measure of the same narrow way of thinking, which we meet
with in this abstract of the Indian journal ; when we fancy the
customs, dress, and manners of other countries are ridiculous and
extravagant, if they do not resemble those of our own.

Hic segetes, illic veniunt felicius uvæ :
Arborei fœtus, alibi, atque injussa virescunt
Gramina. Nonne vides, croceos ut Tmolus odores.
India mittit ebur, molles sua thura Sabœi ?
At Chalybes nudi ferrum, virosaque Pontus.
Castorea, Eliadum palmas Epirus equarum ?
Continuo has leges æternaque fœdera certis
*Imposuit Natura locis——*VIRG.

1. There is no place in the town which I so much love to frequent as the Royal Exchange. It gives me a secret satisfaction and in some measure gratifies my vanity, as I am an Englishman, to see so rich an assembly of countrymen and foreigners consulting together upon the private business of mankind, and making this metropolis a kind of emporium for the whole earth. I must confess that I look upon High Change to be a great council, in which all considerable nations have their representatives. Factors in the trading world are what ambassadors are in the politic world ; they negotiate affairs, conclude treaties, and maintain a good correspondence between those wealthy societies of men that are divided from one another by seas and oceans, or live on different extremities of a continent. I have often been pleased to hear disputes adjusted between an inhabitant of Japan and an Alderman of London, or to see a subject of the Great Mogul entering into a league with one of the Czar of Muscovy. I am infinitely delighted in mixing with these several ministers of commerce, as they are distinguished by their different walks and different languages. Sometimes I am jostled among a body of Armenians ; sometimes I am lost in a crowd of Jews, and sometimes make one in a group of Dutchmen. I am a Dane, Swede, or Frenchman at different

timès ; or rather fancy myself like the old philosopher, who upon being asked what countryman he was, replied, that he was a citizen of the world.

2. Though I very frequently visit this busy multitude of people, I am known to nobody there but my friend, Sir Andrew, who often smiles upon me as he sees me bustling in the crowd, but at the same time connives at my presence without taking any further notice of me. There is indeed a merchant of Egypt, who just knows me by sight, having formerly remitted me some money to Grand Cairo ; but as I am not versed in the modern Coptic, our conferences go no further than a bow and a grimace.

3. This grand scene of business gives me an infinite variety of solid and substantial entertainments. As I am a great lover of mankind, my heart naturally overflows with pleasure at the sight of a prosperous and happy multitude, insomuch that at many public solemnities I cannot forbear expressing my joy with tears that have stolen down my cheeks. For this reason I am wonderfully delighted to see such a body of men thriving in their own private fortunes, and at the same time promoting the public stock, or in other words, raising estates for their own families, by bringing into their country whatever is wanting, and carrying out of it whatever is superfluous.

4. Nature seems to have taken a particular care to disseminate her blessings among the different regions of the world, with an eye to mutual intercourse and traffic among mankind, that the natives of the several parts of the globe might have a kind of dependence upon one another, and be united together by their common interest. Almost every degree produces something peculiar to it. The food often grows in one country and the sauce in another. The fruits of Portugal are corrected by the products of Barbadoes ; the infusion of a China plant sweetened with the pith of an Indian cane. The Philippic Islands give a

flavour to our European bowls. The single dress of a woman of quality is often the product of a hundred climates. The muff and the fan come together from the different ends of the earth. The scarf is sent from the torrid zone, and the tippet from beneath the pole. The brocade petticoat rises out of the mines of Peru, and the diamond necklace out of the bowels of Indostan.

5. If we consider our own country in its natural prospect, without any of the benefits and advantages of commerce, what a barren uncomfortable spot of earth falls to our share ! Natural historians tell us, that no fruit grows originally among us, besides hips and haws, acorns and pig-nuts, with other delicates of the like nature ; that our climate of itself, and without the assistance of art, can make no further advances towards a plum than to a sloe, and carries an apple to no greater perfection than a crab ; that our melons, our peaches, our figs, our apricots, and cherries, are strangers among us, imported in different ages, and naturalized in our English gardens; and that they would all degenerate and fall away into the trash of our own country, if they were wholly neglected by the planter, and left to the mercy of our sun and soil. Nor has traffic more enriched our vegetable world, than it has improved the whole face of nature among us. Our ships are laden with the harvest of every climate. Our tables are stored with spices and oils, and wines. Our rooms are filled with pyramids of china, and adorned with the workmanship of Japan. Our morning's draught comes to us from the remotest corners of the earth. We repair our bodies by the drugs of America, and repose ourselves under Indian canopies. My friend Sir Andrew calls the vineyards of France our gardens, the Spice Islands our hot-beds, the Persians our silk weavers, and the Chinese our potters. Nature indeed furnishes us with the bare necessaries of life, but traffic gives us greater variety of what is useful, and at the same time supplies us with everything that is convenient and ornamental. Nor is it the least part of this our happiness, that whilst we

enjoy the remotest products of the north and south, we are free from those extremities of weather which give them birth ; that our eyes are refreshed with the green fields of Britain, at the same time that our palates are feasted with fruits that rise between the tropics.

6. For these reasons there are no more useful members in a commonwealth than merchants. They knit mankind together in a mutual intercourse of good offices, distribute the gifts of nature, find work for the poor, add wealth to the rich, and magnificence to the great. Our English merchant converts the tin of his own country into gold, and exchanges his wool for rubies. The Mahometans are clothed in our British manufacture, and the inhabitants of the frozen zone warmed with the fleeces of our sheep.

7. When I have been upon the Change, I have often fancied one of our old kings standing in person, where he is represented in effigy, and looking down upon the wealthy concourse of people with which that place is every day filled. In this case how would he be suprised to hear all the languages of Europe spoken in this little spot of his former dominions, and to see so many private men, who in his time would have been the vassals of some powerful baron, negotiating like princes for greater sums of money than were formerly to be met with in the royal treasury ! Trade, without enlarging the British territories, has given us a kind of additional empire. It has multiplied the number of the rich, made our landed estates infinitely more valuable than they were formerly, and added to them an accession of other estates as valuable as the lands themselves.   C.

--------------------*Spatio brevi*
Spem longam reseces ; dum loquimur, fugerit invida
Ætas : carpe diem, quam minimum credula postero.—HOR.

1. We all of us complain of the shortness of time, saith
Seneca, and yet have much more than we know what to do with.
Our lives, says he, are spent either in doing nothing at all, or in
doing nothing to the purpose, or in doing nothing that we ought
to do.   We are always complaining our days are few, and acting
as though there would be no end of them.   That noble philosopher has described our inconsistency with ourselves in this
particular, by all those various turns of expression and thought
which are peculiar to his writings.

2. I often consider mankind as wholly inconsistent with itself
in a point that bears some affinity to the former.   Though we
seem grieved at the shortness of life in general, we are wishing
every period of it at an end.   The minor longs to be at age,
then to be a man of business, then to make up an estate, then
to arrive at honours, then to retire.   Thus although the whole
of life is allowed by every one to be short, the several divisions
of it appear long and tedious.   We are for lengthening our span
in general, but would fain contract the parts of which it is composed.   The usurer would be very well satisfied to have all the
time annihilated that lies between the present moment and next
quarter day.   The politician would be contented to lose three
years in his life, could he place things in the posture which he
fancies they will stand in after such a revolution of time.   The
lover would be glad to strike out of his existence all the
moments that are to pass away before the happy meeting.   Thus
as fast as our time runs, we should be very glad in most parts
of our lives that it ran much faster than it does.   Several hours
of the day hang upon our hands, nay we wish away whole years,

L

and travel through time as through a country filled with many wild and empty wastes, which we would fain hurry over, that we may arrive at those several little settlements or imaginary points of rest which are dispersed up and down in it.

3. If we divide the life of most men into twenty parts, we shall find that at least nineteen of them are mere gaps and chasms which are neither filled with pleasure nor business. I do not however include in this calculation the life of those men who are in a perpetual hurry of affairs, but of those only who are not always engaged in scenes of action ; and I hope I shall not do an unacceptable piece of service to these persons, if I point out to them certain methods for the filling up their empty spaces of life. The methods I shall propose to them are as follow.

4. The first is the exercise of virtue, in the most general acceptation of the word. That particular scheme which comprehends the social virtues, may give employment to the most industrious temper, and find a man in business more than the most active station of life. To advise the ignorant, relieve the needy, comfort the afflicted, are duties that fall in our way almost every day of our lives. A man has frequent opportunities of mitigating the fierceness of a party ; of doing justice to the character of a deserving man ; of softening the envious, quieting the angry, and rectifying the prejudiced ; which are all of them employments suited to a reasonable nature, and bring great satisfaction to the person who can busy himself in them with discretion.

5. There is another kind of virtue that may find employment for those retired hours in which we are altogether left to our selves, and destitute of company and conversation ; I mean that intercourse and communication which every reasonable creature ought to maintain with the great author of his being. The man who lives under an habitual sense of the divine presence keeps up a perpetual cheerfulness of temper, and enjoys every moment

the satisfaction of thinking himself in company with his dearest and best of friends. The time never lies heavy upon him : it is impossible for him to be alone. His thoughts and passions are the most busied at such hours when those of other men are the most inactive ; he no sooner steps out of the world but his heart burns with devotion, swells with hope, and triumphs in the consciousness of that Presence which every where surrounds him ; or, on the contrary, pours out its fears, its sorrows, its apprehensions, to the great supporter of its existence.

6. I have here only considered the necessity of a man's being virtuous, that he may have something to do ; but if we consider further, that the exercise of virtue is not only an amusement for the time it lasts, but that its influence extends to those parts of our existence which lie beyond the grave, and that our whole eternity is to take its colour from those hours which we here employ in virtue or in vice, the argument redoubles upon us, for putting in practice this method of passing away our time.

7. When a man has but a little stock to improve, and has opportunities of turning it all to good account, what shall we think of him if he suffers nineteen parts of it to lie dead, and perhaps employs even the twentieth to his ruin or disadvantage ? But because the mind cannot be always in its fervours, nor strained up to a pitch of virtue, it is necessary to find out proper employments for it in its relaxations.

8. The next method therefore that I would propose to fill up our time, should be useful and innocent diversions. I must confess I think it is below reasonable creatures to be altogether conversant in such diversions as are merely innocent, and have nothing else to recommend them, but that there is no hurt in them. Whether any kind of gaming has even thus much to say for itself, I shall not determine ; but I think it is very wonderful to see persons of the best sense passing away a dozen hours together in shuffling and dividing a pack of cards, with

no other conversation but what is made up of a few game phrases, and no other ideas but those of black or red spots ranged together in different figures. Would not a man laugh to hear any one of this species complaining that life is short?

9. The stage might be made a perpetual source of the most noble and useful entertainments, were it under proper regulations.

10. But the mind never unbends itself so agreeably as in the conversation of a well chosen friend. There is indeed no blessing of life that is any way comparable to the enjoyment of a discreet and virtuous friend. It eases and unloads the mind, clears and improves the understanding, engenders thoughts and knowledge, animates virtue and good resolution, soothes and allays the passions, and finds employment for most of the vacant hours of life.

11. Next to such an intimacy with a particular person, one would endeavour after a more general conversation with such as are able to entertain and improve those with whom they converse, which are qualifications that seldom go asunder.

12. There are many other useful amusements of life, which one would endeavour to multiply, that one might on all occasions have recourse to something rather than suffer the mind to lie idle, or run adrift with any passion that chances to rise in it.

13. A man that has a taste of music, painting, or architecture, is like one that has another sense when compared with such as have no relish of those arts. The florist, the planter, the gardener, the husbandman, when they are only as accomplishments to the man of fortune, are great reliefs to a country life, and many ways useful to those who are possessed of them.

14. But of all the diversions of life, there is none so proper to fill up its empty spaces as the reading of useful and entertaining authors. But this I shall only touch upon, because it in some measure interferes with the third method, which I shall

propose in another paper, for the employment of our dead un-
active hours, and which I shall only mention in general to be
the pursuit of knowledge.

No. 115]   *Thursday, July* 12, 1711.   [*Addison.*

——*Ut sit mens sana in corpore sano.*——JUV.

1. Bodily labour is of two kinds, either that which a man
submits to for his livelihood, or that which he undergoes for his
pleasure. The latter of them generally changes the name of
labour for that of exercise, but differs only from ordinary labour
as it rises from another motive.

2. A country life abounds in both these kinds of labour, and
for that reason gives a man a greater stock of health, and consequently a more perfect enjoyment of himself, than any other
way of life. I consider the body as a system of tubes and glands,
or to use a more rustic phrase, a bundle of pipes and strainers,
fitted to one another after so wonderful a manner as to make a
proper engine for the soul to work with. This description does
not only comprehend the bowels, bones, tendons, veins, nerves,
and arteries, but every muscle and every ligature, which is a
composition of fibres, that are so many imperceptible tubes or
pipes interwoven on all sides with invisible glands or strainers.

3. This general idea of a human body, without considering it
in its niceties of anatomy, lets us see how absolutely necessary

labour is for the right preservation of it. There must be frequent motions and agitations, to mix, digest, and separate the juices contained in it, as well as to clear and cleanse that infinitude of pipes and strainers of which it is composed, and to give their solid parts a more firm and lasting tone. Labour or exercise ferments the humours, casts them into their proper channels, throws off redundancies, and helps nature in those secret distributions, without which the body cannot subsist in its vigour, nor the soul act with cheerfulness.

4. I might here mention the effects which this has upon all the faculties of the mind, by keeping the understanding clear, the imagination untroubled, and refining those spirits that are necessary for the proper exertion of our intellectual faculties, during the present laws of union between soul and body. It is to a neglect in this particular that we must ascribe the spleen, which is so frequent in men of studious and sedentary tempers, as well as the vapours to which those of the other sex are so often subject.

5. Had not exercise been absolutely necessary for our well-being, nature would not have made the body so proper for it, by giving such an activity to the limbs, and such a pliancy to every part as necessarily produce those compressions, extensions, contortions, dilations, and all other kinds of motions that are necessary for the preservation of such a system of tubes and glands as has been before mentioned. And that we might not want inducements to engage us in such an exercise of the body as is proper for its welfare, it is so ordered that nothing valuable can be procured without it. Not to mention riches and honour, even food and raiment are not to be come at without the toil of the hands and sweat of the brows. Providence furnishes materials, but expects that we should work them up ourselves. The earth must be laboured before it gives its increase, and when it is forced into its several products, how many hands must they pass

through before they are fit for use? Manufactures, trade, and
agriculture,' naturally employ more than nineteen parts of the
species in twenty; and as for those who are not obliged to
labour, by the condition in which they are born, they are more
miserable than the rest of mankind, unless they indulge themselves in that voluntary labour which goes by the name of
exercise.

6. My friend Sir Roger has been an indefatigable man in business of this kind, and has hung several parts of his house with
the trophies of his former labours. The walls of his great hall
are covered with the horns of several kinds of deer that he has
killed in the chase, which he thinks the most valuable furniture
of his house, as they afford him frequent topics of discourse, and
shew that he has not been idle. At the lower end of the hall,
is a large otter's skin stuffed with hay, which his mother ordered
to be hung up in that manner, and the knight looks upon with
great satisfaction, because it seems he was but nine years old
when his dog killed him. A little room adjoining to the hall
is a kind of arsenal filled with guns of several sizes and inven-
tions with which the knight has made great havoc in the woods,
and destroyed many thousands of pheasants, partridges and
wood-cocks. His stable doors are patched with noses that belonged to foxes of the knight's own hunting down. Sir Roger
shewed me one of them that for distinction sake has a brass
nail struck through it, which cost him about fifteen hours' riding,
carried him through half a dozen counties, killed him a brace of
geldings, and lost above half his dogs. This the knight looks
upon as one of the greatest exploits of his life. The perverse
widow, whom I have given some account of, was the death of
several foxes; for Sir Roger has told me that in the course of
his amours he patched the western door of his stable. Whenever the widow was cruel, the foxes were sure to pay for it.
In proportion as his passion for the widow abated and old age

came on, he left off fox hunting, but a hare is not yet safe that sits within ten miles of his house.

7. There is no kind of exercise which I would so recommend to my readers of both sexes as this of riding, as there is none which so much conduces to health, and is every way accommodated to the body, according to the idea which I have given of it. Doctor Sydenham is very lavish in its praises ; and if the English reader will see the mechanical effects of it described at length, he may find them in a book published not many years since, under the title of " Medicina Gymnastica." For my own part, when I am in town, for want of these opportunities, I exercise myself an hour every morning upon a dumb bell that is placed in a corner of my room, and pleases me the more because it does every thing I require of it in the most perfect silence. My landlady and her daughters are so well acquainted with my hours of exercise, that they never come into my room to disturb me whilst I am ringing.

8. When I was some years younger than I am at present, I used to employ myself in a more laborious diversion, which I learned from a Latin treatise of exercises that is written with great erudition. It is there called the σκιομαχία, or the fighting with a man's own shadow, and consists in the brandishing of two short sticks grasped in each hand, and loaded with plugs of lead at either end. This opens the chest, exercises the limbs, and gives a man all the pleasure of boxing, without the blows. I could wish that several learned men would lay out that time which they employ in controversies and disputes about nothing, in this method of fighting with their own shadows. It might conduce very much to evaporate the spleen, which makes them uneasy to the public as well as to themselves.

9. To conclude, as I am a compound of soul and body, I consider myself as obliged to a double scheme of duties ; and I think I have not fulfilled the business of the day when I do not thus

employ the one in labour and exercise, as well as the other in study and contemplation. L.

No. 159.] *Saturday, September* 1, 1711. [*Addison.*

—— Omnem quæ nunc obducta tuenti
Mortales hebetat visus tibi, et humida circum
Caligat, nubem eripiam—— Virg.

1. When I was at Grand Cairo, I picked up several oriental manuscripts which I have still by me. Among others I met with one entitled, The Visions of Mirzah, which I have read over with great pleasure. I intend to give it to the public when I have no other entertainment for them ; and shall begin with the first vision, which I have translated word for word as follows.

2. 'On the fifth day of the moon, which according to the cus-
'tom of my forefathers I always keep holy, after having washed
'myself, and offered up my morning devotions, I ascended the
'high hills of Bagdat, in order to pass the rest of the day in
'meditation and prayer. As I was here airing myself on the
'tops of the mountains, I fell into a profound contemplation
'on the vanity of human life ; and passing from one thought to
'another, Surely, said I, man is but a shadow and life a dream.
'Whilst I was thus musing, I cast my eyes towards the summit
'of a rock that was not far from me, where I discovered one in

' the habit of a shepherd, with a little musical instrument in his
' hand. As I looked upon him he applied it to his lips and be-
' gan to play upon it. The sound of it was exceeding sweet,
' and wrought into a variety of tunes that were inexpressibly
' melodious and altogether different from anything I have ever
' heard. They put me in mind of those heavenly airs that are
' played to the departed souls of good men upon their first arrival
' in Paradise, to wear out the impression of the last agonies,
' and qualify them for the pleasures of that happy place. My
' heart melted away in secret raptures.

3. ' I had often been told that the rock before me was the
' haunt of a genius ; and that several had been entertained with
' music that passed by it, but never heard that the musician had
' before made himself visible. When he had raised my thoughts
' by those transporting airs which he played, to taste the
' pleasures of his conversation, as I looked upon him like one
' astonished, he beckoned to me, and by the waving of his hand
' directed me to approach the place where he sat. I drew near
' with that reverence which is due to a superior nature ; and
' as my heart was entirely subdued by the captivating strains I
' had heard, I fell down at his feet and wept. The genius
' smiled upon me with a look of compassion and affability that
' familiarized him to my imagination, and at once dispelled all
' the fears and apprehensions with which I approached him.
' He lifted me from the ground, and taking me by the hand,
' Mirzah, said he, I have heard thee in thy soliloquies ; follow
' me.

4. ' He then led me to the highest pinnacle of the rock, and
' placing me on the top of it, Cast thine eyes eastward, said he,
' and tell me what thou seest. I see, said I, a huge valley, and
' a prodigious tide of water rolling through it. The valley that
' thou seest, said he, is the vale of misery, and the tide of
' water that thou seest is part of the great tide of eternity.

' What is the reason, said I, that the tide I see rises out of a
' thick mist at one end, and again loses itself in a thick mist at
' the other?   What thou seest, said he, is that portion of eter-
' nity which is called time, measured out by the sun, and
' reaching from the beginning of the world to its consummation.
' Examine now, said he, this sea that is bounded with darkness
· at both ends, and tell us what thou discoverest in it.   I see a
' bridge, said I, standing in the midst of the tide.   The bridge
' thou seest, said he, is human life, consider it attentively.   Up-
' on a more leisurely survey of it, I found that it consisted of
' three score and ten entire arches, with several broken arches,
' which, added to those that were entire, made up the number
' about an hundred.   As I was counting the arches, the genius
' told me that this bridge consisted at first of a thousand arches
' but that a great flood swept away the rest, and left the bridge
' in the ruinous condition I now behold it.   But tell me further,
' said he, what thou discoverest on it.   I see multitudes of
' people passing over it, said I, and a black cloud hanging on
' each end of it.   As I looked more attentively, I saw several
' of the passengers dropping through the bridge, into the great
' tide that flowed underneath it; and upon further examination,
' perceived there were innumerable trap-doors that lay concealed
' in the bridge, which the passengers no sooner trod upon, but
' they fell through them into the tide and immediately disappear-
' ed.   These hidden pit-falls were set very thick at the entrance
' to the bridge, so that the throngs of people no sooner broke
' through the cloud, but many of them fell into them.   They
' grew thinner towards the middle, but multiplied and lay
' closer together towards the end of the arches that were entire.

5. ' There were indeed some persons, but their number was
' very small that continued a kind 'of hobbling march on the
' broken arches, but fell through one after another, being quite
' tired and spent with so long a walk.

6. ' I passed some time in the contemplation of this wonderful
' structure, and the great variety of objects which it presented.
' My heart was filled with a deep melancholy to see several
' dropping unexpectedly in the midst of mirth and jollity, and
' catching at everything that stood by them to save themselves.
' Some were looking up towards the heavens in a thoughtful
' posture, and in the midst of a speculation stumbled and fell
' out of sight. Multitudes were very busy in the pursuit . of
' bubbles that glittered in their eyes and danced before them ;
' but often when they thought themselves within the reach of
' them their footing failed them and down they sunk. In this
' confusion of objects, I observed some with scimitars in their
' hands, who ran to and fro upon the bridge, thrusting several
' persons on trap-doors which did not seem to lie in the way,
' and which they might have escaped had they not been forced
' upon them.

7. ' The genius seeing me indulge myself in this melancholy
' prospect, told me I had dwelt long enough upon it ; Take thine
' eyes off the bridge, said he, and tell me if thou yet seest any-
' thing thou dost not comprehend. Then looking up, What
' mean, said I, those great flights of birds that are perpetually
' hovering about the bridge, and settling upon it from time to
' time ? I see vultures, harpies, ravens, cormorants, and among
' many other feathered creatures several little winged boys, that
' perch in great numbers upon the middle arches. Those, said
' the genius, are envy, avarice, superstition, despair, love, with
' the like cares and passions that infest human life.

8. ' I here fetched a deep sigh, Alas, said I, man was made in
' vain ! How is he given away to misery and mortality ! tor-
' tured in life, and swallowed up in death ! The genius being
' moved with compassion towards me bid me quit so uncomfort-
' able a prospect. Look no more, said he, on man in the first
' stage of his existence, in his setting out for eternity ; but cast

' thine eye on that thick mist into which the tide bears the
' several generations of mortals that fall into it. I directed
' my sight as I was ordered, and (whether or no the good genius
' strengthened it with any supernatural force, or dissipated part
' of the mist that was before too thick for the eye to penetrate)
' I saw the valley opening at the further end, and spreading
' forth into an immense ocean, that had a huge rock of ada-
' mant running through the midst of it and dividing it into two
' equal parts. The clouds still rested on one half of it, insomuch
' that I could discover nothing in it. But the other appeared
' to me a vast ocean planted with innumerable islands, that
' were covered with fruits and flowers, and interwoven with
' a thousand little shining seas that ran among them. I
' could see persons dressed in glorious habits with garlands
' upon their heads, passing among the trees, lying down by
' the side of fountains, or resting on beds of flowers ; and
' could hear a confused harmony of singing birds, falling waters
' human voices, and musical instruments. Gladness grew in me
' upon the discovery of so delightful a scene. I wished for the
' wings of an eagle, that I might fly far away to those happy
' seats ; but the genius told me there was no passage to them,
' except through the gates of death that I saw opening every
' moment upon the bridge. The islands, said he, that lie so
' fresh and green before thee and with which the whole face of
' ocean appears spotted as far as thou canst see, are more in
' number than the sands on the sea-shore ; there are myriads of
' islands behind those which thou here discoverest, reaching
' further than thine eye, or even thine imagination can extend
' itself. These are the mansions of good men after death, who
' according to the degree and kinds of virtue in which they ex-
' celled, are distributed among these several islands, which
' abound with pleasures of different kinds and degrees, suitable
' to the relishes and perfections of those who are settled in
' them ; every island is a paradise accommodated to its respective

'inhabitants. Are not these, O Mirzah, habitations worth con-
'tending for? Does life appear so miserable, that gives the
'opportunities of earning such a reward? Is death to be feared
'that will convey thee to so happy an existence? Think not
'man was made in vain, who has such an eternity reserved for
'him. I gazed with inexpressible pleasure on these happy
'islands. At length, said I, Show me now, I beseech thee, the
'secrets that lie hid under those dark clouds which cover the
'ocean on the other side of the rock of adamant. The genius
'making me no answer, I turned about to address myself to him
'a second time, but I found that he had left me. I then
'turned again to the vision which I had been so long contem-
'plating ; but instead of the rolling tide, the arched bridge, and
'the happy island, I saw nothing but the long hollow valley of
'Bagdat, with oxen, sheep, and camels grazing upon the sides
'of it.

9. The end of the first vision of Mirzah. C.

No. 162.] *Wednesday, September 5, 1711.* [*Addison.*

——————Servetur ad imum, ,
Qualis ab incœpto processerit, et sibi constet. - Hor.

1. Nothing that is not a real crime makes a man appear so
contemptible and little in the eyes of the world as inconstancy,
especially when it regards religion or party. In either of
these cases, tho' a man perhaps does but his duty in changing
his side, he not only makes himself hated by those he left, but
is seldom heartily esteemed by those he comes over to.

2. In these great articles of life, therefore, a man's conviction ought to be very strong, and if possible so well timed that worldly advantages may seem to have no share in it, or mankind will be ill-natured enough to think he does not change sides out of principle, but either out of levity of temper or prospects of interest. Converts and renegadoes of all kinds should take particular care to let the world see they act upon honourable motives ; or whatever approbations they may receive from themselves, and applauses from those they converse with, they may be very well assured that they are the scorn of all good men, and the public marks of infamy and derision.

3. Irresolution on the schemes of life which offer themselves to our choice, and inconstancy in pursuing them, are the greatest and most universal causes of all our disquiet and unhappiness. When ambition pulls one way, interest another, inclination a third, and perhaps reason contrary to all, a man is likely to pass his time but ill who has so many different parties to please. When the mind hovers among such a variety of allurements, one had better settle on a way of life that is not the very best we might have chosen, than grow old without determining our choice, and go out of the world, as the greatest part of mankind do, before we have resolved how to live in it. There is but one method of setting ourselves at rest in this particular, and that is by adhering steadfastly to one great end as the chief and ultimate aim of all our pursuits. If we are firmly resolved to live up the dictates of reason, without any regard to wealth, reputation or the like considerations, any more than as they fall in with our principal design, we may go through life with steadiness and pleasure, but if we act by several broken views, and will not only be virtuous, but wealthy, popular and everything that has value set upon it by the world, we shall live and die in misery and repentance.

4. One would take more than ordinary care to guard oneself against this particular imperfection, because it is that which our nature very strongly inclines us to ; for if we examine our understanding, we often embrace and reject the very same opinions ; whereas beings above and beneath us have probably no opinions at all, or at least no wavering and uncertainties in those they have. Our superiors are guided by intuition, and our inferiors by instinct. In respect of our wills, we fall into crimes and recover out of them, are amiable or odious in the eyes of our great judge, and pass our whole life in offending and asking pardon. On the contrary, the beings underneath us are not capable of sinning, nor those above us of repenting. The one is out of the possibilities of duty, and the other fixed in an eternal course of sin, or an eternal course of virtue.

5. There is scarce a state of life or stage in it, which does not produce changes and revolutions in the mind of man. Our schemes of thought in infancy are lost in those of youth ; these too take a different turn in manhood, till old age often leads us back into our former infancy. A new title or an unexpected success throws us out of ourselves, and, in a manner, destroys our identity. A cloudy day, or a little sun-shine, have as great an influence on many constitutions as the most real blessings or misfortunes. A dream varies our being and changes our condition while it lasts, and every passion, not to mention health and sickness, and the greater alterations in body and mind, make us appear almost different creatures. If a man is so distinguished among other beings by this infirmity what can we think of such as make themselves remarkable for it even among their own species ? It is a very trifling character to be one of the most variable beings of the most variable kind, especially if we consider that He who is the great standard of perfection has in him no shadow of change, but is the same yesterday, to-day, and for ever.

6. As this mutability of temper and inconsistency with our-selves is the greatest weakness of human nature, so it makes the person who is remarkable for it in a very particular manner more ridiculous than any other infirmity whatsoever, as it sets him in a greater variety of foolish lights, and distinguishes him from himself by an opposition of party-coloured characters. The most humorous character in Horace is founded upon this un-evenness of temper and irregularity of conduct.

> ————————————Sardus habebat
> Ille Tigellius hoc : Cæsar qui cogere posset
> Si peteret per amicitiam patris, atque suam non
> Quidquam proficeret : si collibuisset, ab ovo
> Usque ad mala citaret, Io Bacche, modo summâ
> Voce, modò hâc, resonat quæ chordis quatuor ima.
> Nil æquale homini fuit illi : sæpe velut qui
> Currebat fugiens hostem : persæpe velut qui
> Junonis sacra ferret : habebat sæpe ducentos,
> Sæpe decem servos : modò reges atque tetrarchas,
> Omnia magna loquens : modó sit mihi mensa tripes, et
> Concha salis puri, et toga, quæ defendere frigus,
> Quamvis crassa, queat. Decies centena dedisses
> Huic parco paucis contento, quinque diebus
> Nil erat in loculis.   Noctes vigilabat ad ipsum
> Manè : diem totam stertebat.   Nil fuit unquam
> Sic impar sibi——. *Hor. Sat. 3, Lib. 1.*

7. Instead of translating this passage in Horace, I shall entertain my English reader with a description of a parallel character that is wonderfully well finished by Mr. Dryden, and raised upon the same foundation :

> In the first rank of these did Zimri stand ;
> A man so various, that he seem'd to be
> Not one, but all mankind's epitome.
> Stiff in opinions, always in the wrong ;
> Was ev'rything by starts and nothing long ;
> But in the course of one revolving moon,
> Was chemist, fiddler, statesman and buffoon ;

M

Then all for women, painting, rhyming, drinking :
Besides ten thousand freaks that died in thinking.
Blest madman, who could ev'ry hour employ,
With something new to wish, or to enjoy !   C.

No. 169.]   *Thursday, Sept.* 13, 1711.   [*Addison.*

Sic vita erat : facile omnes perferre ac pati :
Cum quibus erat cunque una, his sese dedere,
Eorum obseqvi studiis : advorsus nemini ;
Nunquam præponens se aliis : ita facillime
Sine invidia invenias laudem——Ter. And.

1. Man is subject to innumerable pains and sorrows by the very condition of humanity, and yet, as if nature had not sown evils enough in life, we are continually adding grief to grief, and aggravating the common calamity by our cruel treatment of one another. Every man's natural weight of affliction is still made more heavy by the envy, malice, treachery, or injustice of his neighbor. At the same time that the storm beats upon the whole species, we are falling foul upon one another.

2. Half the misery of human life might be extinguished, would men alleviate the general curse they lie under, by mutual offices of compassion, benevolence, and humanity. There is nothing therefore which we ought more to encourage in ourselves and others, than that disposition of mind which in our language goes under the title of good-nature, and which I shall choose for the subject of this day's speculation.

3. Good-nature is more agreeable in conversation than wit, and gives a certain air to the countenance which is more amiable than beauty. It shows virtue in the fairest light, takes off in some measure from the deformity of vice, and makes even folly and impertinence supportable.

4. There is no society or conversation to be kept up in the world without good-nature, or something which must bear its appearance, and supply its place. For this reason mankind have been forced to invent a kind of artificial humanity, which is what we express by the word good-breeding. For if we examine thoroughly the idea of what we call so, we shall find it to be nothing else but an imitation and mimicry of good-nature, or in other terms, affability, complaisance and easiness of temper reduced into an art.

5. These exterior shows and appearances of humanity render a man wonderfully popular and beloved when they are founded upon a real good-nature; but without it are like hypocrisy in religion, or a bare form of holiness, which, when it is discovered, makes a man more detestable than professed impiety.

6. Good-nature is generally born with us. Health, prosperity and kind treatment from the world are great cherishers of it where they find it; but nothing is capable of forcing it up, where it does not grow of itself. It is one of the blessings of a happy constitution, which education may improve but not produce.

7. Xenophon in the life of his imaginary prince, whom he describes as a pattern for real ones, is always celebrating the philanthropy or good-nature of his hero, which he tells us he brought into the world with him, and gives many remarkable instances of it in his childhood, as well as in all the several parts of his life. Nay, on his death-bed, he describes him as being pleased, that while his soul returned to him [who] made

it, his body should incorporate with the great mother of all things, and by that means become beneficial to mankind. For which reason, he gives his sons a positive order not to enshrine it in gold or silver, but to lay it in the earth as soon as the life was gone out of it.

8. An instance of such an overflowing of humanity, such an exuberant love to mankind, could not have entered into the imagination of a writer, who had not a soul filled with great ideas, and a general benevolence to mankind.

9. In that celebrated passage of Sallust, where Cæsar and Cato are placed in such beautiful, but opposite lights, Cæsar's character is chiefly made up of good-nature, as it shewed itself in all its forms towards his friends or his enemies, his servants or dependants, the guilty or the distressed. As for Cato's character, it is rather awful than amiable. Justice seems most agreeable to the nature of God, and mercy to that of man. A being who has nothing to pardon in himself, may reward every man according to his works; but he whose very best actions must be seen with grains of allowance, cannot be too mild, moderate, and forgiving. For this reason, among all the monstrous characters in human nature, there is none so odious, nor indeed so exquisitely ridiculous, as that of a rigid severe temper in a worthless man.

10. This part of good-nature, however, which consists in the pardoning and overlooking of faults, is to be exercised only in doing ourselves justice, and that too in the ordinary commerce and occurrences of life; for in the public administrations of justice, mercy to one may be cruelty to others.

11. It is grown almost into a maxim, that good-natured men are not always men of the most wit. This observation, in my opinion, has no foundation in nature. The greatest wits I have conversed with are men eminent for their humanity. I take

therefore this remark to have been occasioned by two reasons. First, because ill-nature among ordinary observers passes for wit. A spiteful saying gratifies so many little passions in those who hear it, that it generally meets with a good reception. The laugh rises upon it, and the man who utters it is looked upon as a shrewd satirist. This may be one reason, why a great many pleasant companions appear so surprisingly dull, when they have endeavoured to be merry in print; the public being more just than private clubs or assemblies, in distinguishing between what is wit and what is ill-nature.

12. Another reason why the good-natured man may sometimes bring his wit in question, is, perhaps, because he is apt to be moved with compassion for those misfortunes or infirmities, which another would turn into ridicule, and by that means gain the reputation of a wit. The ill-natured man, though but of equal parts, gives himself a larger field to expatiate in; he exposes those failings in human nature which the other would cast a veil over, laughs at vices which the other either excuses or conceals, gives utterance to reflections which the other stifles, falls indifferently upon friends or enemies, exposes the person who has obliged him, and, in short, sticks at nothing that may establish his character of a wit. It is no wonder therefore he succeeds in it better than the man of humanity, as a person who makes use of indirect methods is more likely to grow rich than the fair trader.   L.

Νήπιοι, οἰδ' ἴσασιν ὅσω πλέον ἥμισυ παντός,
Οὐδ' ὅσον ἐν μαλάχῃτε δὲ ἀσφοδέλῳ μέγ' ὄνειαρ. —Hes.

1. There is a story in the Arabian Nights Tales of a king who had long languished under an ill habit of body, and had taken abundance of remedies to no purpose. At length, says the fable, a physician cured him by the following method. He took an hollow ball of wood, and filled it with several drugs; after which he closed it up so artificially that nothing appeared. He likewise took a mall, and after having hollowed the handle, and that part which strikes the ball, he enclosed in them several drugs after the same manner as in the ball itself. He then ordered the Sultan, who was his patient, to exercise himself early in the morning with these rightly prepared instruments, till such time as he should sweat, when, as the story goes, the virtue of the medicaments perspiring through the wood, had so good an influence on the Sultan's constitution, that they cured him of an indisposition which all the compositions he had taken inwardly had not been able to remove. This eastern allegory is finely contrived to shew us how beneficial bodily labour is to health, and that exercise is the most effectual physic. I have described in my hundred and fifteenth paper, from the general structure and mechanism of an human body, how absolutely necessary exercise is for its preservation. I shall in this place recommend another great preservative of health, which in many cases produces the same effects as exercise, and may, in some measure, supply its place, where opportunities of exercise are wanting. The preservative I am speaking of is temperance, which has those particular advantages above all other means of health, that it may be practised by all ranks and conditions, at any season or in any place. It is a kind of regimen into which

every man may put himself, without interruption to business, expense of money, or loss of time. If exercise throws off all superfluities, temperance prevents them; if exercise clears the vessels, temperance neither satiates nor overstrains them; if exercise raises proper ferments in the humours, and promotes the circulation of the blood, temperance gives nature her full play, and enables her to exert herself in all her force and vigour; if exercise dissipates a growing distemper, temperance starves it.

2. Physic, for the most part, is nothing else but the substitute of exercise or temperance. Medicines are indeed absolutely necessary in acute distempers, that cannot wait the slow operations of these two great instruments of health; but did men live in an habitual course of exercise and temperance, there would be but little occasion for them. Accordingly we find that those parts of the world are the most healthy, where they subsist by the chase; and that men lived longest when their lives were employed in hunting, and when they had little food besides what they caught. Blistering, cupping, bleeding, are seldom of use but to the idle and intemperate; as all those inward applications which are so much in practice among us, are for the most part nothing else but expedients to make luxury consistent with health. The apothecary is perpetually employed in countermining the cook and the vintner. It is said of Diogenes, that meeting a young man who was going to a feast, he took him up in the street and carried him home to his friends, as one who was running into imminent danger, had not he prevented him. What would that philosopher have said, had he been present at the gluttony of a modern meal? Would not he have thought the master of a family mad, and have begged his servants to tie down his hands, had he seen him devour fowl, fish, and flesh; swallow oil and vinegar, wines and spices; throw down salads of twenty different herbs, sauces of an hundred ingredients, confections and fruits of numberless sweets

and flavours? What unnatural motions and counterferments must such a medley of intemperance produce in the body? For my part, when I behold a fashionable table set out in all its magnificence, I fancy that I see gouts and dropsies, fevers and lethargies, with other innumerable distempers lying in ambuscade among the dishes.

3. Nature delights in the most plain and simple diet. Every animal, but man, keeps to one dish. Herbs are the food of this species, fish of that, and flesh of a third. Man falls upon every thing that comes in his way, not the smallest fruit or excrescence of the earth, scarce a berry or a mushroom, can escape him.

4. It is impossible to lay down any determinate rule for temperance, because what is luxury in one may be temperance in another; but there are few that have lived any time in the world, who are not judges of their own constitutions, so far as to know what kinds and what proportions of food do best agree with them. Were I to consider my readers as my patients, and to prescribe such a kind of temperance as is accommodated to all persons, and such as is particularly suitable to our climate and way of living, I would copy the following rules of a very eminent physician. Make your whole repast out of one dish. If you indulge in a second, avoid drinking any thing strong, till you have finished your meal; at the same time abstain from all sauces, or at least such as are not the most plain and simple. A man could not be well guilty of gluttony, if he stuck to these few obvious and easy rules. In the first case there would be no variety of tastes to solicit his palate, and occasion excess; nor in the second any artificial provocatives to relieve satiety, and create a false appetite. Were I to prescribe a rule for drinking, it should be formed upon a saying quoted by Sir William Temple; "The first glass for myself, the second for my friends, the third for good humour, and the fourth for mine

enemies." But because it is impossible for one who lives in the world to diet himself always in so philosophical a manner, I think every man should have his days of abstinence, according as his constitution will permit. These are great reliefs to nature, as they qualify her for struggling with hunger and thirst, whenever any distemper or duty of life may put her upon such difficulties; and at the same time give her an opportunity of extricating herself from her oppressions, and recovering the several tones and springs of her distended vessels. Besides that abstinence well timed often kills a sickness in embryo, and destroys the first seeds of an indisposition. It is observed by two or three ancient authors, that Socrates, notwithstanding he lived in Athens during that great plague, which has made so much noise through all ages, and has been celebrated at different times by such eminent hands; I say, notwithstanding that he lived in the time of this devouring pestilence, he never caught the least infection, which those writers unanimously ascribe to that uninterrupted temperance which he always observed.

5. And here I cannot but mention an observation which I have often made, upon reading the lives of the philosophers, and comparing them with any series of kings or great men of the same number. If we consider these ancient sages, a great part of whose philosophy consisted in a temperate and abstemious course of life, one would think the life of a philosopher and the life of a man were of two different dates. For we find that the generality of these wise men were nearer an hundred than sixty years of age at the time of their respective deaths. But the most remarkable instance of the efficacy of temperance towards the procuring of long life, is what we meet with in a little book published by Lewis Cornaro the Venetian; which I the rather mention, because it is of undoubted credit, as the late Venetian ambassador, who was of the same family, attested more than once in conversation, when he resided in England. Cornaro,

who was the author of the little treatise I am mentioning, was of an infirm constitution, till about forty, when by obstinately persisting in an exact course of temperance, he recovered a perfect state of health ; insomuch that at fourscore he published his book, which has been translated into English upon the title of *Sure and certain Methods of attaining a long and healthy Life,* He lived to give a third or fourth edition of it and after having passed his hundredth year, died without pain or agony, and like one who falls asleep. The treatise I mention has been taken notice of by several eminent authors, and is written with such a spirit of cheerfulness, religion, and good sense, as are the natural concomitants of temperance and sobriety. The mixture of the old man in it is rather a recommendation than a discredit to it.

6. Having designed this paper as the sequel to that upon exercise, I have not here considered temperance as it is a moral virtue, which I shall make the subject of a future speculation, but only as it is the means of health.   L.

<hr>

No. 225.]   *Saturday, November* 17, 1711.   [*Addison.*

Nullum numen abest si sit Prudentia—   Juv.

1. I have often thought if the minds of men were laid open, we should see but little difference between that of the wise man and that of the fool. There are infinite reveries, numberless extravagancies, and a perpetual train of vanities which pass through

both. The great difference is that the first knows how to pick and cull his thoughts for conversation, by suppressing some, and communicating others; whereas the other lets them all indifferently fly out in words. This sort of discretion, however, has no place in private conversation between intimate friends. On such occasions the wisest men very often talk like the weakest; for indeed the talking with a friend is nothing else but thinking aloud.

2. Tully has therefore very justly exposed a precept delivered by some ancient writers, that a man should live with his enemy in such a manner that might leave him room to become his friend; and with his friend in such a manner, that if he became his enemy it should not be in his power to hurt him. The first part of this rule which regards our behaviour towards an enemy is indeed very reasonable, as well as very prudential; but the latter part of it which regards our behaviour towards a friend, savours more of cunning than of discretion, and would cut a man off from the greatest pleasures of life, which are the freedoms of conversation with a bosom friend. Besides, that when a friend is turned into an enemy, and (as the son of Sirach calls him) a betrayer of secrets, the world is just enough to accuse the perfidiousness of the friend, rather than the indiscretion of the person who confided in him.

3. Discretion does not always show itself in words, but in all the circumstances of action: and is like an under-agent of Providence to guide and direct us in the ordinary concerns of life.

4. There are many more shining qualities in the mind of man, but there is none so useful as discretion; it is this indeed which gives a value to all the rest, which sets them at work in their proper times and places, and turns them to the advantage of the person who is possessed of them. Without it learning is pedantry, and wit impertinence; virtue itself looks like weakness;

the best parts only qualify a man to be more sprightly in errors, and active to his own prejudice.

5. Nor does discretion only make a man the master of his own parts, but of other men's. The discreet man finds out the talents of those he converses with, and knows how to apply them to proper uses. Accordingly if we look into particular communities and divisions of men, we may observe that it is the discreet man, not the witty, nor the learned, nor the brave, who guides the conversation and gives measures to the society. A man with great talents but void of discretion, is like Polyphemus in the fable, strong and blind, endued with an irresistible force, which for want of sight is of no use to him.

6. Though a man has all other perfections, and wants discretion he will be of no great consequence in the world; but if he has this single talent in perfection, and but a common share of others, he may do what he pleases in his particular station of life.

7. At the same time that I think discretion the most useful talent a man can be master of, I look upon cunning to be the accomplishment of little, mean, ungenerous minds. Discretion points out the noblest ends to us, and pursues the most proper and laudable methods of attaining them. Cunning has only private, selfish aims, and sticks at nothing which may make them succeed. Discretion has large and extended views, and like a well formed eye, commands a whole horizon. Cunning is a kind of short-sightedness, that discovers the minutest objects which are near at hand, but is not able to discern things at a distance. Discretion, the more it is discovered, gives a greater authority to the person who possesses it. Cunning, when it is once detected, loses its force, and makes a man incapable of bringing about even those events which he might have done, had he passed only for a plain man. Discretion is the perfection of reason, and a guide to us in the duties of life; cunning is a kind of instinct,

that only looks out after our immediate interest and welfare. Discretion is only found in men of strong sense and good under- standings. Cunning is often to be met with in brutes them- selves, and in persons who are but the fewest removes from them. In short cunning is only the mimic of discretion, and may pass upon weak men, in the same manner as vivacity is often mistaken for wit, and gravity for wisdom.

8. The cast of mind which is natural to a discreet man, makes him look forward into futurity, and consider what will be his condition millions of ages hence, as well as what it is at present. He knows that the misery or happiness which are reserved for him in another world, lose nothing of their reality by being placed at so great distance from him. The objects do not appear little to him because they are remote. He considers that those pleasures and pains which lie hid in eternity, approach nearer to him every moment, and will be present with him in their full weight and measure, as much as those pains and pleasures which he feels at this very instant. For this reason he is careful to secure to himself that which is the proper happi- ness of his nature, and the ultimate design of his being. He carries his thoughts to the end of every action and considers the most distant as well as the most immediate effects of it. He supersedes every little prospect of gain and advantage which offers itself here, if he does not find it consistent with his views of an hereafter. In a word his hopes are full of immortality, his schemes are large and glorious, and his conduct suitable to one who knows his true interest, and how to pursue it by proper methods.

9. I have, in this essay upon discretion, considered it both as an accomplishment and as a virtue, and have therefore described it in its full extent : not only as it is conversant about worldly affairs, but as it regards our whole existence ; not only as it is the guide of a mortal creature, but as it is in general the direc- tor of a reasonable being. It is in this light that discretion is

represented by the wise man, who sometimes mentions it under
the name of discretion and sometimes under that of wisdom. It
is indeed (as described in the latter part of this paper) the greatest wisdom, but at the same time in the power of every one to
attain. Its advantages are infinite, but its acquisition easy ; or
to speak of her in the words of the apocryphal writer whom I
quoted in last Saturday's Paper, "Wisdom is glorious, and
never fadeth away, yet she is easily seen of them that love her,
and found of such as seek her. She preventeth them that desire her, in making herself first known unto them. He that
seeketh her early, shall have no great travel, for he shall find
her sitting at his doors. To think therefore upon her is perfection of wisdom, and whoso watcheth for her shall quickly be
without care. For she goeth about seeking such as are worthy
of her, sheweth herself favourably unto them in the ways, and
meeteth them in every thought." C.

No. 381.] *Saturday, May 17, 1712.* [*Addison.*

Æquam memento rebus in arduis,
Servare mentem, non secùs in bonis
Ab insolenti temperatam
Lætitiâ, moriture Deli.—Hor.

1. I have always preferred cheerfulness to mirth. The latter
I consider as an act, the former as a habit of the mind. Mirth
is short and transient, cheerfulness fixed and permanent. Those
are often raised into the greatest transports of mirth, who are

subject to the greatest depressions of melancholy ; on the contrary, cheerfulness, though it does not give the mind such an
exquisite gladness, prevents us from falling into any depths of
sorrow. Mirth is like a flash of lightning that breaks through
a gloom of clouds and glitters for a moment ; cheerfulness keeps
up a kind of daylight in the mind, and fills it with a steady
and perpetual serenity.

2. Men of austere principles look upon mirth as too wanton
and dissolute for a state of probation, and as filled with a certain
triumph and insolence of heart, that is inconsistent with a life
which is every moment obnoxious to the greatest dangers.
Writers of this complexion have observed that the sacred Person who was the great pattern of perfection was never seen to
laugh.

3. Cheerfulness of mind is not liable to any of these exceptions;
it is of a serious and composed nature, it does not throw the
mind into a condition improper for the present state of humanity, and is very conspicuous in the characters of those who are
looked upon as the greatest philosophers among the heathens
as well as among those who have been deservedly esteemed as
saints and holy men among Christians.

4. If we consider cheerfulness in three lights, with regard to
ourselves, to those we converse with, and to the great Author
of our being, it will not a little recommend itself on each of
these accounts. The man who is possessed of this excellent
frame of mind, is not only easy in his thoughts, but a perfect
master of all the powers and faculties of his soul : his imagination is always clear, and his judgment undisturbed : his temper is even and unruffled whether in action or in solitude. He
comes with a relish to all those goods which nature has provided for him, tastes all the pleasures of the creation which are
poured about him, and does not feel the full weight of those
accidental evils which may befal him.

5. If we consider him in relation to the persons whom he converses with, it naturally produces love and good-will towards
him.   A cheerful mind is not only disposed to be affable and
obliging, but raises the same good humour in those who come
within its influence.   A man finds himself pleased, he does not
know why, with the cheerfulness of his companion : it is like a
sudden sunshine that awakens a secret delight in the mind without her attending to it.   The heart rejoices of its own accord,
and naturally flows out into friendship and benevolence towards
the person who has so kindly an effect upon it.

6. When I consider this cheerful state of mind in its third relation, I cannot but look upon it as a constant habitual gratitude to the great Author of Nature.   An inward cheerfulness
is an implicit praise and thanksgiving to Providence under all
its dispensations.   It is a kind of acquiescence in the state
wherein we are placed, and a secret approbation of the divine
will in his conduct towards man.

7. There are but two things which, in my opinion, can reasonably deprive us of this cheerfulness of heart.   The first of these
is the sense of guilt.   A man who lives in a state of impeni-
tence, can have no title to that evenness and tranquillity of
mind which is the health of the soul, and the natural effect of
virtue and innocence.   Cheerfulness in an ill man deserves a
harder name than language can furnish us with, and is many
degrees beyond what we commonly call folly or madness.

8. Atheism, by which I mean a disbelief of a Supreme Being,
and consequently of a future state, under whatsoever titles it
shelters itself, may likewise very reasonably deprive a man of
this cheerfulness of temper.   There is something so particularly gloomy and offensive to human nature in the prospect of
non-existence, that I cannot but wonder, with many excellent
writers, how it is possible for a man to outlive the expectation
of it.   For my own part I think the being of a God is so little

to be doubted, that it is almost the only truth we are sure of, and such a truth as we meet with in every object, in every occurrence, and in every thought. If we look into the characters of the tribe of infidels, we generally find they are made up of pride, spleen and cavil : it is, indeed, no wonder that men, who are uneasy to themselves should be so to the rest of the world ; and how is it posssible for a man to be otherwise than uneasy in himself, who is in danger every moment of losing his entire existence, and dropping into nothing ?

9. The vicious man and atheist have, therefore, no pretence to cheerfulness and would act very unreasonably should they endeavour after it. It is impossible for any one to live in good humour, and enjoy his present existence who is apprehensive either of torment or of annihilation ; of being miserable, or of not being at all.

10. After having mentioned these two great principles, which are destructive of cheerfulness in their own nature, as well as in right reason, I cannot think of any other that ought to banish this happy temper from a virtuous mind. Pain and sickness, shame and reproach, poverty and old age, nay death itself, considering the shortness of their duration, and the advantage we may reap from them do not deserve the name of evils. A good mind may bear up under them with fortitude, with indolence, and with cheerfulness of heart. The tossing of a tempest does not discompose him, which he is sure will bring him to a joyful harbour.

11. A man who uses his best endeavors to live according to the dictates of virtue and right reason has two perpetual sources of cheerfulness ; in the consideration of his own nature, and of that being on whom he has a dependence ; if he looks into himself he cannot but rejoice in that existence which is so lately bestowed upon him, and which, after millions of ages, will be still new and still in its beginning. How many self-congratulations

N

naturally arise in the mind, when it reflects on this its entrance
into eternity, when it takes a view of those improvable faculties, which in a few years, and even at its first setting out have
made so considerable a progress, and which will be still receiving an increase of perfection, and consequently an increase of
happiness? The consciousness of such a being spreads a perpetual diffusion of joy through the soul of a virtuous man and
makes him look upon himself every moment as more happy
than he knows how to conceive.

12. The second source of cheerfulness to a good mind is its
consideration of that Being on whom we have our dependence,
and in whom, though we behold him as yet but in the first
faint discoveries of his perfection, we see everything that
we can imagine as great, glorious, or amiable. We find
ourselves everywhere upheld by his goodness and surrounded
with an immensity of love and mercy. In short, we depend upon a being, whose power qualifies him to make us
happy by an infinity of means, whose goodness and truth engage him to make those happy who desire it of him, and
whose unchangeableness will secure us in this happiness to all
eternity.

13. Such considerations, which every one should perpetually
cherish in his thoughts, will banish from us all that secret
heaviness of heart which unthinking men are subject to when
they lie under no real affliction, all that anguish which we may
feel from any evil that actually oppresses us, to which I may
likewise add those little cracklings of mirth and folly that are
apter to betray virtue than support it, and establish in us such
an even and cheerful temper as makes us pleasing to ourselves,
to those with whom we converse, and to him whom we were
made to please.   I.

Quid purè tranquillet—— Hor.

1. In my last Saturday's paper I spoke of cheerfulness as it is a moral habit of the mind, and accordingly mentioned such moral motives as are apt to cherish and keep alive this happy temper in the soul of man. I shall now consider cheerfulness in its natural state, and reflect on those motives to it, which are indifferent either as to virtue or vice.

2. Cheerfulness is, in the first place, the best promoter of health. Repinings and secret murmurs of heart, give imperceptible strokes to those delicate fibres of which the vital parts are composed, and wear out the machine insensibly ; not to mention those violent ferments which they stir up in the blood, and those irregular disturbed motions, which they raise in the animal spirits. I scarce remember, in my own observation, to have met with many old men, or with such, who (to use our English phrase) wear well, that had not at least a certain indolence in their humour, if not a more than ordinary gaiety and cheerfulness of heart. The truth of it is, health and cheerfulness mutually beget each other ; with this difference that we seldom meet with a great degree of health which is not attended with a certain cheerfulness, but very often see cheerfulness where there is no great degree of health.

3. Cheerfulness bears the same friendly regard to the mind as to the body. It banishes all anxious care and discontent, soothes and composes the passions, and keeps the soul in a perpetual calm. But having already touched on this last consideration, I shall here take notice, that the world, in which we are placed, is filled with innumerable objects that are proper to raise and keep alive this happy temper of mind.

4. If we consider the world in its subserviency to man, one would think it was made for our use; but if we consider it in its natural beauty and harmony, one would be apt to conclude it was made for our pleasure. The sun, which is as the great soul of the universe, and produces all the necessaries of life, has a particular influence in cheering the mind of man and making the heart glad.

5. Those several living creatures which are made for our service or sustenance at the same time either fill the woods with their music, furnish us with game, or raise pleasing ideas in us by the delightfulness of their appearance. Fountains, lakes, and rivers are as refreshing to the imagination, as to the soil through which they pass.

6. There are writers of great distinction, who have made it an argument for providence, that the whole earth is covered with green rather than any other colour, as being such a right mixture of light and shade, that it comforts and strengthens the eye instead of weakening or grieving it. For this reason several painters have a green cloth hanging near them to ease the eye upon, after too great an application to their colouring. A famous modern philosopher accounts for it in the following manner. All colours that are more luminous overpower and dissipate the animal spirits which are employed in sight; on the contrary, those that are more obscure do not give the animal spirits a sufficient exercise; whereas the rays that produce in us the idea of green, fall upon the eye in such a due proportion, that they give the animal spirits their proper play, and by keeping up the struggle in a just balance, excite a very pleasing and agreeable sensation. Let the cause be what it will, the effect is certain, for which reason the poets ascribe to this particular colour the epithet of cheerful.

7. To consider further this double end in the works of nature, and how they are at the same time both useful and entertaining, we find that the most important parts in the vegetable world are those which are most beautiful. These are the seeds by which the several races of plants are propagated and continued, and which are always lodged in flowers or blossoms. Nature seems to hide her principal design, and to be industrious in making the earth gay and delightful, while she is carrying on her great work, and intent upon her own preservation. The husbandman after the same manner is employed in laying out the whole country into a kind of garden or landscape and making everything smile about him, whilst in reality he thinks of nothing but of the harvest, and increase which is to arise from it.

8. We may further observe how providence has taken care to keep up this cheerfulness in the mind of man, by having formed it after such a manner, as to make it capable of conceiving delight from several objects which seem to have very little use in them ; as from the wildness of rocks and deserts, and the like grotesque parts of nature. Those who are versed in philosophy may still carry this consideration higher by observing that if matter had appeared to us endowed only with those real qualities which it actually possesses, it would have made but a very joyless and uncomfortable figure ; and why has providence given it a power of producing in us such imaginary qualities as tastes and colours, sounds and smells, heat and cold, but that man, while he is conversant in the lower stations of nature, might have his mind cheered and delighted with agreeable sensations. In short, the whole universe is a kind of theatre filled with objects that either raise in us pleasure, amusement or admiration.

9. The reader's own thoughts will suggest to him the vicissitude of day and night, the change of seasons, with all that

variety of scenes which diversify the face of nature, and fill the mind with a perpetual succession of beautiful and pleasing images.

10. I shall not here mention the several entertainments of art, with the pleasures of friendship, books, conversation, and other accidental diversions of life, because I would only take notice of such incitements to a cheerful temper, as offer themselves to persons of all ranks and conditions, and which may sufficiently show us that providence did not design this world should be filled with murmurs and repinings, or that the heart of man should be involved in gloom and melancholy.

11. I the more inculcate this cheerfulness of temper, as it is a virtue in which our countrymen are observed to be more deficient than any other nation. Melancholy is a kind of demon that haunts our island, and often conveys herself to us in an easterly wind. A celebrated French novelist, in opposition to those who begin their romances with the flowery season of the year, enters on his story thus : " In the gloomy month of November, when the people of England hang and drown themselves, a disconsolate lover walked out into the fields, &c."

12. Every one ought to fence against the temper of his climate or constitution, and frequently to indulge in himself those considerations which may give him a serenity of mind, and enable him to bear up cheerfully against those little evils and misfortunes which are common to human nature, and which by a right improvement of them will produce a satiety of joy, and an uninterrupted happiness.

13. At the same time that I would engage my reader to consider the world in its most agreeable lights, I must own there are many evils which naturally spring up amidst the entertainments that are provided for us : but these, if rightly considered should be far from overcasting the mind with sorrow, or des-

troying that cheerfulness of temper which I have been recom-
mending. This interspersion of evil with good, and pain with
pleasure, in the works of nature, is very truly ascribed by Mr.
Locke, in his essay on Human Understanding, to a moral reason, in the following words :

14. Beyond all this, we may find another reason why God
hath scattered up and down several degrees of pleasure and
pain, in all the things that environ and affect us, and blended
them together, in almost all that our thoughts and senses have
to do with ; that we finding imperfection, dissatisfaction, and
want of complete happiness in all the enjoyments which the
creatures can afford us, might be led to seek it in the enjoyment of him, with whom there is fulness of joy, and at whose
right hand are pleasures for evermore.   L.

No. 458.]   *Friday, August* 15, 1712.   [*Addison.*

[Αἰδὼς οὐκ ἀγάθη ——————— Hes.]
——*Pudor malus* ——————Hor.

1. I could not smile at the account that was yesterday given
me of a modest young gentleman, who being invited to an
entertainment, though he was not used to drink, had not the
confidence to refuse his glass in his turn, when on a sudden he
grew so flustered that he took all the talk of the table into his
own hands, abused every one of the company, and flung a bottle
at the gentleman's head who treated him. This has given me

occasion to reflect upon the ill effects of a vicious modesty, and to remember the saying of Brutus, as it is quoted by Plutarch, that the person has had but an ill education, who has not been taught to deny anything. This false kind of modesty has, perhaps, betrayed both sexes into as many vices as the most abandoned impudence, and is the more inexcusable to reason, because it acts to gratify others rather than itself, and is punished with a kind of remorse, not only like other vicious habits when the crime is over, but even at the very time that it is committed.

2. Nothing is more amiable than true modesty, and nothing is more contemptible than the false. The one guards virtue, the other betrays it. True modesty is ashamed to do anything that is repugnant to the rules of right reason : false modesty is ashamed to do anything that is opposite to the humour of the company. True modesty avoids everything that is criminal, false modesty everything that is unfashionable. The latter is only a general undetermined instinct ; the former is that instinct, limited and circumscribed by the rules of prudence and religion.

3. We may conclude that modesty to be false and vicious, which engages a man to do anything that is ill or indiscreet, or which restrains him from doing anything that is of a contrary nature. How many men, in the common concerns of life, lend sums of money which they are not able to spare, are bound for persons whom they have little friendship for, give recommendatory characters of men whom they are not acquainted with, bestow places on those whom they do not esteem, live in such a manner as they themselves do not approve, and all this merely because they have not the confidence to resist solicitation, importunity or example ?

4. Nor does this false modesty expose us only to such actions as are indiscreet, but very often to such as are highly criminal. When Xenophanes was called timorous, because he would not

venture his money in a game of dice: "I confess," said he, "that I am exceeding timorous, for I dare not do any ill thing." On the contrary, a man of vicious modesty complies with every thing, and is only fearful of doing what may look singular in the company where he is engaged. He falls in with the torrent, and lets himself go to every action or discourse, however unjustifiable in itself, so it be in vogue amongst the present party. This, tho' one of the most common, is one of the most ridiculous dispositions in human nature, that men should not be ashamed of speaking or acting in a dissolute or irrational manner, but that one who is in their company should be ashamed of governing himself by the principles of reason and virtue.

5. In the second place we are to consider false modesty, as it restrains a man from doing what is good and laudable. My reader's own thoughts will suggest to him many instances and examples under this head. I shall only dwell upon one reflection, which I cannot make without a secret concern. We have in England a particular bashfulness in everything that regards religion. A well-bred man is obliged to conceal any serious sentiment of this nature, and very often to appear a greater libertine than he is, that he may keep himself in countenance among the men of mode. Our excess of modesty makes us shamefaced in all the exercises of piety and devotion. This humour prevails upon us daily: insomuch, that at many well-bred tables, the master of the house is so very modest a man, that he has not the confidence to say grace at his own table: a custom which is not only practised by all the nations about us, but was never omitted by the heathens themselves. English gentlemen who travel into Roman Catholic countries, are not a little surprised to meet with people of the best quality kneeling in their churches, and engaged in their private devotions, though it be not at the hours of public worship. An officer of the army, or a man of wit and pleasure in those countries, would be afraid of passing not only for an irreligious,

but an ill-bred man, should he be seen to go to bed, or sit down at table, without offering up his devotions on such occasions. The same show of religion appears in all the foreign reformed churches, and enters so much into their ordinary conversation, that an Englishman is apt to term them hypocritical and precise.

6. This little appearance of a religious deportment in our nation, may proceed in some measure from that modesty which is natural to us, but the great occasion of it is certainly this. Those swarms of sectaries that overran the nation in the time of the great rebellion, carried their hypocrisy so high, that they had converted our whole language into a jargon of enthusiasm ; insomuch that upon the Restoration men thought they could not recede too far from the behaviour and practice of those persons, who had made religion a cloak to so many villanies. This led them into the other extreme, every appearance of devotion was looked upon as Puritanical, and falling into the hands of the ridiculers who flourished in that reign, and attacked everything that was serious, it has ever since been out of countenance among us.   By this means we are gradually fallen into that vicious modesty which has in some measure worn out from among us the appearance of Christianity in ordinary life and conversation, and which distinguishes us from all our neighbours.

7. Hypocrisy cannot indeed be too much detested, but at the same time is to be preferred to open impiety. They are both equally destructive to the person who is possessed with them ; but in regard to others, hypocrisy is not so pernicious as barefaced irreligion.   The due mean to be observed is to be sincerely virtuous, and at the same time to let the world see we are so. I do not know a more dreadful menace in the Holy Writings than that which is pronounced against those who have this perverted modesty, to be ashamed before men in a particular of such unspeakable importance.   C.

Nec Deus intersit nisi dignus vindice nodus
Inciderit——————— , Hor.

1. We cannot be guilty of a greater act of uncharitableness, than to interpret the afflictions which befall our neighbours, as punishments and judgments. It aggravates the evil to ·him who suffers, when he looks upon himself as the mark of divine vengeance, and abates the compassion of those towards him, who regard him in so dreadful a light. This humour of turning every misfortune into a judgment, proceeds from wrong notions of religion, which, in its own nature, produces good-will towards men, and puts the mildest construction upon every accident that befalls them. In this case, therefore, it is not religion that sours a man's temper, but it is his temper that sours his religion : people of gloomy uncheerful imaginations, or of envious malignant tempers, whatever kind of life they are engaged in, will discover their natural tincture of mind in all their thoughts, words, and actions. As the finest wines have often the taste of the soil, so even the most religious thoughts often draw something that is particular from the constitution of the mind in which they arise. When folly or superstition strike in with this natural depravity of temper, it is not in the power even of religion itself, to preserve the character of the person who is possessed with it, from appearing highly absurd and ridiculous.

2. An old maiden gentlewoman, whom I shall conceal under the name of Nemesis, is the greatest discoverer of judgments that I have met with. She can tell you what sin it was that set such a man's house on fire, or blew down his barns. Talk to her of an unfortunate young lady that lost her beauty by the

small-pox, she fetches a deep sigh, and tells you, that when she had a fine face she was always looking on it in her glass. Tell her of a piece of good fortune that has befallen one of her acquaintance; and she wishes it may prosper with her, but her mother used one of her nieces very barbarously. Her usual remarks turn upon people who had great estates, but never enjoyed them, by reason of some .flaw in their own, or their father's behaviour. She can give you the reason why such an one died childless : why such an one was cut off in the flower of his youth : why such an one was unhappy in her marriage : why one broke his leg on such a particular spot of ground, and why another was killed with a back-sword, rather than with any other kind of weapon. She has a crime for every misfortune that can befall any of her acquaintance, and when she hears of a robbery that has been made, or a murder that has been committed, enlarges more on the guilt of the suffering person than on that of the thief, or the assassin. In short, she is so good a Christian, that whatever happens to herself is a trial, and whatever happens to her neighbours is a judgment.

3. The very description of this folly, in ordinary life, is sufficient to expose it; but when it appears in a pomp and dignity of style, it is very apt to amuse and terrify the mind of the reader. Herodotus and Plutarch very often apply their judgments as impertinently as the old woman I have before mentioned, though their manner of relating them makes the folly itself appear venerable. Indeed, most historians, as well Christian as pagan, have fallen into this idle superstition, and spoken of ill success, unforeseen disasters, and terrible events, as if they had been let into the secrets of providence, and made acquainted with that private conduct by which the world is governed. One would think several of our own historians in particular had many revelations of this kind made to them. Our old English monks seldom let any of their kings depart in peace,

who had endeavoured to diminish the power or wealth of which
the ecclesiastics were in those times possessed. William the
Conqueror's race generally found their judgments in the New
Forest, where their fathers had pulled down churches and
monasteries. In short, read one of the chronicles written by
an author of this frame of mind, and you would think you were
reading an history of the kings of Israel or Judah, where the
historians were actually inspired, and where, by a particular
scheme of providence, the kings were distinguished by judgments or blessings, according as they promoted idolatry or the
worship of the true God.

4. I cannot but look upon this manner of judging upon misfortunes, not only to be very uncharitable, in regard to the
person whom they befall, but very presumptuous in regard to
him who is supposed to inflict them. It is a strong argument
for a state of retribution hereafter, that in this world virtuous
persons are very often unfortunate, and vicious persons prosperous; which is wholly repugnant to the nature of a being
who appears infinitely wise and good in all his works, unless we
may suppose that such a promiscuous and undistinguishing dis-
tribution of good and evil, which was necessary for carrying
on the designs of providence in this life, will be rectified and
made amends for in another. We are not therefore to expect
that fire should fall from heaven in the ordinary course of providence; nor when we see triumphant guilt or depressed virtue
in particular persons, that omnipotence will make bare its holy
arm in the defence of the one, or punishment of the other. It
is sufficient that there is a day set apart for the hearing and
requiting of both according to their respective merits.

5. The folly of ascribing temporal judgments to any particular crimes, may appear from several considerations. I shall
only mention two: first, that generally speaking, there is no
calamity or affliction, which is supposed to have happened as a

judgment to a vicious man, which does not sometimes happen to men of approved religion and virtue. When Diagoras the atheist was on board one of the Athenian ships, there arose a very violent tempest; upon which the mariners told him, that it was a just judgment upon them for having taken so impious a man on board. Diagoras begged them to look upon the rest of the ships that were in the same distress, and asked them whether or no Diagoras was on board every vessel in the fleet. We are all involved in the same calamities, and subject to the same accidents : and when we see any one of the species under any particular oppression, we should look upon it as arising from the common lot of human nature, rather than from the guilt of the person who suffers.

6. Another consideration that may check our presumption in putting such a construction upon a misfortune, is this, that it is impossible for us to know what are calamities, and what are blessings. How many accidents have passed for misfortunes, which have turned to the welfare and prosperity of the persons in whose lot they have fallen? How many disappointments have in their consequences, saved a man from ruin? If we could look into the effects of every thing, we might be allowed to pronounce boldly upon blessings and judgments; but for a man to give his opinion of what he sees but in part, and in its beginnings, is an unjustifiable piece of rashness and folly. The story of Biton and Clitobus, which was in great reputation among the heathens, (for we see it quoted by all the ancient authors, both Greek and Latin, who have written upon the immortality of the soul), may teach us a caution in this matter. These two brothers, being the sons of a lady who was priestess to Juno, drew their mother's chariot to the temple at the time of a great solemnity, the persons being absent who by their office were to have drawn her chariot on that occasion. The mother was so transported with this instance of filial duty, that she petitioned her goddess to bestow upon them the greatest gift

that could be given to men; upon which they were both cast into a deep sleep, and the next morning found dead in the temple. This was such an event, as would have been construed into a judgment, had it happened to the two brothers after an act of disobedience, and would doubtless have been represented as such by any ancient historian who had given us an account of it.   O.

No. 574.]   FRIDAY, *July* 30, 1714.   [*Addison.*

Non possidentem multa vocaveris
Rectè beatum, rectiùs occupat
Nomen beati, qui deorum
Muneribus sapienter uti
Duramque callet pauperiem pati.—Hor.

1. I was once engaged in discourse with a Rosicrusian about the great secret. As this kind of men (I mean those of them who are not professed cheats) are over-run with enthusiasm and philosophy, it was very amusing to hear this religious adept descanting on his pretended discovery. He talked of the secret as of a spirit which lived within an emerald, and converted everything that was near it to the highest perfection it is capable of. It gives lustre, says he, to the sun and water to the diamond. It irradiates every metal, and enriches lead with all the properties of gold. It heightens smoke into flame, flame into light, and light into glory. He further added that a single

ray of it dissipates pain, and care, and melancholy from the person on whom it falls.   In short, says he, its presence naturally changes every place into a kind of heaven.   After he had gone on for some time in this unintelligible cant, I found that he jumbled natural and moral ideas together into the same discourse, and that his great secret was nothing else but content.

2. This virtue does indeed produce, in some measure, all those effects which the alchymist usually ascribes to what he calls the philosopher's stone ; and, if it does not bring riches, it does the same thing by banishing the desire of them.   If it cannot remove the disquietudes arising out of a man's mind, body, or fortune, it makes him easy under them.   It has, indeed, a kindly influence on the soul of man, in respect of every being to whom he stands related.   It extinguishes all murmur, repining, and ingratitude towards that being who has allotted him his part to act in this world.   It destroys all inordinate ambition, and every tendency to corruption with regard to the community wherein he is placed.   It gives sweetness to his conversation, and a perpetual serenity to all his thoughts.

3. Among the many methods which might be made use of for the acquiring of this virtue, I shall only mention the two following.   First of all, a man should always consider how much he has more than he wants ; and secondly, how much more unhappy he might be than he really is.

4. First of all, a man should always consider how much he has more than he wants.   I am wonderfully pleased with the reply which Aristippus made to one who condoled him upon the loss of a farm, "Why," said he, "I have three farms still, and you have but one, so that I ought rather to be afflicted for you than you for me."   On the contrary, foolish men are more apt to consider what they have lost than what they possess ; and to fix their eyes upon those who are richer than themselves, rather than on those who are under greater difficulties.   All the real

pleasures and conveniences of life lie in a narrow compass ; but it is the humour of mankind to be always looking forward and straining after one who has got the start of them in wealth and honour. For this reason, as there are none can properly be called rich, who have not more than they want ; there are few rich men in any of the politer nations but among the middle sort of people, who keep their wishes within their fortunes, and have more wealth than they know how to enjoy. Persons of a higher rank live in a splendid kind of poverty, and are perpetually wanting, because instead of acquiescing in the solid pleasures of life, they endeavour to outvie one another in shadows and appearances. Men of sense have at all times beheld with a great deal of mirth this silly game that is playing over their heads, and by contracting their desires, enjoy all that secret satisfaction which others are always in quest of. The truth is this ridiculous chase after imaginary pleasures cannot be sufficiently exposed, as it is the great source of those evils which generally undo a nation. Let a man's estate be what it will, he is a poor man if he does not live within it, and naturally sets himself to sale to any one that can give him his price. When Pittacus, after the death of his brother, who had left him a good estate, was offered a great sum of money by the King of Lydia, he thanked him for his kindness, but told him he had already more by half than he knew what to do with. In short, content is equivalent to wealth, and luxury to poverty ; or, to give the thought a more agreeable turn, " Content is natural wealth," says Socrates ; to which I shall add " Luxury is artificial poverty." I shall, therefore, recommend to the consideration of those who are always aiming after superfluous and imaginary enjoyments, and will not be at the trouble of contracting their desires, an excellent saying of Bion, the philosopher ; namely, " That no man has so much care as he who endeavours after the most happiness."

o

5. In the second place, every one ought to reflect how much more unhappy he might be than he really is. The former consideration took in all those who are sufficiently provided with the means to make themselves easy ; this regards such as actually lie under some pressure or misfortune. These may receive great alleviation from such a comparison as the unhappy person may make between himself and others, or between the misfortune which he suffers, and the greater misfortunes which might have befallen him.

6. I like the story of the honest Dutchman, who, upon breaking his leg by a fall from the mainmast, told the standers-by it was a great mercy that it was not his neck. To which, since I am got into quotations, give me leave to add the saying of an old philosopher, who, after having invited some of his friends to dine with him, was ruffled by his wife that came into the room in a passion, and threw down the table that stood before them. " Every one," says he, " has his calamity, and he is a happy man that has no greater than this." We find an instance to the same purpose in the life of Dr. Hammond, written by Bishop Fell. As this good man was troubled with a complication of distempers, when he had the gout upon him, he used to thank God that it was not the stone ; and when he had the stone that he had not both these distempers on him at the same time.

7. I cannot conclude this essay without observing that there was never any system besides that of Christianity, which could effectually produce in the mind of man the virtue I have hitherto been speaking of. In order to make us content with our present condition many of the ancient philosophers tell us that our discontent only hurts ourselves, without being able to make any alteration in our circumstances ; others that whatever evil befalls us is derived to us by a fatal necessity to which the gods themselves are subject ; whilst others very

gravely tell the man who is miserable that it is necessary he should be so to keep up the harmony of the universe, and that the scheme of providence would be troubled and perverted were he otherwise. These, and the like considerations rather silence than satisfy a man. They may show him that his dis. content is unreasonable, but are by no means sufficient to relieve it. They rather give despair than consolation. In a word, a man might reply to one of these comforters as Augustus did to his friend, who advised him not to grieve for the death of a person whom he loved, because his grief could not fetch him again. "It is for that very reason," said the Emperor, "that I grieve."

8. On the contrary, religion bears a more tender regard to human nature. It prescribes to every miserable man the means of bettering his condition ; nay, it shows him that the bearing of his afflictions as he ought to do will naturally end in the removal of them ; it makes him easy here, because it can make him happy hereafter.

9. Upon the whole, a contented mind is the greatest blessing a man can enjoy in this world ; and if in the present life his happiness arises from the subduing of his desires, it will arise in the next from the gratification of them.

No. 583.]   FRIDAY, *August* 20, 1714.   [*Addison.*

Ipse thymum pinosque ferens de montibus altis,
Tecta serat late circum, cui talia curœ :
Ipse labore manum duro terat, ipse feraces
Figat humo plantas, et amicos irriget imbres.   Virg.

---

1. Every station of life has duties which are proper to it. Those who are determined by choice to any particular kind of business, are indeed more happy than those who are determined

by necessity, but both are under equal obligation of fixing on employments, which may be either useful to themselves or beneficial to others. No one of the sons of Adam ought to think himself exempt from that labour and industry which were denounced to our first parent, and in him to all his posterity. Those to whom birth or fortune may seem to make such an application unnecessary, ought to find out some calling or profession for themselves, that they may not lie as a burden on the species, and be the only useless parts of the creation.

2. Many of our country gentlemen in their busy hours apply themselves wholly to the chase, or to some other diversion which they find in the fields and woods. This gave occasion to one of our most eminent English writers to represent every one of them as lying under a kind of curse pronounced to them in the words of Goliah, " I will give thee to the fowls of the air, and to the beasts of the field."

3. Though exercises of this kind, when indulged with moderation, may have a good influence both on the mind and body, the country affords many other amusements of a more noble kind.

4. Among these I know none more delightful in itself, and beneficial to the public, than that of planting. I could mention a nobleman whose fortune has placed him in several parts of England, and who has always left these visible marks behind him, which show he has been there. He never hired a house in his life, without leaving all about it the seeds of wealth, and bestowing legacies on the posterity of the owner. Had all the gentlemen of England made the same improvements upon their estates, our whole country would have been at this time as one great garden. Nor ought such an employment to be looked upon as too inglorious for men of the highest rank. There have been heroes in this art, as well as in others. We are told in particular of Cyrus the great, that he planted all the lesser

Asia. There is indeed something truly magnificent in this kind of amusement. It gives a nobler air to several parts of nature; it fills the earth with a variety of beautiful scenes, and has something in it like creation, For this reason the pleasure of one who plants is something like that of a poet, who, as Aristotle observes, is more delighted with his productions than any other writer or artist whatsoever.

5. Plantations have one advantage in them which is not to be found in most other works, as they give a pleasure of a more lasting date, and continually improve in the eye of the planter. When you have finished a building or any other undertaking of the like nature, it immediately decays upon your hands; you see it brought to its utmost point of perfection; and from that time hastening to its ruin. On the contrary, when you have finished your plantations, they are still arriving at greater degrees of perfection as long as you live, and appear more delightful in every succeeding year than they did in the foregoing.

6. But I do not only recommend this art to men of estates as a pleasing amusement, but as it is a kind of virtuous employment, and may therefore be inculcated by moral motives; particularly from the love which we ought to have for our country, and the regard which we ought to bear to our posterity. As for the first, I need only mention what is frequently observed by others, that the increase of forest-trees does by no means bear a proportion to the destruction of them, insomuch that in a few ages the nation may be at a loss to supply itself with timber sufficient for the fleets of England. I know when a man talks of posterity in matters of this nature, he is looked upon with an eye of ridicule by the cunning and selfish part of mankind. Most people are of the humour of an old fellow of a college, who, when he was pressed by the society to come into something that might redound to the good of their successors, grew very peevish. "We are always doing," says he, "something for posterity, but I would fain see posterity do something for us."

7. But I think men are inexcusable, who fail in a duty of this nature, since it is so easily discharged. When a man considers that the putting a few twigs into the ground, is doing good to one who will make his appearance in the world about fifty years hence, or that he is perhaps making one of his descendants easy or rich, by so inconsiderable an expense, if he finds himself averse to it, he must conclude that he has a poor and base heart, void of all generous principles and love to mankind.

8. There is one consideration, which may very much enforce what I have here said. Many honest minds that are naturally disposed to do good in the world, and become beneficial to mankind, complain within themselves that they have not talents for it. This therefore is a good office, which is suited to the meanest capacities, and which may be performed by multitudes, who have not abilities sufficient to deserve well of their country and to recommend themselves to their posterity, by any other method. It is the phrase of a friend of mine, when any useful country neighbour dies, that you may trace him : which I look upon as a good funeral oration, at the death of an honest husbandman, who hath left the impressions of his industry behind him, in the place where he has lived.

9. Upon the foregoing considerations, I can scarce forbear representing the subject of this paper as a kind of moral virtue : which, as I have already shown, recommends itself likewise by the pleasure that attends it. It must be confessed, that this is none of those turbulent pleasures which is apt to gratify a man in the heats of youth ; but if it be not so tumultuous, it is more lasting. Nothing can be more delightful than to entertain ourselves with prospects of our own making, and to walk under those shades which our own industry has raised. Amusements of this nature compose the mind, and lay at rest all those passions which are uneasy to the soul of man, besides that they naturally engender good thoughts, and dispose us to laudable

contemplations. Many of the old philosophers passed away the greatest parts of their lives among their gardens. Epicurus himself could not think sensual pleasure attainable in any other scene. Every reader who is acquainted with Homer, Virgil and Horace, the greatest geniuses of all antiquity, knows very well with how much rapture they have spoken on this subject; and that Virgil in particular has written a whole book on the art of planting.

10. This art seems to have been more especially adapted to the nature of man in his primeval state, when he had life enough to see his productions flourish in their utmost beauty, and gradually decay with him. One who lived before the flood might have seen a wood of the tallest oaks in the acorn. But I only mention this particular, in order to introduce in my next paper, a history which I have found among the accounts of China, and which may be looked upon as an antediluvian novel.

No. 598.] *Friday, Sept.* 24, 1724. [*Addison.*

Jamne igitur laudas, quod de sapientibus alter
Ridebat, quoties a limine moverat unum
Protuleratque pedem: flebat contrarius alter ?—Juv.

1. Mankind may be divided into the merry and the serious, who, both of them, make a very good figure in the species, so long as they keep their respective humours from degenerating into the neighbouring extreme; there being a natural tendency

in the one to a melancholy moroseness, and in the other to a fantastic levity.

2. The merry part of the world are very amiable, whilst they diffuse a cheerfulness through conversion at proper seasons and on proper occasions; but on the contary, a great grievance to society, when they infect every discourse with insipid mirth, and turn into ridicule such subjects as are not suited to it. For though laughter is looked upon by the philosophers as the property of reason, the excess of it has been always considered as the mark of folly.

3. On the other side, seriousness has its beauty whilst it is attended with cheerfulness and humanity, and does not come in unseasonably to pall the good humour of those with whom we converse.

4. These two sets of men, notwitstanding they each of them shine in their respective characters, are apt to bear a natural aversion and antipathy to one another.

5. What is more usual, than to hear men of serious tempers and austere morals, enlarging upon the vanities and follies of the young and gay part of the species; whilst they look with a kind of horror upon such pomps and diversions as are innocent in themselves and only culpable when they draw the mind too much?

6. I could not but smile upon reading a passage in the account which Mr. Baxter gives of his own life, wherein he represents it as a great blessing, that in his youth he very narrowly escaped getting a place at Court.

7. It must indeed be confessed that levity of temper takes a man off his guard, and opens a pass to his soul for any temptation that assaults it. It favours all the approaches of vice, and weakens all the resistance of virtue. For which reason a renowned statesman in Queen Elizabeth's days, after having retired from Court and public business, in order to give himself up to the

duties of religion; when any of his old friends used to visit him, had still this word of advice in his mouth, *Be serious.*

8. An eminent Italian author of this cast of mind, speaking of the great advantage of a serious and composed temper, wishes very gravely, that for the benefit of mankind he had Trophonius's cave in his possession; which says he, would contribute more to the reformation of manners than all the workhouses and bridewells in Europe.

9. We have a very particular description of this cave in Pausanias, who tells us, that it was made in the form of a huge oven, and had many particular circumstances, which disposed the person who was in it to be more pensive and thoughtful than ordinary; insomuch that no man was ever observed to laugh all his life after, who had once made his entry into this cave. It was usual in those times, when anyone carried a more than ordinary gloominess in his features, to tell him that he looked like one just come out of Trophonius's cave.

10. On the other hand writers of a more merry complexion have been no less severe on the opposite party; and have had one advantage above them, that they have attacked them with more turns of wit and humour.

11. After all if a man's temper were at his own disposal, I think he would not choose to be of either of these parties; since the most perfect character is that which is formed out of both of them. A man would neither choose to be a hermit nor a buffoon; human nature is not so miserable, as that we should be always melancholy; nor so happy, as that we should be always merry. In a word, a man should not live as if there was no God in the world; nor at the same time, as if there were no men in it.

LITERARY AND PERSONAL.	GENERAL.
1672. Addison born.	Test Act (1673) Habeas Corpus, Act, 1679.
1685. Addison at the Charterhouse.	Monmouth's rebellion.
1687. Addison enters Queen's Coll. Newton's *Principia*.	Revolution (1688). Declaration of Rights.
1693. Addison's verses to Dryden.	Massacre of Glencoe (1692).
1695. Addison's *Poem to His Majesty*.	Capture of Namur.
1697. Dryden's *Virgil*. Hogarth born.	Treaty of Ryswick.
1701. Addison's *Letter from Italy*. Steele's *Christian Hero*. Dryden died.	Act of Settlement.
1704. *The Campaign. Tale of a Tub*. Defoe's *Review*.	Blenheim, Capture of Gibraltar.
1706. Addison under Secretary of State.	Ramillies, Union Act (1707).
1709. A. chief Sec. for Ireland. *Tatler*. Johnson born.	Malplaquet, Sacheverell's Trial (1710).
1711. *Spectator* begun. *Essay on Criticism*.	Dismissal of Marlborough, 1712.
1713. *Englishman. Guardian. Cato. Rape of the Lock*. Sterne born.	Treaty of Utrecht.
1716. Addison's marriage. Garrick and Gray born.	Septennial Act.
1717. Addison Sec. of State.	Triple Alliance.
1719. *Old Whig. Robinson Crusoe*. Addison died.	
1721. Burnet's *History of Our Own Times*.	Walpole's Ministry.
1725. Pope's *Iliad. The Gentle Shepherd*.	
1726. *Gulliver's Travels*. Thompson's *Winter*.	
1729. Steele and Congreve died. *The Dunciad*.	Methodists at Oxford.
1733. *Essay on Man*.	Walpole's Excise Bill.
1740. *Pamela*.	Wesley and Whitefield separate.

LITERARY AND PERSONAL.

1741. Garrrick on stage. Hume's *Essays. Joseph Andrews.*
1744. Pope died. *Night Thoughts.*
1746. *Ode on the Passions.*
1748. *Castle of Indolence. Clarissa Harlowe.*
1750. *The Rambler. The Elegy.*
1758. *The Idler.*
1759. Robertson's *Hist. of Scotland. Rasselas. Tristram Shandy.*
1760. *Ossian.* Churchill's *Rosciad.*
1761. *The Citizen of the World.*
1762. *Fingal.*
1764. *The Traveller.* Walpole's *Otranto.*
1765. Percy's *Reliques.*
1766. *Vicar of Wakefield.*
1769. *Letters of Junius.* Chatterton's forgeries.
1770. *The Deserted Village.*
1771. Beattie's *Minstrel.* Sc tt born.
1773. *She Stoops to Conquer.*
1774. Warton's *History of Poetry.*
1776. *Wealth of Nations. Decline and Fall of Rom. Emp.*
1777. *School for Scandal.*
1781. *Lives of the Poets.* Crabbe's *Library.*
1783. Crabbe's *Village.*
1784. Johnson died.
1785. *The Task.*—1786. Burns' 1st Volume.
1788. Byron born. First issue of *The Times.*
1790. Burke's *Reflections.*
1992. *Pleasures of Memory.* Shelley born.
1793. Wordsworth's *Evening Walk.*
1794. Keats born. — 1796. Burns died.

GENERAL.

Walpole resigns (1742). Dettingen (1743).
Fontenoy. The 45.
Culloden.
Tr. of Aix la Chapelle.

1757. Plassey, Byng shot.
Capture of Quebec.

Wilkes and the *North Briton.*

The Stamp Act.

The Boston " tea-party."
Lexington and Bunker Hill (1775).
Declaration of Independence.

Burgoyne's Surrender.
Surrender of Cornwallis.

Treaty of Versailles.
Pitt Premier, " India Bill."

Hastings' Trial. — 1789. French Revolution.

" Reign of Terror."

LITERARY AND PERSONAL.	GENERAL.
1798. Wordsworth's *Lyrical Ballads.*	Irish Rebellion.
1799. *Pleasures of Hope.*	
1801. Southey's *Thalaba.*	Union of Ir. and Eng. Parl.
1802.	Treaty of Amiens.
1805. *Lay of the Last Minstrel.* Byron at Cambridge. `	Trafalgar. Austerlitz, 1806 — Jena. " Berlin Decrees."
1807. *Hours of Idleness. Parish Register.*	
1808. *Marmion.*	Peninsular War (1808-14).
1809. *English Bards and Scotch Reviewers.* Byron goes to the Continent. Shelley's *Queen Mab.*	Battle of Corunna.
1810. *Lady of the Lake.*	
1812. *Childe Harold,* 1st and 2nd Cantos.	War with United States.
1813. *Giaour.* Hogg's *Poems. Life of Lord Nelson.*	
1814. *Corsair. Waverley. The Excursion.*	Treaty of Ghent. Napoleon goes to Elba.
1815. Shelley's *Alastor.*	Waterloo.
1817. *Revolt of Islam. Lalla Rookh.*	
1818. *Childe Harold. Don Juan. Endymion.*	
1822. Shelley died. —1824. Byron died.	

POETRY AND PROSE.*

1. It is archaic and non-colloquial.

(*a*) Poetry, being less conversational than prose, is less affected by the changes of a living language, and more influenced by the language and traditions of the poetry of past ages.

(*b*) Not all words are adapted for metre.

(*c*) Certain words and forms of expression being repeated by successive poets, acquire poetic associations and become part of the common inheritance of poets.

2. It is more picturesque than prose.

(*a*) It prefers specific, concrete, and vivid terms to generic, abstract and vague ones.

(*b*) It often substitutes an epithet for the thing denoted.

Note.—Distinguish carefully between *ornamental* epithets, added merely to give color, interest and life to the picture ; and *essential* epithets, necessary to convey the proper meaning.

3. It is averse to lengthiness.

(*a*) It omits conjunctions, relative pronouns, and auxiliaries, and makes free use of absolute and participial constructions.

(*b*) It substitutes epithets and compounds for phrases and clauses.

(*c*) It makes a free use of ellipsis.

(*d*) It avoids long, commonplace words.

Note.—Sometimes, however, for eupheony, euphemism or picturesqueness, it substitutes a periphrasis for a word.

4. It pays more regard to euphony than prose does.

5. It allows inversions and grammatical constructions not used in prose.

6. It employs figures of speech much more freely than prose.

THE ELEMENTS OF STYLE.

The elements of Style are Vocabulary, Sentences, Paragraphs, and Figures of Speech.

VOCABULARY.

Under this head are included the choice and the use of words. The requisites of a good vocabulary are purity, aptness (propriety and precision), copiousness and variety.

* Compiled from various sources.

Sentences may be considered with reference to the choice, number, arrangement, and sound of the words.

The chief reasons for varying the order of words in a sentence are :

1. To make the meaning clear.
2. To give emphasis to certain words or phrases.
3. To make the sentence more euphonious.

A well constructed sentence should be characterized by

1. Unity of Thought.　This may be injured or destroyed by
   (a) Change of subject.
   (b) Coupling of unconnected thoughts.
   (c) Use of long parentheses.
   (d) Addition of a supplementary clause.

2. Clearness of meaning.　The faults to be avoided are : Obscurity and Ambiguity, which may be caused by
   (a) Long or involved sentences.
   (b) Bad arrangement.
   (c) The use of ambiguous words.
   (d) The careless use of pronouns.
   (e) Ellipsis.
   (f) Punctuation, or the want of it.

3. Strength of expression.　The faults to be avoided are :
   (a) Use of unnecessary words.
   (b) Too many connectives.
   (c) Loose Structure.
   (d) Weak endings.

4. Melody of Sound.　The faults to be avoided are :
   (a) A succession of a number of unaccented syllables or words.
   (b) The use of harsh combinations of consonant sounds.
   (c) Repetition of same or similar sounds.

Sentences may be classified according to
   (a) Their length, into Short and Long.
   (b) Their Structure, into Periodic, Loose, Balanced.

PARAGRAPHS.

The chief requisites of the paragraph are Unity of Subject, and Continuity of Thought.

The rules or laws for its construction are :

1. The law of the subject or topic sentence.　Unless obviously preparatory, the opening sentence should indicate the subject of the paragraph.

2. The law of continuity. The several thoughts should follow one another in their natural and logical order.

3. The law of explicit reference. The connection of each sentence with what precedes should be clear and explicit. This is usually attained by the use of (1) *Connectives*, such as conjunctions, pronouns, adverbs, adverbial phrases ; (2) *Repetitions ;* (3) *Inversions.*

4. The law of unity. Every statement should be subservient to one principal affirmation, *viz.* that in the topic sentence.

5. The law of parallel construction. When two or more consecutive sentences iterate or illustrate the same idea, they should, as far as possible, be similarly constructed.

6. The law of due proportion. Everything should have prominence according to its importance. Principal statements should not be outweighed by subordinate ones.

FIGURES OF SPEECH.

Figures of speech are used for clearness, force or ornament. They may be divided into—

1. Figures of Diction.

(*a*) Founded on Similarity. Simile, Metaphor, Allegory, Personification, Hyperbole.

(*b*) Founded on Contiguity. Metonymy, Synecdoche, Transferred Epithet.

(*c*) Founded on Contrast. Antithesis, Epigram, Innuendo, Irony, Oxymoron.

2. Figures of Thought. Interrogation, Exclamation, Apostrophe, Vision, Climax.

The chief faults in the use of figurative language are :

1. The use of inappropriate, far-fetched or extravagant figures.

2. Carrying a figure too far.

3. The mingling of literal statements and figurative ones.

4. The mixing of metaphors.

QUALITIES OF STYLE.

The qualities of Style may be divided into

1. Intellectual, including—

Clearness,—opposed to Obscurity and Ambiguity,

Simplicity,—opposed to Abstruseness,

Impressiveness, and Picturesqueness.

2. Emotional, including Strength, Force, Feeling (Pathos). The Ludicrous (Wit, Humor, Satire.)

3. Æsthetic, including Melody, Harmony (of sound and sense) Taste.

The chief forms of prose composition are Description, Narration and Exposition.

The general principles governing these are :

1. In all communications of knowledge we must proceed on a basis of the known.

2. All statements bearing on the same topic should be kept together.

3. What is subordinate or incidental should not interfere with the prominence of the principal.

4. Unnecessary adjuncts are to be avoided.

5. In Exposition the chief devices for aiding the understanding are Example, Contrast, Repetition.

The parts of a Composition are :

1. Essential.—The Proposition and the Discussion.

2. Non-Essential.—The Introduction and the Conclusion.

NOTES.

———o———

ESSAY 21.

For translation of the mottoes, see list at the end.

Of the nine paragraphs which this Essay contains—

1.—Gives the general subject ; then follow the sub-divisions, 2 referring to the church, 3, 4 and 5 to law, 6 and 7 to medicine ; while 8 and 9 set forth the remedy for the evil. Paragraph 1 is well adapted for its purpose, being short and clear. Note the loose structure.

" Practitioners" does not go very well with "divinity."

" Ingenious," in its original meaning of " possessed of genius," " in - tellect."

" That starve one another," wittily and pithily sums up the conse- quence.

2. **All that wear scarfs.**—Elsewhere (Essay 609) he laughs at the wearing of scarfs by young divines who came up to London from the University, to make people think they were D.D's. He calls the scarf- decoration " venerable foppery."

Give more modern words for " notwithstanding," " strict," " ex- ceeding," " converting," " insomuch," " by the splitting of."

Of late years.—Where might this phrase be better placed, and why ?

Prebendary.—In old times in cathedral or college churches the daily services were performed by prebendaries, who got food and drink (*prebenda*) at the expense of the institution.

Lutestring.—A shiny silk cloth—a corruption of " lustring."

Splitting of their freeholds.—Cut up their glebes and tithes into 40-shilling freeholds, and so make more votes in the Counties. Com- pare the creation at the present day of what are called " fagot-votes."

Derive the words " clergy," " laity," " bishop" and " dean," and give the corresponding adjectives.

3. " Prodigious" and " litigious" in close succession are scarcely harmonious.

P

Westminster Hall.—Till lately the head-quarters of the legal profession in England. Compare Osgoode Hall, in Toronto.

Term-time.—The time during which the superior law courts are open for the trial of cases, now often called "sittings."

Full of humor.—Shew why it is so.

Passionate.—The use of an epithet specially applicable to quantity of words, *e.g.*, "volubly," would have given the sentence balance; both clauses now refer to "Anger," and the second alone is sufficient, being more concrete.

"To the reader."—Is the phrase needed?

"Above," for "more than," is going out of use, but should be retained, being pithy and unambiguous.

Is "only" (l. 36) correctly placed?

The student may condense this paragraph considerably by substitutions and omissions, but heed must be paid to ease of utterance and harmony.

4. This and 5 might well be put together in one, as they relate to the same subject, and their united length would not be too great.

"Accomplish," *i.e.*, "make accomplished," or "fit," a meaning which has become obsolete.

Is "rather" correctly placed?

The last sentence is an exquisite one for unity, balance and emphasis, as well as for its humorous satire.

5. The first sentence is periodic down to "Westminster Hall;" it then becomes loose, and well so, as giving a specific additon

Inns of Court.—Colleges in which students of law reside and are instructed. The four principal are the Inner Temple, the Middle Temple, Lincoln's Inn and Gray's Inn.

Play-house.—Going out of use, but the common name in Addison's day.

Why is "in all—except" better than "in all other—than a Court of Justice?"

"Conveyances" is redundant. Why?

Is "palliate" properly used here? Can you suggest a better word?

"Chamber practice." The practice of a barrister who gives advice in his office, *i. e.*, his "chambers," but does not advocate cases in court.

How are the two sentences of the paragraph connected?

6. A characteristic paragraph. Note the seeming paradox stated in the epigrammatic or pointed manner—"when a nation abounds in

physicians it grows thin of people." Note, too, the humorous idea of the great publicist's ignorance of so simple a cause.

Sir William Temple.—Famed as the author of the Triple Alliance, 1668. Was Ambassador at the Hague for years, and brought about the marriage of William III. His plans of a Privy Council of thirty (1679-80) would not work. The allusion in this essay is to his *Observations on the United Provinces.* He was a patron of Swift's.

Explain the reference in "Goths and Vandals," "Thor and Woden."

"And that this science . . . . at present." Improve this clause if you can, giving reasons for any changes you make.

"In our country" seems redundant; it might perhaps be better to change "country" to "time" or "day."

Stragglers.—Not chosen with Addison's usual taste, as stragglers are not usually combatants, but deserters or laggards. What other word can you substitute? The student may attempt changes in construction in this paragraph, but it cannot easily be improved, being easy and yet pointed.

7. "Retainer."—This word does not now signify a "hanger-on" or "apprentice," which is Addison's meaning. What are its two modern meanings?

Give the term of Latin origin for "cutting up alive."

Note the sort of anti-climax.

8. "Each—are."—Account for the error. The first sentence is periodic, has unity, and is exceedingly melodious.

"Of the science," *i. e.,* who know but have nothing to do.

"In them" and "of them" might well be left out.

Is "rather" correctly placed?

Humour.—"Whim" or "disposition."

This paragraph is symmetrical in its division with the whole essay. The second sentence deals with the church, the third with physic, and the fourth with law. They should therefore be parallel in construction. Are they so?

Discuss the substitution of "at the same time" for "withal," "plenty" for "abundance," "abilities" for "parts," "mind" for "apprehension."

"Venturing."—To trust; a rare and questionable use of the word.

Note the alliteration in sentence three. What are the conditions of melodious structure?

Combine the last two sentences in periodic form.

"Genius."—Bent, or natural aptitude for certain callings.

9. Make the first sentence a periodic one. What are the advantages
of the period ? Which form is better here ?

" By multitudes."—Explain why ?

Criticise the use of " hands" and " professors."

Squadrons.—Properly detachments of vessels of war, and therefore
does not harmonize well with " vend" and " sloops," otherwise the
metaphor is good, and gives us a picturesque conclusion.

Chapmen.—Itinerant dealers ; from the same root as " cheap."

What are the phrases which serve to give unity to this paragraph ? The
last sentence might perhaps be more closely connected with the preceding
one by beginning it "Our merchantmen are but," etc. ; or the second
and third sentence might be transposed, and then the paragraph would
end as it began, with a reference to all three professions.

ESSAY 23.

1.—The first sentence might be made shorter and more emphatic for a
topic sentence by omitting " there is," and writing " giving a man's
reputation secret stabs." Note that Addison regularly says " the
doing of " for " doing," but sometimes omits " the" or " of." The
older form is now seldom used. See *H. S. Gr.* xvii.

Sentence 2 is connected in *sense* with sentence 1, being illustrative,
giving more definite information as to the manner of infliction.

Lampoon.—Distinguish from " satire." " These personal and scandalous libels, carried to excess in the reign of Charles II., acquired the
name ' lampoon ' from the burden sung to them, ' Lampone, camerada,
lampone,' ' guzzler, guzzler, my fellow guzzler.' "—SIR WALTER SCOTT.

Ill-natured.—*Habitual* bad temper. Not quite the opposite of
" good-natured."

How would it affect the sense to omit "a" before " greater " and
" barbarous " in sentence 4 ?

Note the balance of the infinitive phrases, " to stir....derision." Do
they observe the rule of " gradation " in meaning or force ? The meaning of " uneasiness " is a little obscure. We should expect " strife."
The last part might be shortened to " while he remains."

Sentence 5 may be strengthened and improved by contracting to " if
besides being witty and ill-natured, a man is also vicious." The adverb
before " vicious " gives greater point ; " in addition " would do, but
" into the bargain " seems to deprive the sentence of its dignity.

Civil.—Civilized, as opposed to barbarous. Comp. "Civil Service."
What additional idea does "vicious" join to "ill-natured"

Sentences 6 and 7 might well be combined.

Sentence 8 is a good example of Addison's redundancy. Show how it may be shortened.

Sentence 9.—Correct the syntax and account for the error if you can.

"A *considerable* sum of money" seems a weak and rather ridiculous comparison with "even life itself." Substitute some phrase like "all they have in the world." Omit "not" before "rather."

"A mark."—Would "marks" be better? Is "of" the proper preposition? What other expression might be substituted?

Sentence 10.—The connection is a little obscure. The concluding sentence of a paragraph should sum up the general tenor of it (unity) and thus impress the idea of the topical sentence, or else suggest the coming paragraph. The last part of 9 ("but, &c.") and 10 are considerations opposed to the first part of 9. A possible emendation would be to begin a new sentence after "murder" and combine the last with it, thus : "At the same time how many there are who would lose all they have in the world, or even life itself, rather than be set up as a mark of infamy and derision ; and besides in this case a writer should consider," &c. Is "not" in its proper place in sentence 10?

Socrates.—The great Athenian philosopher (469—399 B.C.). He effected a revolution in the subject-matter of philosophy, declaring the proper study of mankind to be *man*. He shewed the necessity of accurate definition and classification in the use of general and abstract terms ; his chief doctrine was that virtue consisted in knowledge. He was indicted in 399 for not worshipping the gods and for corrupting the youth ; was condemned to death and compelled to drink the hemlock.

Aristophanes.—The greatest comic poet of Athens, who in his plays boldly launched his satire against his contemporaries. In the *Clouds* (423 B.C.) he falsely attacked *Socrates* as the representative of that pernicious sect of innovators in religion and morals, the *Sophists*, and also Alcibiades as his pupil in iniquity. This had considerable influence in preparing the way for Socrates' accusation and death.

Anguish.—Is this the right word here?

Passage in, *i.e.*, in the account of, as given in Plato's *Phædon.*

Sentence 3 might perhaps be improved by writing, "*entertains*....soul, *and* at his entering upon it says."

Any.—Suggest a better word.

Glances upon.—"Refers to."

Buffoonery.—The jokes and antic gestures of the comic actor (buffo) in an opera.

We say now "equally moved at," or "moved by," but never "resentment of."

In sentence 6 we would now say, "I submit that, etc."

Discover.—Note the old meaning, now uncommon except in poetry. Show how the two meanings are connected.

Catullus.—A Roman poet (87–39 B.C.), a writer of lyrics and epigrams much admired by competent judges. He attacked Julius Cæsar and his favourite (Mamurra) in one of his poems No. 29.* According to Morley the story in the text that Cæsar forgave him for his father's sake is of doubtful authority.

Mazarin.—Cardinal and Chief Minister of France during the minority of Louis XIV., and successor to Richelieu and his policy. Crafty and unscrupulous, but fairly tolerant and liberal, under him the foreign influence of France increased, but the domestic government in the departments of justice and finance was corrupt and wasteful, being inferior to Richelieu's. He was secretly married to the Queen-mother, Anne of Austria. Died in 1661.

Expostulations.—Is "upon" the proper preposition?

Fall—*i.e.*, fall vacant.

4. **Pasquin.**—A tailor or cobbler, who lived in Rome at the end of the 15th century, noted for his wit and sarcasm. After his death a mutilated fragment of ancient statuary was dug up under his shop, was set up, and to it the tailor's name was given, because witty and sarcastic criticisms of the popes and cardinals were affixed to it, a free expression of opinion being impossible. On a rival statue (Marforio) questions and replies were posted up. Hence the term *pasquinade.* It was not the sister of Sixtus (Camilla) that was the laundress ; it was his aunt.

Pietro Aretino.—*i. e.*, of Arretium, now Arezzo, a celebrated satirist, who assailed the traffic in indulgences of Leo XI. He steered clear of persecution in spite of his bitter writing, got a gold chain from Francis I., and a pension from Charles V.

Sophi.—About the year 1500 Ismail Sofi founded the 12th dynasty (the Sophis) of Persia. Sophi means pure or holy. The grandfather earned his sanctity by his asceticism, and the grandson (Ismail) got the benefit.

In sentence 3—" in which " would be better than " that." The whole paragraph is well-constructed, being smooth and well-connected.

Paragraphs 2, 3 and 4 are parallel illustrations of the topical sentence of 2.

5. Resumes the general consideration of the topic.

Note the recurring phrases, "secret wounds," "barbarous and in-human."

Discuss the substitution of "collected" for "drawn together," "sensitive to" for "sensitive of," "to shame" for "out of countenance."

Very differently.—Not from each other, but from the wits who had reproached them. Omit "of the age."

For the use of "shall" in sentences 4 and 7, see *H. S. Gr.*, *viii.*, *117*

An unhappy feature.—Some unfortunate deformity or peculiarity of face. This sentence and sentences 5 and 6 would be better joined by semicolons.

Temperate.—In its older sense of moderate in opinions and conduct.

Representation.—He means wrong representation, ·*i. e.*, misrepresentation.

6. **Of distinguishing.**—What would be the usual expression ?

The last part of the sentence, "as it were," etc., is rather loosely joined to what precedes. What is the grammatical relation of its clauses ?

"For which reason," "as the former," etc. What words would now l e used in place of "which" and "as ? "

Sir Roger L'Estrange was a violent Tory of the reign of Charles II., and in 1663 was appointed sole licenser of newspapers. He published a volume of fables, translated from various sources. This one of Æsop's Addison copied *verbatim*. Sir Roger had died but a few years before.

Still as.—Whenever or as often as.

7. **Set apart.**—Easter in 1711 fell on the first of April.

Set apart (for) and dedicated (to).

Speculations.—Meditations.

Settling, etc.—We now say "Bringing ourselves into a frame of mind." For the grammatical form see note on the first paragraph.

ESSAY 26.

1. **Westminster Abbey.**—This great structure, famed for its extent and the beauty of its architecture, is now in the metropolis. At one time the burial place of the kings, it has become a national honor to be interred within its walls. In the eastern aisle of the south transept is Poet's Corner. After Dean Stanley became connected with the Abbey,

much improvement was made. Also within the limits of the old city of Westminster is William Rufus Hall, in which the Inns of Court were till lately held.

Note Addison's manner of beginning so many essays with a " when" clause.

What previous phrase justifies the words " not disagreeable ? "

Cloisters.—Covered walks surrounding the open quadrangle in monastic or collegiate buildings, and generally separated from it only by a row of pillars. Used for study and recreation.

Amusing.—Note the change in the meaning of the word.

Sentence 4. **Them,** themselves.—Distinguish " other than" and " other but."

In what consists the humor of sentence 5 ?

Holy Writ.—The reference is to the *Apocrypha.*

2. **Human.**—Addison wrote "humane," but with the same meaning.

The second sentence is a very fine one. Note the change in the order of the contrasted words in the last clause, and suggest, if you can, a reason for it.

Magazine.—Not a good word, being suggestive of incongruous ideas. Suggest a substitute for it.

Fabric.—Not much used now in this sense. What is the usual meaning ?

Deliver the character.—A somewhat uncommon expression.

Greek or Hebrew.—Some one has humorously suggested the thought that when England's glory shall have passed away, and the antiquarians of 3000 years hence are unearthing her monuments, they will conclude that our tongue was Greek or Latin, instead of English. This practice of inscribing Latin epithets, once so common, is happily dying out.

Uninhabited.—Note the transferred epithet. Give an equivalent term of classical origin for an " empty tomb."

4. **Politeness.**—Then had the meaning of culture or elegance.

Turn.—Explain : how do you reconcile it with both " monuments" and " inscriptions ? "

Put in execution.—Would " into" do here ? Express in other words the meaning of this phrase, and of " conceive an idea."

Periwig.—Wig or peruke, corrupted from F. *perruque.* See No. 129 and No. 58 of the *Spectator* for descriptions.

Canopy.—What was the original meaning ?·

Answerable to.—Correspond to, is in keeping with.

Manner of death.—Shovel, who rose by his merit from cabin boy to admiral, was cast away on the Scilly islands on returning from an unsuccessful attack on Toulon. His body was robbed of a ring by a fisherman, and buried in the sand. This ring led to his disinterment and burial in Westminster Abbey.—MORLEY.

Taste of antiquity.—Is this a correct expression? The student will notice Addison's many differences from modern usage in the employment of prepositions.

Like themselves.—In their true character.

Rostral.—Like a ship's beak (rostrum). Explain the origin of the phrase " mount the rostrum" (properly rostra).

5. Which is better, " repository" or " depository?"

" Serious amusement."—In the modern sense of the latter word would be an *oxymoron*.

Sentence 5.—A fine example of a balanced sentence. Could you vary the order of the clauses so as to better the climax? The whole essay is considered one of Addison's finest, both as to structure and the "serious humour" it displays. The student should go carefully over the essay, noting the connection of the paragraphs, their arrangement, whether wholly appropriate and suited for the best effect. It has been said that if you take care of the paragraphs the composition will take care of itself. However true this may be, the correct structure of the sentences will not ensure the correct structure of the paragraphs. The sentences in this essay will be found to exhibit fewer of Addison's faults (looseness, redundancy, confusion) than usual, and the words are well chosen for meaning and melody.

ESSAY 47.

1. Hobbes' (1588-1679).—His greatest work is his *Leviathan* (1651).

What is the subject of this essay, and where is it indicated?

Re-write Hobbes' sentence in modern phraseology.

Curious.—Elaborate with art, rare ; The word has now taken on an unfavorable meaning, like *notorious*. See *H. S. Gr. IV.*, 40, d.

2. **Observations.**—He should have used "circumstances" or "proofs," as he immediately recounts some.

Tame.—Domesticated or trained.

Paragraph 3 is too short, and might well be joined to 2, being an example under sentence 3 of it.

4. **Boileau.**—"In his 4th Satire, John Dennis was at this time the leading critic of the French school, to whom Pope afterwards attached

lasting ridicule."—MORLEY. In the *Dunciad.* He was the only one who assailed *Cato :* see life of Addison.

Loll.—To rest or lean lazily ; it is still a word much used by common people.

People above mentioned.—Who are meant ?

Understanding.—Not used now as an adjective.

5. **Droll.**—A comical fellow, a wag (Fr. drôle), not much used now as a *noun.*

"According to the old proverb." Where might this phrase be better placed.

Circumforaneous.—One who goes from one market to another. This word has not lived through to our time.

Fool's coat.—*i.e.*, a fool's manner and appearance, to create laughter.

6. "Triumph of the understanding." What and where mentioned ? See paragraph 1.

Sentence 2 is ambiguous. The probable meaning would be made clear by writing, "As there are more follies discovered on this day, so there is more laughter raised on it," etc.

"Makes his boasts" must have been a correct expression then, or Addison would never have written so unmusical a phrase.

Inkle.—A kind of broad linen tape used by shoemakers. The poor half-wit sent on this errand got sometimes the shoemaker's stirrup across the back, they calling it *stirrup-oil.*

Sleeveless.—Useless. Obsolete in this sense now.

8. "In the main." Supply "part."

The meaning of the last part of the last sentence is not quite plain, but is perhaps this : "If a person wishes to acquire and to keep the character of a wag, he must be content to occupy the place of inferiority (in some respects) into which the laughter at his follies or witticims puts him."

Addison's theory is a very poor one, and between paragraph 6 and paragraph 9 there appears to be little correspondence. As to the motive of the laughter, certainly admiration of the wit's character may co-exist with our laughter.

9. **Abstracted.**—We would now say "abstract."

Has laughter always for its basis a principle belonging to the malevolent or selfish side of our nature ? If so, the product very often destroys the principle that gave it life. Laughter, whatever its source may be, often brings good humor in its train. We suppose Addison would say, however, that we are then pleased with "some eminency in ourselves in comparison with the infirmity of others," and so by vanity made kindly disposed.

10. "Turn of humour," "cast in person." Give equivalent expressions.

"Only fit for." Is "only" correctly placed? If not, account for its position.

The quotation is from the 2nd. part of *Henry IV.*, Act I., sc. 2.

ESSAY 50.

1. "The *Spectator* is written by Steele with Addison's help. It is often very pretty. Yesterday 'twas made of a noble hint I gave him long ago for his *Tatler*, about an Indian supposed to write his travels into England. I repent he had it. I intended to have written a book on that subject." Swift to Stella, April 28, 1711. Swift was in error as to the writer. Goldsmith carried out such an idea in the *Citizen of the World ;* Swift's took the form of *Gulliver's Travels*.

Indian Kings.—" Four Iroquois chiefs, induced by the Colonists to visit England, see Queen Anne and prove for themselves the falsity of the Jesuits' assertion that England and all other nations were vassals of France. They were said also to have been told that the Saviour was born in France and crucified in England."—MORLEY. "They went to see *Macbeth* at the Haymarket ; the gods in the gallery became uproarious, and were appeased by their majesties taking chairs on the stage, which they good humoredly did."—ARNOLD.

St. Paul's.—Begun by Sir Christopher Wren in the reign of Charles II., finished in that of Anne.

3. "Same day with the sun," "by the best information I am apt to think," "fashioned by tools." Discuss the correctness of these expressions. Can you give any rule for the proper use of "by" and "with" after passive verbs ?

Curiously.—May mean here either "singularly" or "with elaborate care."

Surface of a pebble.—The original reading was "as polished marble." Suggest a reason for the change.

Garlands.—Refers to the ornaments of the *capitals* of the pillars ; the trunks of trees gave, no doubt, the first idea for the supports of a roof.

State the subject of the last paragraph in this essay.

What two subjects in this paragraph (3)? Where does the second begin?

The last sentence should be divided by a period after " behaviour."

4. Knock us down.—The Tories accused the Whigs of driving away their lawful kings and setting up unlawful ones in their stead.

5. Foreigners.—The Tories are represented by Addison as much more opposed to foreigners and their ways than the Whigs. The insular prejudices of both parties are well known. Note as instances the feeling against the Dutch favoritism of William III., the articles in the Act of Settlement, etc.

Secret.—Mysterious. The original meaning was lonely, apart, remote. Cp. Milton, " The secret top of Oreb or of Sinai."

Monster.—Means here not a being "of large size," but " unnatural in form,"=monstrosity.

6. Cunning.—The old and Biblical sense had not in it the idea of sinister or fox-like wisdom—but Bacon uses it with its modern meaning.

Covered rooms.—Sedan-chairs take their name from Sedan (Fr.), wrongly said to have been introduced by Buckingham into England; they became very common during the reign of Charles II.; they are now little used except for invalids.

" About the neck." Is this a necessary addition to "strangle themselves ? "

What circumstances may justify tautology ?

Bush of hair.—These monstrous wigs were in full fashion during the 17th and most of the 18th century. Then they were superseded by the long queue and hair powder.

Correct " as if it was," " hoped to have seen," giving your reasons.

Make the last clause similar to the preceding one.

7. " Persons of . . . among them." The original reading was, " men of the greatest perfection in their country."

8. Back spots.—The custom of wearing patches on the face was then in vogue, and they were often of fantastic shapes. One is mentioned as being cut to the figure of a coach and six. The " Citizen of the World" tells us that they might be placed anywhere but on the tip of the nose. Pope gives us the armament of a lady of fashion—" Puffs, powders, patches, Bibles, billet-doux." For an amusing account of the use of patches in party warfare, see No. 81 of the *Spectator*.

9. Criticize and improve the order of words in "I cannot likewise forbear observing."

Abstract of.—Should be "from." Why?

Point out expressions in this essay that strike you as old-fashioned. Show that it contains both humor and satire.

ESSAY 69.

Royal Exchange.—The first Royal Exchange, modelled after the Antwerp Bourse, was built by Sir Thomas Gresham, and finished in 1567. It was burned in the Great Fire, was re-built, but was again burned down in 1838. The present structure has not the statues of the Kings of England as ornaments, which the previous ones had.

High Change.—On Tuesdays and Fridays the throng is greatest, and these are specially known as 'Change days.

Factors.—Agents employed by merchants to buy or sell on commission.

Substitute explanatory or more modern phrases for "politic world," "affairs," "correspondence," "live on," "ministers," "walks."

Great Mogul.—The Emperor of Hindostan, with capital at Delhi. The reigning mogul at that time was the son of the great Aurungzebe.

Old philosopher.—Diogenes, the cynic, who lived in a tub, and who wanted nothing from Alexander the Great but that he should get out of his sunshine.

Give a word of classical origin for "citizen of the world."

2. **Sir Andrew Freeport.**—The merchant member of the *Spectator's* Club; see introduction.

Connive.—What is the literal meaning of the word?

Grand Cairo.—A reference to his visit to that city, mentioned in No. 1.

Coptic.—The language of the Copts, Christian descendants of the ancient Egyptians. The language had not been *spoken* for many centuries before Addison's time, Arabic having supplanted it.

3. **For the reason.**—Explain the reference, and show how it might have been made clearer by inserting a word.

Public stock.—What is meant? Exemplify other uses of "stock."

4. **Disseminate.**—Would "distribute" be a better word? Why? Do you see any redundance in the first sentence?

Point out any example of *metaphor* and *metonymy* in the paragraph ; and explain the different geographical allusions.

The single dress.—The dress alone : " dress" being used of course in its wide sense.

The sentences from " The food" to " bowels, "and from " The muff " to " Indostan," although, as they ought to be, similarly constructed, are too short, and would be better separated by semi-colons, as they are merely particular illustrations of the general statements of the preceding sentence. No words of explicit reference are needed, the connection in meaning being so close. What three sentences keep the main idea of the paragraph before the reader ?

The different ends.—Would opposite be better ? Why ?

5. **Grows originally.**—What is meant ? Is the expression a correct one ?

Delicate.—How used ? The word is not in use now.

Than to a sloe.—Omit " to," the meaning being " than a sloe is."

The topic is " In a state of nature (natural prospect) our soil and climate have few advantages ; the first is barren, the second unculti-vated. Commerce supplies these deficiencies."

Sentence 2 puts more prominence on the naturalization and cultivation that are the indirect effect of commerce, than on the fruits themselves. The sentence might perhaps be rearranged so as to end with " English gardens." The words of explicit reference, " more enriched," would then have a closer connection, and the main idea would be kept more in sight.

The whole face of Nature.—This does not seem to be the expres-sion required here, for he proceeds to give a list of products of *art* and luxury, and not of improvements of the face of Nature. Perhaps " than it has added to the comfort and convenience of our households," would be an improvement.

"Extremities of weather." What do we say now ?

Vegetable world carries us back to the barren soil and the fruits ; the other phrase seems meant to revive the idea in " uncomfortable."

Explain the reference in " morning's draught," "drugs of America," " Indian canopies."

Sentence 10 is a re-statement, and a clear one, of the topic. It and the last sentence are a fine termination of the paragraph, the first part of which is weak and not very clear. They are of good length, well balanced, and the language is well chosen and well arranged for pre-cision, picturesqueness and melody.

Point out examples of parallel construction in the paragraph.

6. **For these reasons.**—State them briefly in your own words. If the phrase were omitted there would still be a sense reference in the word "merchants." But Addison, on account of his desire for an easy style, seldom omits words or phrases of explicit reference, except in short enumerating sentences. See paragraphs 4 and 5.

7. **Effigy.**—There were about twenty statues.
The reference, "in this case," may be omitted with advantage. Why?
The third sentence might perhaps be improved by beginning it with some such clause as "Thus it is that," or "Thus we see that."
Point out any redundance in the last sentence.
The whole paragraph is, however, not capable of much improvement, and it forms an excellent conclusion to the essay.

ESSAY 93.

1. What statements of this paragraph are discussed in the remainder of the essay, and where?

2. Which is the topical sentence of par. 2, and what sentence of par. 1 does it in substance repeat?
Note that sentences 4 and 5 are practically the same in meaning, differing only in expression : they might be expunged, and then sentences 3, 6, 7, 8 would fall into more orderly arrangement as illustrations of the general principle. The last two sentences reiterate it and prepare the way for the next paragraph.

3. What are the words of explicit reference to the last paragraph?
The first part of sentence 2 seems unnecessary, the word "most" sufficiently indicating that there are exceptions; if retained, accent "always."
What word in the first sentence is misplaced?
Enumerate in a tabulated form the different methods he proposes, and the subdivisions of those he deals with in this essay. Note carefully also the additional motives he suggests for the practice of each method.

4. " Find a man in business "—Is " in business " an adjunct of
" man " or " find ?" Express the meaning in other words and write
out the " than " clause in full.

" Rectifying."—A rare, if not incorrect use of the word as applied to
persons. Exemplify its ordinary use.

5. Notice the accumulation of phrases of nearly equivalent meanings ;
" retired " and " in which . . . ourselves," " company " and " con-
vention," " intercourse " and " communication."

Such hours when.—To what does "such" refer ? Would " the hours
when " convey the same meaning ?

No sooner....but—Is this correct ?

6. Are " only " and " not only " correctly placed ?

Redoubles upon us—Is doubly strong.

7. " Nor strained up to a pitch "—Expand the metaphor.

8. **Should be**—Would " is " be better ?

Below—What should we say now ?

Hurt—This word is now concrete in its meaning.

Which is better, " thus much " or " this much ?"

9. By " proper regulations " Addison means regulations which would
secure decency and respect for ordinary morality. The reformation of
the English stage had begun but had not yet advanced very far. The
plays of Wycherley were still on the stage. Congreve was a celebrity.

11. " Endeavour after," "go asunder," give modern equivalent
phrases for these.

12. Would " should endeavour " be an improvement ?
Develop the comparison implied in " run adrift."

13. Is " taste of music " correct ?

Sense—Exemplify different meanings and uses of this word.

Florist, &c.—Show that the meaning is awkwardly if not obscurely
expressed, and improve the sentence.

14. **Empty**—Would " void " or " vacant " do as well ?
What phrase in the last sentence might be better placed, and where ?

ESSAY 115.

1. Can you point out any distinction between "submits" and "undergoes?"

Show how the second sentence might be improved by shortening it, and by altering the position of "only." •

2. Give synonymous expressions for "stock," "phrase," "engine," "composition," "interwoven."

Distinguish "veins and arteries," "muscles and tendons," "rustic" and "rural."

Ligatures—Seems to be incorrectly used for "ligaments," the white, solid, inelastic substance that connects bones. Exemplify the correct use of "ligature." .

Note and criticise the use of "more perfect," and the position of "not only."

The first sentence of this paragraph, although closely connected with the preceding one, is rather out of place, and would come better perhaps at the end of paragraph 3, or even later. In its present position it anticipates too soon the subject of the excellence of a country life. The real subject of the paragraph is the body and should stand first in it.

3. An excellent paragraph—Give synonyms for "juices," "humorous," "infinitude," "redundancies," "distributions."

4. An example of Addison's indefiniteness and confusion of ideas—What are the "spirits" but the understanding and the imagination? And what is "refining" but making clear and "untroubled?"

Spleen—This organ of the body, whose functions are still somewhat in doubt, was anciently supposed to be the seat or cause of ill-humour and melancholy. Hence the latter are frequently called the spleen.

Vapours—A disease (of women) marked by nervous weakness and depression of spirits, in which strange freaks and fancies come into the mind, and strange images float before the eyes, etc. The term is now seldom used.

5. What is the topical sentence?—Show that the train of thought is uninterrupted throughout.

Without destroying the literary form substitute synonymous expressions for "proper for," "be come at," "be laboured," "it is forced into."

Name the periodic sentences in the paragraph. How would you class the rest?

Q

Note Addison's method of proving that exercise is necessary.

State briefly the three arguments by which he supports his opinion.

" Are more miserable." Would be more miserable.—Why ?

Par. 6 is an exemplification of the last sentence of par. 5. What words in the paragraph show the humor and sarcasm of Addison's writing.

Distinguish "trophy" and "prize," "the chase" and "hunting," "topic" and "subject," "perverse" and "wayward," "exploit" and "feat," "arsenal" and "magazine," "discourse," "converse," and "conversation."

What should we write now for " otter's skin," "distinction sake ?"

Note the difference in the use of "furniture" and "patched" from modern usage.

Note also the economy and consequent energy in the words "earned —killed—lost."

Sit—The hare is said to sit in its " form" during the day, going out to feed at night.

7. **The idea**—What idea and where given ?

Will see—Note the use of "will," not as a mere auxiliary or tense form, but an independent verb, "wills" or "wishes" to see.

Exercise upon—What preposition would be used now ?

Ringing a dumb bell is a pleasant conceit or pun.

8. Substitute equivalent expressions in present use for "loaden," "either," "evaporate the spleen," "uneasy."

This Essay is throughout characteristic of Addison's lighter vein of pleasant humour and easy, good tempered ridicule. The paragraphs are, with the exception of the 2nd, well arranged and related ; the interest which culminates in par. 6 is skilfully led up to. Criticise the last para-graph as to its relation to the preceding.

ESSAY 159.

This Essay is but a short Allegory ; in other words it is a comparison by metaphors carried on and sustained through many details. The student must look out for the correspondence between the pictures called up and the things they represent, but he must remember that if there is a strong *general* impression and a vividness of conception, he should be satisfied. Of course where there is a continuation of metaphors the danger of straining them, *i.e.*, going into irrelevant particulars, is very great. We may note other celebrated allegories, as the *Fairie Queen, Pilgrim's Progress, Tale of a Tub, Gulliver's Travels.* Many of the parables are allegories. Be careful to distinguish a parable from an an example or illustration. An allegory or true parable contains two distinct meanings, the literal (as it reads) and the figurative (as it is applied). In the Vision of Mirzah, the parallelism of the two lines of meaning descends to the details pretty minutely. The resemblances should be so close as to be *easily* grasped. The criticism of an allegory (except as to the mere form) must depend upon what is the main consideration, the illustration of the subject, the interest of the narrative, or the picturesqueness of the description, etc. This vision is judged highly because it quite effectively unites these.

1. The name Mirza (Persian *emir, zadeh,* prince's son), the locality, Bagdat, once the capital of a Mohammedan empire, and the appearance of the genius may have been suggested by the *Arabian Nights' Entertainments,* which were published about this time.

Translated—From what language? Derive the word, also "Oriental" and "manuscripts."

What is A's object in representing the vision as a translation from an Eastern manuscript?

Washed—Washing and morning devotion are characteristics of the Mahometans.

Notice the artful antithesis between "tops of mountains" and "fell into a profound contemplation."

What is the subject of the vision as mentioned in the second sentence, and how does the remainder of the Essay carry it out?

The Genii of the Eastern Mythology are a sort of fairies, are mortal, marry and give in marriage, and were formed out of the "smokeless fire" of the simoom several thousand years before Adam. As they paid no heed to the prophets sent to instruct them, they were driven from the earth to the island regions. They were not guardian or attendant spirits like the Roman Genii but were fallen angels and hostile to man. man.—*Brewer.*

The last three sentences of this paragraph are a fine example of fancy; the music had the magical power of causing forgetfulness of the agonies of death, and of so entrancing and elevating the mind above the grossness of earthly sense as to give him for the time the powers of an immortal.

2. Notice that at first he feels *rapture,* then, as he approaches, *astonishment* and *fear* mingle with it. This is not the natural order in

meetings with supernatural beings. What sentence justifies the order given?

Give from its derivation the literal meaning of *rapture,* and compare that of *transports* and of *ecstasy.*

To taste—So as to be able to taste.

Is there any distinction between "fears" and "apprehension?"

Heart subdued—What is meant? Has it the same force as "heart melted away" in the preceding paragraph?

4. The Allegory proper begins here.

Mist—The two great questions that agitate the religious world are "What was our origin?" and "Whither are we going?" Thousands of years of speculation have brought us no nearer to the true answer to these. Revelation can be our only guide.

What other terms does he use to describe the mist?

Consummation—Would "end" do as well?

Write explanatory notes on "three score and ten," "broken arches," "one thousand arches," "ruinous condition," "trap-doors."

Distinguish "entire" and "complete."

"No sooner trod upon but they fell."—What should this be?

Entrance—It has often been said that of all that are born, one-third die before they are seven years of age.

What are the periods of life specially fatal?

What are the two subjects of this paragraph?

6. Give in general terms the subject of this paragraph.

Speculation—In its old sense ; meditation.

Bubbles—Show the appropriateness of the term.

Scimitars—War is thus symbolized as a great cause of death.

7. The Vultures, Harpies, etc., are embodiments of evil spirits or passions ; the metaphor is pushed a little too far. Associating them with the winged boys (Cupids) seems incongruous, as mingling the fancies of the heathen mythologies with our ideas of the forms that evil spirits assume.

Assort if you can the different passions to the birds, etc., symbolizing them, *e.g.,* a Harpy to Avarice, etc.

According to the classical mythology the Harpies were ravenous, disgusting, winged monsters, with the head of a woman, and the body of a bird.

Why are these creatures spoken of as on "the *middle* arches?"

8. **Fetch a sigh**—An old form of expression. What is now the usual word?

Adamant—What is the literal meaning? "Diamond" is but another form of it.

Islands—The "Islands of the Blest" of the classical writers, supposed to lie somewhere in the Atlantic.

Degree—Some might object to the use of this word as indicating a graduated scale of rewards (and consequently punishments); but Addison is not writing a treatise on theology.

This paragraph (3) and No. 4 bear away the palm for correctness of comparison, for beauty of thought, and for picturesqueness. Notice the varied length of the sentences, and the forcible interrogation in the three successive sentences near the end. Notice too, the artful abrupt ending of the vision, implying (1) That it *was* all a dream or vision; (2) The reluctance of the kind genius to unfold the miseries behind the rock of adamant. In the last sentence he selects the three prominent parts of his vision as in sudden contrast with the ordinary prospect of every day life.

ESSAY 162.

1. What is the subject of this Essay?

Our system of party government has led to especial fear of being termed a "turncoat," and a renegade is visited with peculiar hatred by those he deserts.

2. **Articles of life**—What are meant?

Out of—What is the more common preposition?

Levity—Give the literal meaning and show how that of "fickleness" has come from it.

Renegadoes—The old form. Derive. Note that the word had not necessarily the bad meaning which we now associate with it.

3. **Schemes**—*Plan* is the better and more common word.

Notice the accumulation in "greatest" and "most universal," "disquiet" and "unhappiness." The expression would be stronger if "most universal," and "disquiet" were omitted. What other objection is there to "most universal?"

Parties—To what does this refer?

"Hovers," "settle on."—What is the comparison implied?

"One had....we might."—How would you improve this?

Does not the exceptive clause "any more....design," rather empha-size and approve the "principle of expediency?"

By several, etc.—In accordance with several wavering plans of life, and *wish* not only to be, etc.

Substitute an adjective if you can for "everything....world," so as to balance the sentence better.

We might try a change in last line, "live in misery and die repent-ing."

4. **Would**—Ought this to be "should?"

Show the balance existing in the various sentences of this paragraph?

5. **Schemes of thought**—Ways of thinking.

Former infancy—Recalls Shakespeare's 7th age:

"Sans teeth, sans eyes, sans taste, sans everything."

"A Man"—Omit "a." Why?

Trifling—Trivial, of slight value.

Shadow of change—St. James, Chap. I : 17.

6. "In a.... manner"—An example of the "squinting construc-tion." Show how the ambiguity may be removed.

Are there any words or phrases in this paragraph that may with advantage be omitted?

7. The passage is from *Absalom and Achitophel*, and gives the character of Villiers, Duke of Buckingham.

ESSAY 169.

1. **Calamity**—Distinguish "calamity," "misfortune," "evil."

Foul upon—What do we now say?

Notice that "injustice" is a word less specific in its meaning than "malice," "envy," "treachery," and including them. When and how does this contribute to *strength?* Does it in this case?

2. The offices (duties) of compassion *are* benevolence and humanity.

Distinguish "compasssion" and "pity," "benevolence" and "hu-manity."

3. **Wit.**—Is malevolence a necessary element in wit?

Nothing can be more true than the sentiments here expressed. If one be a genial, good-natured fellow a score of gross and even nauseous vices are often tolerated.

Note that "humanity" is used in its old sense of "culture." Compare its use in the Scotch universities still, *e.g.*, Professor of Humanity *i.e.* of the Latin language and literature.

4. Discuss Addison's definition of good breeding.

5. Is there tautology in this sentence, and if so is it defensible?

6. **Born**—*i.e.*, like poetical genius, *nascitur non fit.*
Constitution—He means of mind.

7. **Life**—*Cyropædia*, Book VIII : Chap. 6.
Incorporate—Usually transitive. Give the literal meaning.
Enshrine—*i.e.*, not to cremate him and preserve his ashes in the urn
Par. 8 should be joined to par. 7....The student would find it a good exercise to combine the preceding paragraphs : 3, 4, 5, may be joined and somewhat shortened ; also 6, 7, and 8. Is there any rule as to the length of paragraphs other than the preservation of Unity?

9. **Passage**—Sallust's *Catilina*, Chap. 54.
"Seen with grains of allowance," would be better "judged with, etc." Compare the common expression "*cum grano salis.*"

10. "That part" would be better than "this."

11. Distinguish "maxim" and "proverb."

12. The first sentence refers to sentence 1 of par. 11, and should recall the maxim a little more distinctly by using a somewhat similar form. Say "Another reason why good-natured men are not esteemed men of the most wit, is that perhaps they, etc.
Are the last 2 clauses of this sentence properly co-ordinated?
Sentence 2 is of excellent construction, well *balanced* and *energetic* : few words could be omitted or introduced or changed with advantage.
The last sentence would conclude better with the word "humanity," leaving the reader to supply the cause. The illustration "who.... methods," does not illustrate, and the resemblance between the "indirect methods" and the acts mentioned in the sentence is not *at once* apparent.
"Indirect" means "dishonest," a sense in which it is seldom if ever used now.

ESSAY 195.

Story—The story of the Greek King and the Physician, told by the Fisherman to the Genie.

An hollow—Note that Addison uses *an* before many words, where we would use *a*.

Is there any difference between English and American usage in this respect?

Artificially—Artfully. Not used now in this sense.

A new paragraph might well begin at " This Eastern allegory."

What qualities of style does the last sentence exhibit?

One might almost think from the last line that with A. temperance meant abstemiousness.

2. What difference might there be between the "substitute *of* exercise " and "*for* exercise."

Cupping—The word might be left out as "cupping" is but a method of bleeding by exhausting the air in the cupping glass.

Countermining — What comparison is suggested? Express the meaning of the sentence in your own words. What terms do we ordinarily use instead of "apothecary " and "vintner?"

Salads—From the same root (Lat. *sal.* salt) as "sauce," the primary idea of each being something to give a relish to other food.

Dropsies—Give the original form and the derivation of the word, also any examples of similar changes. See *H. S. Gr. IV.*, 45, d.

3. " Berry," " mushroom."—Specific examples of the preceding general terms.

4. **Determinate**—We now say "fixed."

To what do the words "first case " and " second" refer?

" Solicit his palate " and " create a false appetite," are phrases of like meaning ; so farther on, " sickness in embryo " and " first seeds of indisposition."

Rule for drinking—Sir William's seems liberal enough, to our ideas.

Note the anacoluthon in the last sentence, account for it, and show how it can be removed.

5. **Of two different dates**—What is meant?

Addison seems to imply 60 as the common limit for his time ; these philosophers were over 80. What would he have said if he had seen men like Gladstone, Palmerston, Disraeli, and even our own Sir John, carrying on heavy political work in the seventies and eighties.

Recovered—Do you see any objection to the use of this word here? Express in other words the meaning of "the efficacy of temperance towards the procuring of long life," "it is of undoubted credit," "the mixture of the old man in it."

ESSAY 225.

1. **Cull** originally meant to gather (Fr. cueillir), but its later use is "to select the best."

2. **Tully**—Now commonly if not always spoken of as Cicero (Marcus Tullius Cicero). The word "expose" is here used in its modern sense of fault-finding. Show how the meaning is connected with the derivation.

Son of Sirach—In the *Apocrypha*. The wisdom of Jesus, the son of Sirach, or *Ecclesiasticus*. The quotation at the end of the Essay is from another work of the *Apocrypha*, *The Wisdom of Solomon*.

Bewrayer—The same in meaning as "betrayer," but of a different origin.

Paragraphs 3 and 4 should be joined ; also 5 and 6.

5. The words "the discreet man" might perhaps be moved with advantage to a more emphatic position after "brave."

Polyphemus—A great one-eyed giant that lived in Sicily. He made captive Ulysses and twelve of his crew and ate six of them, but Ulysses by a stratagem put out his one eye, and thus escaped. See *Odyssey*, Book *IX*.

6. Either "though" should be "if," or "and wants" should be "yet if he wants."

The seventh paragraph shows well what Addison was capable of in employing the balanced and pointed style.

Give the meaning of "indifferently" (1), "may pass upon" (7), "supersedes" (8), "preventeth" (9) ; and correct the syntax of sentence 2 of paragraph 8.

The student should look at the Essay as a whole composition and see whether it is a model for imitation in the orderly and logical development of its parts.

ESSAY 381.

1. The third sentence might be improved in balance by giving it greater similarity of form, thus ; " Mirth often raises into the greatest transports those who, etc." This is bringing the first part into form similar to the second. Try also changing the second part ; (1) To bring it into agreement with the first ; (2) So that "mirth" and "cheerfulness" shall occupy positions close to each other in the middle of the sentence ; (3) So they shall occupy the extreme ends of the sentence.

What are the different forms and uses of the balanced sentence, and what are the cautions to be observed in its use ?

2. Notice that the topic words " mirth " and " to laugh " occupy the positions of emphasis, the beginning and the end.

Obnoxious—In its original Latin meaning of "exposed to."

3. **Exceptions**—In the sense of "objections."

Present state—To what clause of paragraph 2 does this refer ?

This paragraph is one of Addison's unsuccessful loose sentences. The three phrases with "among," are unusually harsh....Arrange thus "cheerfulness....and does not....humanity. It is very conspicuous—those among the heathen who....philosophers as well as those among Christians who....men."

This arrangement improves the balance, and reduces the length and looseness of the sentence.

4. What is the general character of the sentences in this paragraph ?

6. Why is it better to begin with " If we consider ? "

7. In what sense are the words "title " and " ill" respectively used ?

8. The first sentence might be divided into two ; (1) " Atheism may, etc." (2) " By Atheism I mean, under whatever title it may shelter itself, a disbelief, etc." This would make the connection with the preceding paragraph closer, and bring out more clearly the relation of the adjunct "under whatever title."

Disbelief of—What is the more common preposition ?

" To out-live the expectation of it."—To expect such a thing and still live on.

Tribe—A word chosen as expressive of some contempt.

Infidels--Infidels, disbelievers in *revelation*. Atheists, disbelievers in the existence of God.

This paragraph ends with an interrogation. What intellectual or emotional qualities of style is this form of sentence useful for ; (1) if the interrogation be answered ; (2) if not?

10. Improve if you can the arrangement of the first sentence, giving your reason for any change you make.

"Pain" and "sickness," "shame" and "reproach," are too close in meaning.

We might try, "shame, disease, poverty, old age, nay death itself," or, keeping the pairs of words, "shame and sickness, pain and reproach, poverty and old age, nay, etc."

Considering—Turn into a "when" clause, and place it at the end of the sentence, or join it at the end of the next sentence by beginning, "for if we consider."

Indolence—In its root meaning (Lat. *in, doleo*) "without grief or pain."

Point out the awkwardness of the last sentence and reconstruct if you can so as to remove it.

11. In Addison's best manner.

The third sentence should end with ! instead of ? as it is really exclamatory. It is rather long for either of these too varieties of sentence.

Criticise "increase of perfection" and "spreads a diffusion."

12. In the last sentence can "to all eternity" be changed in position with advantage ?

13. The clause "to which I may....it" is an awkward parenthesis, and arrests the movement of what is otherwise a fine concluding sentence.

Made to please—To accent "made" does away partly with the harshness of "please," following so close upon "pleasing." A possible variation would be "glorify" for "please."

ESSAY 387.

1. He seems to confound the terms "soul" and "mind."

Natural—In the sense of "physical."

Improve the form of expression, "indifferent either as to virtue or vice," and express the meaning in other words.

2. Distinguish "repinings" and "secret murmurs of heart."

Spirits—Exemplify the various meanings of this word.

"I scarce remember to have met with such who, etc." Improve the form.

Indolence—See note on paragraph 10, of No. 381.

3. "Our use," "our pleasure."—"His" would perhaps be better.
"As the great soul."—Omit "as" or say "as it were."

5. Should be joined to 4.

"Furnish us with game."—Is considered in its relation to pleasure, and not to utility.

In the original text there is only a comma after "appearance," but in that case there should clearly be an "and" before the next clause.

6. "As being....shade."—Give the connection and parse "being." It would be better to expand the phrase into a clause.

Invert "grieving" and "weakening."—Why? Grieving is rarely if ever used now of producing physical pain.

Philosopher—Sir Isaac Newton.

Struggle—Between what?

7. **To consider**—A conditional clause would be better as in par. 3.

Landscape—The original has "landskip," i.e., "land-shape."

But of the harvest—Omit "of."

8. "Grotesqueness" is not like "wildness;" each can exist without the other.

Imaginary qualities—Perhaps he is thinking about Locke's secondary qualities, "looked upon as real qualities in the things thus affecting us; but are only the *powers* existent in bodies to produce in us the ideas of colours, tastes, sounds, smells, etc."

It would be better to have begun a new sentence after "figure," introducing it with some such clause as "It may also be asked."

It is not quite clear what he means by "conversant in the lower stations of nature."

9. Would be better joined to 8.

Vicissitude—In its original meaning (Lat. *vicis*, change). Exemplify its present use.

Notice the constant recurrence of the same phrases for words when Addison treats of similar subjects, "beautiful and pleasing images," "murmurs and repinings."

11. Sentence 2 is a sort of epigram associating the east wind and melancholy as cause and direct consequence. The difficulty of at once seeing the connection gives us a slight shock of surprise.

Cowper speaks of the "aguish east," Thompson of the "biting east." How do you account for these frequent references to its unfavorable influence on health?

12. "Fence against," etc. —Express the meaning in other words.

ESSAY 458.

What is the subject of the Essay and where is it indicated?

1. The clause "though .... drink" is a good illustration of the "squinting construction;" see *H. S. Gr.* xviii. 5; say "who was.... and though, etc.," or perhaps better "and unaccustomed (or unused) to drink." As the object of the next clause ("when, etc."), is not to tell the "time" but the consequence, say "and thus on a sudden, etc.;" also "head of the gentleman."

What is the difference between "vicious" and "false modesty?"

Which is better "false kind of modesty," or "kind of false modesty?"

3. "Of a contrary nature."—We might fill out the comparison by substituting "good or well-timed."

What prominent feature of style in this paragraph? ("Balance, giving clearness, simplicity, point and pleasure to the ear.")

It might better be an exclamatory sentence than interrogative.... Give evidences of energy of expression in the paragraph. Are there any words whose excision would lend still more force?

4. "Dare to do no ill."—Why is this called an epigrammatic way of speaking?

Torrent—What is the more common expression?

So it be—"So" is rarely used in this way now. In the last sentence consider the effect of the following changes; for "men" read "a company," and for "their company" read "that company."

5. Point out any instances of tautology in this paragraph in the use of pairs of words meaning about the same.

Shamefaced—Note that the spelling is due to a wrong idea of the derivation. The word is properly "shamefast."

Give examples of similar errors in spelling, see *II. S. Gr.* iv. 46.

Is Addison speaking seriously or ironically in what he says here of Englishmen's modesty in religious matters?

At his own table—The repetition of table is inelegant. Show if you can how it may be avoided.

Give more modern expressions for " men of mode," " best quality."

6. **Little appearance**—Say " lack " or " want ; " also say " our natural modesty."

We see that by vicious modesty he means the modesty that fears to be thought puritanical ; he shows, however, that it is really the modesty that tends to vice.

7. **Menace**—See *St. Luke IX.*, 26.

Show how the paragraphs of this Essay are connected, stating the subject of each, and discuss whether the Essay as a complete composition is characterized by *unity* and *symmetry* of *treatment*.

Are the leading principles of exposition duly employed? if so, point out where.

ESSAY 483.

What is the subject of the Essay?

1. Are there any words, phrases, or clauses, in this paragraph, that may with advantage be omitted or shortened?

The student should not forget the principle underlying effective brevity. The mind derives pleasure from action, if easy and not too long sustained. Speeches and writings are sometimes wearisome because the point aimed at is seen long before it is reached, and hence we are impatient to get on.

Substitute equivalent expressions for " discover their natural tincture," " strike in with."

" Draw something particular," — *i. e.*, " derive or contract a bias from."

Do you see anything faulty in the grammar of the last sentence?

2. A charming paragraph.—Note the familiar, colloquial phraseology, *e.g.*, " she can tell you," " talk to her," " when she had a fine face," etc. Note also the whimsical associations of supposed cause and effect.

Nemesis—A female deity of the Greeks — the personification of retribution or the righteous anger of the Deity.

Back-sword --Probably the same as what was also called "single-stick," a cudgel with a basket handle (like a sword), used by the rustics in trials of strength and skill.

That has been made—We do not now speak of "making a robbery." The second "that" clause would do for "robbery" also ; or indeed both might well be omitted.

3. " Very."—What other words could be substituted ?

"Amuse and terrify."—As "amusement," (even in the older meaning of the word) and "terror" cannot exist together, we must put "or" for "and," or write "if it does not terrify."

Impertinently—In its original meaning, "not pertinently ; " very different from "impertinently " as commonly employed.

" As well Christian as Pagan."—How would this be written now ?

Conduct—Method of management.

Had....made—Better "had had....made," or "had received."

Particular scheme—Special design.

4. Is "not only " in its proper place in the first sentence ?

The second sentence would perhaps be improved by substituting "for this " for the first " which ; " and the third by supplying the verb between "nor" and "when."

5. Diagoras was an Athenian who attacked the popular religion and was driven from the city, 411, B.C. To the sailors he was the Jonah on board.

6. The parenthesis in sentence five is rather long, and interferes with the unity of the sentence. It might perhaps be dispensed with by omitting the preceding clause, thus ; " the story of Biton and Clitobus, which is quoted by all the ancient authors who have, etc." The student may try other methods of improving the passage.

The last sentence is loosely constructed and might with advantage be made shorter and more periodic, thus ; "Had such an event (result or fate) happened to the two brothers after an act of disobedience, it would have been construed into a judgment, and would doubtless have been represented as such by any ancient historian."

The student will find it an excellent exercise to write out in outline the plan of an Essay. The following is offered not as the best but as a suggestion :

(1) Definition of the failing—its double evil—its origin—a comparison.

(2) A humorous example—showing its absurd side.

(3) Examples from ancient and modern history, showing its serious side. The arguments against such a belief in judgments are in the following paragraph.

(4) Presumptuous and contrary to the doctrine of future reward and punishment.

(5) Foolish (a) Calamities happen to both the vicious and the virtuous.

(6)   (b) We know not what are calamities and what are blessings—with illustrations.

By this means the sufficiency and arrangement of the paragraph topics can be easily discussed.

ESSAY 574.

1. **Rosicrucian**—Not from *rosa crux* (rosy cross), but *ros crux* (dew cross). Dew was considered by the ancient alchemists as the most powerful solvent of gold ; and cross in alchemy is the synonym of light, because any figure of a cross contains the three letters L. V. X. (light). *Lux* is the menstruum of the red dragon (gross or corporal light) and this light properly digested produces gold, and dew is the digester. Hence the Rosicrucians are those who use dew for digesting light, for the purpose of coming at the philosopher's stone.—*Brewer's Hand-book*.

They formed a secret society during the 16th, 17th, and perhaps the 18th centuries, and had many mummeries and pretended mysteries.

Adept—Learned in religious ceremonial.

Water—*i.e.*, "lustre," as in the phrases, "diamond of the first water," "watered silk."

Cant.—Hypocritical jargon whiningly delivered.

4. **Condole**—Aristippus's position is that to have more than necessary is an affliction. What peculiarity in the use of "condole" here.

Got the start of—This colloquialism has lasted till our day.

Splendid poverty—Note the epigram ; so below:
"Luxury is artificial poverty."

6. Note the old forms of expression, "standers by," "am got into."

7. Note that Addison is in this Essay, as in all others, thoroughly orthodox as to the essentials of religion.

Derived—(*de rivus*) turned from its regular course.

ESSAY 583.

1. **Equal obligation**.—Both are obliged perhaps, but not equally.
If choice determine how can obligation have force? Explain.
Omit "industry," as being in some measure voluntary and not inconsistent with pleasure.
Denounced to—Express the meaning in other words.
Distinguish calling, business, profession.

2. The second sentence furnishes a good example of the Pun—the point depending on the meaning attached to the word "give."

3. Would be better joined to 2.

4. Is the "who" clause in the last sentence restrictive or descriptive?

5. Condense this paragraph by omissions and substitutions.

6. The repetition of "but" has an awkward effect. How might it be avoided? Is there any other change needed in the first clause?
Come into something—*i.e.*, to join them in some scheme.

7. Can you suggest better positions for the phrase, "by....expense," and the clause "if he....to it?"

9. Point out and correct any faulty syntax in sentence 2.

10. "Life enough"—*i.e.*, long enough.
What is the subject of this Essay?
Whole book—*Georgics, Bk. II.*

ESSAY 598.

In this Essay the parts are somewhat out of proportion; paragraphs 5, 6, 7, 8, 9, are devoted to showing the aversion of the serious to the merry, while the aversion of the merry to the serious is scarcely more than a mere general statement, and occupies only a few lines (par. 10).

7. **For which reason**—This use of "which" (a Latinism) as a connective of sentences is scarcely met with now.

8. **Cave of Trophonius**—Was one of the celebrated oracles of Greece. The entrance was so small that the consulter had to be completely supine, when he was dragged in by the heels by some unseen interior

R

power, and afterwards ejected in a similar way, ghastly pale and generally shaken up.

Bridewell—The Holy well of St. Bride or St. Bridget. It was
originally a hospital built over a holy well of medicinal water in Black-
friars, London. It was presented by Edward VI. to the City and turned
into a penitentiary.

Compare the similar origin of "bedlam."

9. **Pausanias**—A Greek traveller and geographer, who lived in the
reign of the Roman Emperor, Marcus Aurelius, and wrote a geography
or itinerary of Greece in ten books.

11. Comment on anything faulty in "would neither....buffoon,"
"not so miserable as that," "if there was no God."

TRANSLATIONS OF THE MOTTOES.

For the convenience of non-classical teachers and students, who may wish to know the meaning of the mottoes prefixed to the Essays, the translations given in Morley's *Spectator* are copied below. It may be added that they vary greatly in merit and that several are paraphrases rather than translations.

ESSAY 21.—*Horace, I. Epode, V.* 28 :
"There's room enough, and each may bring his friend."—*Creech.*

ESSAY 23.—*Virgil Aeneid, IX.* 420 :
"Fierce Volscens foams with rage, and gazing round,
Descried not him who gave the fatal wound ;
Nor knew to fix revenge."—*Dryden.*

ESSAY 26.—*Hor. 1., Od. IV.* 13 :
"With equal foot, rich friend, impartial fate
Knocks at the cottage and the palace gate ;
Life's span forbids thee to extend thy cares,
And stretch thy hopes beyond thy years ;
Night soon will seize, and you must quickly go
To storied ghosts, and Pluto's house below."—*Creech.*

ESSAY 47.—*Martial* :
"Laugh, if you are wise."

ESSAY 50.—*Juv. Sat. XIX.* 321 :
"Good taste and nature always speak the same."

ESSAY 69.—*Virg. Georgics, I.* 54 :
"This ground with Bacchus, that with Ceres suits ;
That other loads the happy trees with fruits,
A fourth with grass, unbidden, decks the ground ;
Thus Tmolus is with yellow saffron crowned ;
India black ebon and white ivory bears ;
And soft Idume weeps her odorous tears ;
Thus Pontus sends her beaver stones from far ;
And naked Spaniards temper steel for war ;
Epirus for the Elean chariot breeds
(In hope of palms) a race of running steeds.
This is the original contract ; these the laws,
Imposed by nature, and by nature's cause."—*Dryden.*

ESSAY 93.—*Hor.* 1., *Od. XI.* 6 :

> " Thy lengthened hopes with prudence bound,
>   Proportioned to the flying hour ;
>   While thus we talk in careless ease,
>   The envious moments wing their flight ;
>   Instant the fleeting pleasure seize,
>   Nor trust to-morrow's doubtful light."—*Francis.*

ESSAY 115.—*Juv. Sat. X.* 356 :

> " Pray for a sound mind in a sound body."

ESSAY 159.—*Virg. Aen. II.* 604 :

> " The cloud, which, intercepting the clear light,
>   Hangs o'er thy eyes, and blunts thy mortal sight,
>   I will remove."

ESSAY 162.—*Hor. Ars. Poet,* 126 :

> " Keep one consistent plan from end to end."

ESSAY 169.—*Ter. Andria, Act 1, Sc. 1 :*

> " His manner of life was this : to bear with everybody's humors ; to comply with the inclinations and pursuits of those he conversed with ; to contradict nobody ; never to assume a superiority over others. This is the ready way to gain applause without exciting envy."

ESSAY 195.—*Hesiod :*

> " Fools not to know that half exceeds the whole,
>   How blest the sparing meal and temperate bowl ! "

ESSAY 225.—*Juv. Sat. X.* 365 :

> " Prudence supplies the want of every good."

ESSAY 381.—*Hor.* 2, *Od. III.* 1 :

> " Be calm, my Dellius, and serene,
>   However fortune change the scene ;
>   In thy most dejected state,
>   Sink not underneath the weight ;
>   Nor yet when happy days begin,
>   And the full tide comes rolling in,
>   Let a fierce, unruly joy
>   The settled quiet of thy mind destroy."

ESSAY 387.—*Hor.* 1, *Ep. XVIII.* 102 :

> " What calms the breast and makes the mind serene."

ESSAY 458.—*Hor.* :

"False modesty."

ESSAY 483.—*Hor. Ars. Poet*, 191 :

"Never presume to make a god appear,
But for a business worthy of a god."—*Roscommon.*

ESSAY 574.—*Hor.* 4, *Od. IX.* 45 :

"Believe not those that lands possess,
    And shining heaps of useless ore,
    The only lords of happiness ;
    But rather those that know
    For what kind fates bestow,
    And have the heart to use the store
    That have the generous skill to bear
    The hated weight of poverty."—*Creech.*

ESSAY 583.—*Virg. Georg. IV.* 112 :

"With his own hand the guardian of the bees,
    For slips of pines may search the mountain trees,
    And with wild thyme and savory plant the plain,
    Till his hard horny fingers ache with pain ;
    And deck with fruitful trees the fields around,
    And with refreshing waters drench the ground."—*Dryden.*

ESSAY 598.—*Juv. Sat. X.* 28 :

"Will ye not now the pair of sages praise,
    Who the same end pursued by several ways ?
    One pitied, one condemned the woful times ;
    One laughed at follies, one lamented crimes."—*Dryden.*

THE COPP, CLARK COMPANY, LIMITED, PRINTERS, COLBORNE STREET, TORONTO.